Praise for *Settler's Mine* by Mechele Armstrong

The Rivals

"Once again, Ms. Armstrong brings us another captivating tale of romance, suspense and plenty of action. This story will definitely keep you intrigued to the very end."

– Anya, *Enchanting Reviews*

The Lovers

"*The Lovers* is a fun and steamy sci-fi ménage romance. I found myself by turns frustrated, anxious and flushed from passion by the intrigue and love shared between Amory, Zelda and Bren."

– Bella, *Two Lips Reviews*

The Woman

"Mechele Armstrong's third book in the *Settler's Mine* series is absolutely fabulous. The passion and richness of this story makes it even better than the last. These characters truly are amazing and the writing top-notch."

– Kimberley Spinney, *eCataromance*

"With intriguing characters, exciting erotic play, and a fantastic plot, *The Woman* doesn't lack in its ability to sustain your attention. Throw in a dash of suspense and action and you've just been given a book that will keep you entertained and enthralled."

– *Literary Nymphs*

Loose Id®

ISBN 13: 978-1-59632-817-4
THE WOMAN: SETTLER'S MINE 3
Copyright © July 2009 by Mechele Armstrong
Originally released in e-book format in April 2008

Cover Art and Layout by April Martinez

All rights reserved. Except for use of brief quotations in any review or critical article, the reproduction or utilization of this work in whole or in part in any form by any electronic, mechanical or other means, now known or hereafter invented, including xerography, photocopying and recording, or in any information storage or retrieval is forbidden without the prior written permission of Loose Id LLC, 870 Market St, Suite 1201, San Francisco CA 94102-2907. http://www.loose-id.com

DISCLAIMER: Many of the acts described in our BDSM/fetish titles can be dangerous. Please do not try any new sexual practice, whether it be fire, rope, or whip play, without the guidance of an experienced practitioner. Neither Loose Id nor its authors will be responsible for any loss, harm, injury or death resulting from use of the information contained in any of its titles.

This book is an original publication of Loose Id. Each individual story herein was previously published in e-book format only by Loose Id and is a work of fiction. Any similarity to actual persons, events or existing locations is entirely coincidental.

Printed in the U.S.A. by
Lightning Source, Inc.
1246 Heil Quaker Blvd
La Vergne TN 37086
www.lightningsource.com

THE WOMAN
SETTLER'S MINE 3

Chapter One

"What are we doing?" Jax groused as he waited to board the small gray shuttle with twenty other people.

Tam tied back his hair with a leather strip to get the strands out of his face. "You know my answer to that." How many times now had he woken up from a dream where they'd returned to Settler's Mine? Or lost himself in a daydream? Too many to count. The urge to go back there had been overwhelming. Two days after the initial dream and many more visions, he'd convinced himself that he needed to go. Or go crazy from the longing.

"I don't understand why your gift can't pick some fun destination. Like the beaches of Pompay. The Garse Gardens of Niobeline. At least there, we'd have some fun. The aphrodisiac qualities of the Garse plant are well documented." Jax surveyed the people they waited alongside with a bored look.

"Like we need an aphrodisiac. I don't tell my dreams what to see. The visions come to me." They always had. Whatever they suggested compelled him to follow through or go mad from the stirred up feelings inside him. He paid the price of being half Ebolian. At times he had cursed that part of his heritage.

Ebolians were a race of seers. He had the sight. Had since he'd been a little boy. He'd learned to deal with his urges by giving in to them. Jax didn't understand how he was unable to resist his premonitions. It was hard on anyone who wasn't Ebolian to comprehend how strong they were. Was the dreaming even worse for those of pure blood? He didn't have anyone in his life to ask that question.

"But why Settler's Mine? Not as if we need to go back there. Either of us." Jax shifted closer to Tam, and his heartstone lit up with ruby fire.

Tam's heartstone answered, glowing in time with Jax's stone. Heartstones glowed during moments of intense emotions between mates. Heat bolted along his chest where the stone touched. The glowing of their stones together never failed to fill his heart with wonder.

A rarity.

Two males selected to be together without a uniting female. They were one of the rarest pairings in the galaxy. He'd been paired with a Native. One of the most no-nonsense races in the quadrant. Jax had Native qualities in spades. Yep, the Fates had a broad sense of humor.

"I wish I knew. I only know...I need to go there. *Now.*" Why remained to be seen. The reason must be important. His longings had never been this intense. Urgency continued to boil up in him and would until he reached his destination.

"Be glad you give good head." Jax stepped onto the gangplank without a look back.

Tam couldn't help but smile. His cock tented his pants, despite the early-morning quickie they'd already shared before coming here. There'd been no time for more if they'd wanted to leave on this morning's shuttle. The compulsion had been building to the point that walking had started to sound good if he couldn't get a shuttle transport. It was a long journey through space—with no oxygen—to get to Settler's Mine. That thinking had sealed the decision to leave today and not wait a minute longer. "I know you are."

Jax waggled his brows as they ducked under the low shuttle doorway. Tam had to duck more than Jax. Reaching the seats listed on their tickets, Jax shoved their bag of gear in a stowaway hatch above their seats before taking the position by the shuttle window. Jax had claustrophobia and needed to see open spaces when vehicles enclosed him. He always got the window seat because of his reactions.

Tam sat carefully beside him, peering to see the dock they'd left. His hand crept out to his lover's. They were on their way. He had to give Jax credit. The man hadn't protested much over the use of their funds to take this trip. He hadn't asked a lot of questions, instead accepting Tam's pronouncement they needed to go. Some lovers wouldn't have jumped because of a vision. Jax, for all his bluster, made a good mate for him. One day, he'd make this up to Jax. In pleasurable ways.

Their stones ignited in a pool of fire again.

"You're jumpier than I've ever seen you." Jax traced Tam's hand with his thumb. No one could see their clutched hands, which explained why Jax allowed the contact. He also probably maintained it because he sensed Tam's nervousness and his need to be touching him. Jax would do anything for him, a fact that told Tam much more than the logical man's words could ever say.

Tam couldn't contain the shiver at the movement of Jax's fingers across his skin. He always reacted this way to

Jax's touch. He craved his mate's skin to be alongside his at all times. It was the way of mates, especially with him. Super-sized emotions did have their drawbacks, but on the whole, he enjoyed them germinating. Some said Ebolians acted on pure emotion. While he used his intelligence, his internalizations drove him in most situations.

A harsh-faced woman caught their attention by waving a hand in front of Tam's face. "Hey, you two. Those are our seats." A harsher-looking man and a doe-eyed, petite woman, dressed in the primmest item of clothing he'd ever seen, followed the first woman. Severe didn't begin to describe the threesome. "Get out of them."

Jax frowned. "I'm afraid you're mistaken. These are ours." He pulled out the tickets as if to display them for proof.

Natives were big on rules and regulations. Some said they were the most logical race in the galaxy. Jax made most Natives look like criminals when it came to sticking to the rules.

These people in front of them weren't logical.

The man with the frown, standing behind the woman, raised a hand. "How dare you question us!" Then he added a few unintelligible syllables.

The woman grabbed his arm. "I'll take care of this." She turned her attention back to Jax and Tam. "I think this trumps whatever you think you might have." She pulled out an ID card around her neck.

A Union Alliance-given ID. She must be an agent of the commonwealth.

Tam's blood froze. Trouble with Union Alliance never brought good things. This woman had decided their seats were better than any other unoccupied ones. Probably because she wanted to flex her muscles and show she was top bitch.

She continued, "Not to mention, I'm part of a threesome." Her lips curved in a sneer. "A prized threesome. Unlike the *two* of you."

The man snarled. "Now, beat it."

Jax's hand tightened on Tam's. He was about to make a scene. They couldn't afford that. Not with the odds stacked against them, which was all the time, but especially not right now.

Tam leaned forward as if studying the ID. "That's you, all right." He stood up, looking for another pair of seats and tugged on Jax to follow.

The pilot watched them intently. Looked ready to jump forward and intervene. No question whose side he'd come in on. Not Tam and Jax's.

"Tam, they have no…"

He squeezed his hand around Jax's. Technically, these people didn't have the right, no matter what the woman's designation. Or mated status. But the truth didn't back up that assertion. A woman in a prized threesome, besides being an agent for Union Alliance, would be able to get away with this. Especially against a pair not prized by the Alliance.

Male mated pairs were rare. They weren't the prized mating that ménages were, especially these people's type. That kind of threesome received all sorts of perks from the

Union Alliance. Damn, even one woman-two men ménages received special treatment. Neither was too common, though they were prized. But God forbid you be a male mated pair. They weren't coddled or protected at every turn. Men in mated threesomes fared even worse.

Tam willed Jax to be quiet. He moved his head forward to indicate the pilot, who had his hand on his phaser. Last thing they needed was to get shot. Or worse.

Jax's mouth pursed as he saw what Tam had noticed. "But…"

Damn Jax for his adherence to the letter of the law. "There's another pair of seats." Tam moved up to grab their gear from the compartment. "Come on, Jax." *Don't cause a fight.* They'd be on the losing end.

"Uh-huh. Go on." The woman looked triumphant, along with a nastiness evident on her face. Her sneer could cover continents, along with her eager joy. Yep, this action had been to display her power.

Tam wanted to wipe her face clean of that look. And he could. But he'd get in trouble for doing anything to her. Best to walk away with his body and his mate intact. He had no desire to be in a Union Alliance holding cell being questioned for hours.

They moved to the new seats, and Tam stowed their gear. He motioned Jax to sit by the window.

After they'd settled themselves, Jax whispered, "Why did we do that? Give up our seats? They had no right to do that." His voice went high in his aggravation.

"You know as well as I do, whether they had the right or not, that's incidental. They will do what they do regardless of the law." Hard for Jax to swallow, but something Tam understood too well. Jax saw things in shades of white and black. He always had. Things never seemed that well-defined to Tam.

"It wasn't right."

Tam reached over to stroke Jax's face, ignoring the dirty look the woman, who'd booted them from their seats, shot him. "I know, *perlin*. But this was easier." Tempted to do more groping to piss the woman off, he refrained. He wouldn't lower himself to do things for her annoyance. Not with his wonderful mate, who deserved attention for what he was, not for retaliation.

"I could have taken them." Jax leaned into his touch, rubbing his cheek against Tam's hand, like a *psi-cat*, an Ebolian pet, seeking affection. Then, as if he'd remembered they were in public, Jax moved away. Public displays of affection beyond holding hands were gaudy in his eyes. Tam always warmed when Jax forgot where they were when his touch overcame his usual disapproval on the subject.

His cock rehardened, making him want Jax all the more. Soon as they arrived at Settler's Mine, he'd take advantage of his lover. "I know you could." Tam put his hand down in his lap. "Of that, I have no doubt. But, we need to get where we're going. Not be stopped here because of some jerks that have no couth."

"What will we find at Settler's Mine anyway? What do you hope to locate?" Jax leaned back in his seat. "Do you have any idea?"

The words that came out of Tam's mouth surprised even him. "Our future." Once they left his tongue, they were so right he almost shivered at the import of them. He leaned back, peering around Jax's solid frame.

Their future lay at the mine that had given them each other, due to the finding of their stones. He could be sure of nothing else but that.

* * *

Kiann walked through the throngs of people. She pushed her backpack farther up on her shoulder. Time to check in.

She went over to a counter and waited in line. The same way she'd been doing all day long. What was one more line to wait in?

She leaned wearily against a post.

Would she find what she sought here?

As if in answer, her mind slammed down into a vision of epic proportions. Red danced across her mind like a spinning ballerina doing pirouettes across the stage.

Yes, she'd find what she sought here. Every time she asked the question, the answer came in spades. She needed to stop asking herself the question, especially if she didn't want to faint. Her time was short to find what she sought, meaning the spells had to stop. The visions better help her accomplish what she was here for before she was dragged back to where she'd come from.

Her knees knocked together from the strength of her daydream. Good thing she'd leaned against the pole, or she would have ended up on the floor.

What did red have to do with anything?

She didn't have that answer. Her brows drew together in vexation. If only she knew what the dreams meant.

"Hey, you. It's your turn." The person behind her poked her in the side.

She'd missed the man behind the counter calling, "Next."

On shaking legs, she approached from the front of the line.

A big man, standing nearby, frowned. He took a step toward her, his concern evident on his face. "Are you okay, miss?"

She nodded, pushing wispy hairs behind her ears.

His gaze appraised her. "You sure? You don't look so good."

"Fine. I'm just tired." She took another step, and her legs almost gave way. The visions left her weak, and she wasn't in the condition to deal with their wear on her body. She clutched the counter to keep herself upright. "I need to dig for my heartstone." A stupid thing to say. No other reason existed for her to be here. They could figure that out on their own. Swallowing, she piled platinum on the counter. *Pull yourself together, woman. You can do this.*

The clerk behind the counter looked harried. "Name?"

"Kiann." Good thing her real name had no traces of her identity.

"Race?"

"Ebolian." She tightened her hands on the counter, trying not to sway. *Take my money, and let me get the hell away from here.* Only pure will kept her upright on unsteady legs.

"Vita." The big man had come to her side when she hadn't been paying attention and now spoke to the clerk. "I'll take this one over from here."

Vita nodded, looking relieved, and belted out, "Next!"

"I'm fine, really." She tried to assert her position to the big man, but she'd already been dismissed by the clerk helping her. Her face drooped. She couldn't wait in that line again, so she'd better go along.

The man took her arm, handed her back her platinum, and propelled her toward a door. A door to an office.

She froze, trying to drag her heels. Maybe he had other objectives than concern for her health. Maybe he knew who she was. What she was. She should resist more, but she weakened inside. Her legs elasticized as if they'd been made of rubber, giving out on her.

No. He couldn't know her identity. She'd covered her tracks. Marses's duplicity ensured that few knew Kiann's true identity. First time she'd been grateful for that.

"Come on." The man's concerned brown eyes stared into hers. "I'll get you checked in and get you something to eat. You look as if a brisk wind will knock you over."

She continued to resist, which didn't impede him from guiding her. "Who are you? What do you want from me?" If only she were stronger. Then, she could plow her fist right into his face and get away from whatever purpose he intended. She was too delicate. Always had been. One of

Marses's chief complaints. Self-loathing filled her, along with fear.

She didn't trust this man. She'd been betrayed too many times for that.

"I'm Bren." His lips curled up into a big smile to match his stature. "Perhaps you've heard of me."

Everyone had. He was Zelda's mate. Well, one of Zelda's mates. They ran the mine. Her breathing hiked up a notch. "What do you want with me?" Nothing could be worse than garnering his attention. He could do anything he wanted to with her, and no one would question him. He made the law on Settler's Mine.

"Look, you almost passed out in my line. You had a vision, and it weakened you. I didn't want you to injure yourself or anyone else. That's all." He took one meaty hand and made the sign of the Etruscan vow. "Promise."

How did he know that sign? Everyone knew the vow could be trusted beyond all else. For that matter, how did he know she'd had a vision?

She'd announced her race to the clerk. Bren had put the evidence together. Ebolians were well-known for their sight, despite being reclusive. "Why help me?"

No one was known around the galaxy for helping out of the goodness of their hearts, least of all the owners of Settler's Mine. Platinum made the galaxy go around. Zelda had a reputation for being a greedy bitch.

Kiann had been trying to go in under their radar. The last thing she needed was for them to realize who she was and try to profit from her identity. Profit could be made from betraying her whereabouts. Large profits that would run the mine for ages. A temptation a greedy bitch would jump on too quickly. Now Kiann had walked right into the snare. She'd have to tread carefully to extricate herself.

"You're Ebolian, aren't you? I heard you say that. And you have the look of the species."

Kiann's heart stopped for a second before traveling on a roller coaster. No sense denying her nationality. She had the classic looks of her race and had admitted what she was. The key was who she was. Did Bren know? "Yes."

They continued into a small office. He propelled her to a seat.

"What does my being Ebolian have to do with anything?" Had Marses publicized her running away? Surely he wouldn't, when he hadn't publicized any other points of her existence. He wouldn't risk the embarrassment her escape would cause. No, he would have kept her disappearance quiet. Which made Bren's comment puzzling. He couldn't know anything about her true identity. Which meant he wanted something else. What could it be?

"You have visions."

"Yes." All the time. She'd had a persistent one months before she'd planned to come here. She'd tried to talk to Marses about her dream seeing, tell him why she needed to come to Settler's Mine, but he hadn't listened. He never listened. She'd had to do the best thing for herself, even if leaving had been against the rules of her life. A small smile graced her lips in spite of the dangerous man in front of her. She'd broken herself out. Marses didn't think she'd have the foresight or the guts. "What does that have to do with anything?"

"Promise to share any visions that come to you about Settler's Mine while you're onboard. Or about Zelda, Amory, or me." He nodded to her. "That's all I'm asking. Not a lot for what you get."

That explained his interest. He wanted information. How bad for him that he didn't understand Ebolian visions. Few did. Their race didn't travel extensively or publicize the extent of their gifts to the galaxy. Ebolian visions were linked intrinsically to one's intimate circle. Few visions expanded out of that family unit. Bren and Zelda weren't even in her social arena, much less family or friends. But Bren didn't know that. What he didn't know wouldn't hurt him. Only deny him a reward that he didn't know if he'd collect or not. "I will." She'd agreed to share visions she wouldn't have for a speedy check-in. Her extensive hunger ate up her guilt at duping him.

He picked up a com. "What do you like to eat? I doubt we have any standard Ebolian fare. But I can get you most anything else you'd like."

"Parsnips with potatoes. It's an Etruscan dish…"

"I know the food well." Bren made a face, indicating his dislike of what she'd requested. He must have dealings with an Etruscan. Rumors said that Amory, their third mate, sported Etruscan heritage. Bren spoke into the com and ordered her a meal to be brought to his office.

She reached in her pocket for her limited funds.

He shook his head. "You have to pay for your mining. The rest of your meals will be on you, too. I'll catch this one."

"How much is the down payment on mining?" Yes, he'd do this one in the hopes she'd give him some vital piece of information about his future. While unlikely to happen, her seeing abilities had gotten her a free meal along with personal service. She wouldn't argue or complain. Hunger ate pride every time.

He quoted an amount.

She slowly counted out the platinum needed to find her place to dig. "Do you have any sections with red rock?"

Bren's full lips crinkled. "No. It's all pretty much gray stone around here. Everywhere is gray."

The mine had been carved from the rock itself. Everything in the mine had been hollowed out of the mountains and caverns that were rich with heartstones and other jewels. "You're sure?" Lack of red rock made no sense with the red hue she kept seeing in her visions. There had to be a connection. She'd assumed the color had been because of a pocket of red rock. That the red would tell her where to dig. Would have made things easier. *Should have known better. This is my life.* Nothing from the time she'd been born had been easy. She'd heard too many times how she hadn't wanted to be born and had taken forever.

What the hell was up with the red in her visions if it wasn't telling her where to dig?

"I know the mine inside and out. No red stone." A knock came on the door, and a man shepherded in her dinner. "Sure I shouldn't have Dr. Bennett come take a look at you?"

"No. I'll eat and be fine." With shaking hands, she ate.

She wolfed the food down with gusto, trying not to think she didn't know what to do next. Something would come up. Her visions wouldn't have led her here if it hadn't been important. She clung to that small hope, her lifeline.

Bren chuckled as she polished down the last bite in only minutes. "Good to see you have an appetite."

Not eating for several days would do it every time. "Yes. I better get settled in my quarters. Find my spot to stake my claim."

Bren stood up to see her out. "And you'd best set up a time to go through all the found heartstones."

Another flash of red came across her vision. Her sitting position helped her manage not to quake or fall. With food in her belly, she could handle the weakness that the daydream caused. "Found heartstones?"

He nodded. "We have lots of unclaimed heartstones. Best to start there before you dig. You might get lucky, and find your stone has already been mined."

Could she be that lucky? She'd never had luck before. Could this be the turning tide she needed? The vision had to be trying to tell her something. Her heart pulsated. "I'd like to go do that first."

"You got enough to eat? Why don't you first set down your gear in your quarters? Then, you can head over to the sort. There will be a nominal fee for a found stone there, of course. Since it's already been mined."

Of course. Nothing came for free. She couldn't fault them. Their livelihood came from people like her at the mine. "That sounds good."

He handed over a small machine. "Map of the mine. That will help you find everything. Your quarters number has been marked on the front."

She stood up and managed not to sway. The eating had helped drive off some of the off-balance feelings she had, but wooziness still infected her core. No vision had ever done to her what these did. They grew in intensity with each unanswered flash of her mind. The dreams had to be about her greatest desires. About finding her heartstone. Another hope she clung to.

Bren offered his hand. "Good luck, Kiann."

"Thanks." She took his hand and shook it brusquely. He had a harsh grip. Odd custom for such a big man.

She marched out of Bren's office with renewed determination. Pumped herself up with every thought.

A man bowled her over.

He caught her before she slammed to the floor. "Damn. I didn't see you there. You okay?"

She looked up into features that she recognized as that of her own race. Dark obsidian eyes stared at her. A prominent nose. Long dark hair. Full ruby lips. A dark black tattoo of spiraling bands wound down his neck.

Another man arrived in a flash. "Tam, you okay? And you, miss? You knocked together hard." A Native man. With hair down past his shoulders. Flaxen hair. Lavender eyes. Strong shoulders. Big arms.

Red flashed across her vision. Deep red. A crimson tide rolled with oceanic force across her. All red phased across her vision, bringing her to her knees even as the stones of the men in front of her grew a deep reddish hue.

Chapter Two

Tam put out his hands awkwardly to break the woman's fall. He looked down curiously at her.

With a swoosh of his long jacket, Jax rushed to his side. "You always did have a way with women. Now you have them falling at your feet."

Tam snorted. As if. Women had always been a whole other species to him. His mother had passed away when he was small. Same with Jax, who'd grown up with an all-male family after his mother died. Neither of them had been disappointed to be mated to another male because they didn't know much about women. "Help me get her to the side." He looked down at the delicate woman they supported between them. A red haze crowded his vision for a second. He shook but managed to stay upright.

"Are you okay? Don't you faint, too." Jax shot him a concerned look. "I'm not carrying your big self to the side of the path."

"I'm fine." Tam blinked as his vision cleared. What had happened? He'd never had a reaction to anyone, especially one this strong. He scanned the woman's features and froze.

"What now?" Jax sounded irritated.

As they'd been heading to try out their room when they'd been interrupted by the woman, Tam could predict his lover's mood. Pissed and horny. But what he saw in front of him superseded that. "She's Ebolian."

"I thought you said they don't come out much."

"I said they stick to themselves." Which was true. Pure chance had mated his mother and father. Ebolians didn't leave home often or associate with others of Quatar descent. "I've never…well, besides my mother, I've never seen an Ebolian." Not close up, not far away, not ever, at least in person. Only on brief news snippets he managed to catch once in a parsec. His mother had passed to the next world when he'd been little. All he had left of her were pictures.

From the looks of this woman, she possessed full blood. Not a half mix like him. Long, shimmery hair, which was as dark as a night sky. Matching eyes he'd noticed before she'd closed them. Full ruby lips had parted slightly from her state of consciousness. A black tattoo ran up her neck. Ebolians received their life tattoo at birth. The mark grew with them like a web. His mother had followed the old ways and tattooed him before he could walk.

A shiver raced up him. One of his own race lay before him. He remembered the swath of red that had clouded his vision as he'd looked at her and frowned. Everything about her screamed unusual.

"Well, this one is out. And out of it."

Tam leaned down to pat her on the face. The instant his fingers touched, the sensation hit of dipping them into molten lava. He drew back his hand. His fingers continued to tingle.

"Is she hot?" Jax watched him quietly. "Maybe she's sick."

The woman swallowed deeply but didn't open her eyes. "I'm not sick." Her voice sounded deep and throaty.

He watched as the woman's eyes fluttered once, twice, then opened.

Pure black stared back at him. Nothing escaped through those eyes. The vastness of space couldn't look any different from her irises and pupils. They were nothing he'd be able to read. His own eyes stared back at him. He'd never expected to see eyes the same as his, especially here and now. "What are you, then?"

"Clumsy." She moved to sit up. "Least I picked someone nice to fall on this time. It's always bad when I fall on someone who gets mad." Her husky voice ran along Tam's skin like lubricating oil. Silky. Deep. He'd never heard a tone quite like hers. He shivered at the sound of her.

She lied. Ebolians had grace. That was one respect in which they were similar to Natives. Why lie? Unless, she'd been having a vision. Something else that his people kept tightly under wraps. She wouldn't reveal the content of her visions to them or anyone she considered strangers. Many misconceptions existed about Ebolians' gift of sight because they were closed-mouthed about the talent. "I can't imagine you fall a lot."

She drew herself up as if trying to make herself smaller and go into a ball to hide. "Well, I do." She pushed up to her feet with a pensive luxury that he found vaguely familiar. "Sorry about that. Thanks for catching me." Her arm brushed his on the way up. More tingling sensations ran across him.

His cock bulged.

Jax cleared his throat. "Glad you're okay." Jax had noticed Tam's reactions. A quick look down revealed a definite bulge in Jax's pants. Did he anticipate their tryst? Or did he have the same reaction Tam did to the woman? Tam became more puzzled the longer they stayed in her company.

"Yep." Tam moved closer to the slight woman in front of him. "No harm, no foul. Glad I could keep you from the hard stone floor."

A slight smile moved across her face. Her features softened. What a lovely creature. One who stole Tam's breath away. "Me, too. You two have a great afternoon." Her face pinched miserably.

Somehow Tam didn't want to leave her. But why? They were strangers.

His heartstone glowed in sync with Jax's. Not intense, but enough to display an emotional reaction to her comments. Did Jax not want her to leave, either?

"You two are mates."

"Yeah." Jax straightened up rigidly. "Yeah, we are." His voice sounded irritated at the question. Many people questioned them about being together, as if they didn't believe two men would ever be mated.

"Your stones glow red." Her words came carefully as though she chose them with precision.

Tam fingered his carefully. The stone still warmed around his touch. "Yep, they do."

"Do all heartstones glow red?" She bit her lip. A nervous habit.

That's when he noticed the absence of a heartstone around her neck. Since he'd had Jax, he never checked others any more. He had his mate, had no need to look. This explained why she came to Settler's Mine. Every race of Quatar descent looked for their heartstone. Males couldn't even fuck anyone until they located theirs. The Union Alliance had mandated no sex until one found his or her heartstone. Despite this and the fact that screwing without sexual desire wasn't as fun as with the emotion, some got desperate enough they were willing to try sex anyway. Most important of all, true mates could only be determined by the shimmery piece of rock. All those things made finding one's stone a priority for everyone of Quatar descent.

Tam continued to hold his stone. "No, they glow in a variety of colors. The whole rainbow, in fact."

Her face deflated. "The whole spectrum of colors? Not only red?" Her disappointment showed in every pore.

Why did that piece of information devastate her? Tam frowned as he mulled over the matter. Better yet, how come she didn't know that?

"Yeah." Jax motioned to the rock, which hung around his neck from a black cord. "Blue, red, violet, yellow. The list goes on. There is quite a variety. Why do you want to know, Miss…"

"Kiann. My name is Kiann. And—" She broke off. "I'm curious." She acted as nervous as a six tailed Feton cat in a room full of rocking chairs.

There existed more behind her question. What it was, Tam couldn't say. But he'd do his best to find out what stories surrounded this intriguing woman.

* * *

"What are your names?" The woman quietly asked as she surveyed them warily. Her mind shifted to running away, evidenced by her eyes darting around.

"I'm Tamalak." Tam didn't look at ease, either. He had reacted fully to this woman with shivers and an erection bulging. Why? Why would Tam react to a woman this way? He already had a mate.

Not to mention, why was Jax having his own set of reactions to this small female, who was a stranger to them? The experience didn't make logical sense. Jax's throat closed up before he managed to get out his answer to her question. "I'm Jax." His voice sounded hoarse and deep even to his own ears. After speaking, he bowed formally in the Native tradition.

Tam slightly opened his mouth as if he were going speak, then stopped, though he looked as if he wanted to comment.

Jax glared at him. He'd greeted her in a traditional way, the logical thing to do. He hadn't lost his traditions from living with an Ebolian any more than the Ebolian had lost his divining talents. He might be rusty, but the protocols were still there. Curse him if the woman in front of him didn't make him want to pull them all out and flaunt them.

Not a typical reaction. He hadn't even acted that way when he and Tam had mated.

Kiann looked back and forth between them before stuffing her hands in her pants pockets. Such small hands. Her feet were tiny, even encased in big boots. The boots looked worn, as did her clothes. Rough. Her knee peeked through a hole in the pants. The elbows of her shirt were threadbare. She must have had a hard time.

His heart swelled, wanting to somehow protect her. He didn't understand why he'd reacted to her this way, either.

"Well, anyway, see you around. Thanks for catching me." She moved to walk away, which would bring her between them. She swallowed softly at how closely she'd have to pass by them both.

Neither of them moved. Later, when he could think, Jax would ask himself why they hadn't moved. Maybe they'd wanted that touch, however brief.

She continued forward slowly. One side of her brushed each of them.

A short glance at Tam confirmed he wanted her touch. A look of craving had moved across his face. Had a similar one moved across Jax's at the moment her body brushed his?

Jax's heart rate boomed. The sound echoed in his ears. From one small touch in passing. A full-contact touch might cause his heart to explode.

Who was this witch that she could affect them this way? Did her being fully Ebolian play a part? Not that Jax had met others beyond Tam to know how they affected the two of them, but he couldn't see why her mere race would do this.

Were there other deep-seated reasons? What could the reasons be? He had no answers. No solution put out any form of logic, which bothered him on many levels.

She moved away from them. Her steps picked up the pace as though she hurried to escape them.

Jax watched her swishing butt. The muscles moving under the tight material were pleasing to the eye.

What was he doing? He was mated, for curse's sake. With his mate by his side.

He turned his head to Tam. His gaze remained riveted to where Jax's had been. On the woman's retreating form.

Only when she turned a corner did Tam pull his gaze away to meet Jax's. While he looked a little sheepish at being caught, he didn't display embarrassment.

Jax had never caught him checking out anyone else before. Nor had Jax checked out anyone but Tam. "What was that all about?"

Tam met Jax's gaze full on. As usual, his eyes revealed nothing about what he felt. But his face gave everything away. Jax could read Tam. He'd never had any trouble figuring out Tam's emotions. "I don't know." He turned in the direction of their quarters. "I have no idea what that was about."

"Neither do I." Jax fell into step with him.

"What was the bow for?" Tam sounded incredulous as though he couldn't believe Jax had done one.

Jax could hardly believe his reaction himself. "I...it seemed appropriate to greet her formally." Not anything he'd planned. Had anyone else asked but Tam, he'd have told them to bug off. "I haven't lost my ancestry, you know. That was a Native formal greeting."

"You've never done that for me." Nothing sounded hurt in Tam's voice. But Jax could tell the action bothered him. As it did Jax. Why had he done such for the woman, when he hadn't for his long-standing mate? It made no sense.

He ignored Tam's comment and changed subjects. "That vision you had. Could she be the reason we're here? Maybe we're supposed to help her?" He didn't want to think on the bow and why he'd done such a thing. Better to change the focus.

Tam stopped suddenly. Jax continued one step ahead of him before he realized Tam had stopped. He quickly turned round to face Tam.

Tam took a step as if to start walking again, but stopped as he realized how close Jax was. Their bodies touched with the contact. "That could be the answer. You might be onto something. Maybe we're supposed to help her. Did you see how nervous she acted? I would wager a vision took her down when she ran into me."

"I noticed." Jax enjoyed the touch of Tam against him. Not a public display of affection but a bump. Accidental, but enjoyable.

"Did you see how unsure she seemed while asking us questions? Her clothes were ratty. She's spent all her money to come here." Tam continued talking, not pulling away, seemingly oblivious to the contact of their bodies.

Jax made a noncommittal noise. How close were they to their cabin?

"I bet…" Tam turned, his face lighter than it had been since the visions had started. The look made him appear younger than his years. Amazing how his face could light up so much. And thrilling. His mate acting happy never ceased to make Jax aroused. "Maybe we're supposed to help her find her heartstone."

"What?" Jax took a step back from his lover to create some distance and pull back his arousal. While he enjoyed seeing Tam excited, certain parts of him were enjoying it a little too much. He didn't want everyone to notice his erection. And he needed blood to think, which wouldn't happen as long as Tam touched him. "What do you mean?"

"She wore no heartstone. Didn't you notice?"

Jax hadn't been able to move his eyes beyond her face or her small breasts, until she'd turned around, and he'd stared at her butt. He'd not noticed much else. "No. I didn't." Why had Tam been looking for her heartstone? Tam already had a mate. Only Tam's looking didn't bother him as much as it should have. As much as Tam's actions would have with any other person. He frowned. Why was that?

"I noticed after she asked us the question about heartstones glowing red for everyone. She didn't have one." Tam moved forward again.

Well, that explained the whole situation. Logic dictated that there must be a reason for the visions that had necessitated their trip to Settler's Mine. "I bet we are supposed to help her find hers." Made sense. They could do that and then go home. Get back to their routine and simple life.

Tam stopped again.

"What's wrong now?" Jax didn't continue on this time, but stopped in line with him, having been paying better attention.

"There's only one problem with that."

"What's that?" Leave it to his mate to find a problem with the logical solution. Tam hated logic.

"I only have visions about those who are close to me." His mouth twisted. "I don't know her intimately."

* * *

Kiann shivered, pulling her arms around herself as she rounded the corner of the mine shaft away from the men she'd met.

The men's gaze burned her, yet she shivered. What was the logic in that? Never had eyes gleamed as warmly as Jax's. Never had a mouth parted as sensuously as Tam's.

Logic didn't normally become a question her mind had to ask. Not everything had to make ordered sense.

Now, Jax, she could tell he liked order.

His golden hair stretched past his shoulders. His violet eyes saw everything. They noticed everything. She'd never expected a Native man to be this…developed. While she'd studied many races a long time ago in anticipation of what she might become—before Marses—she'd never met many of them. Luckily, she possessed a good memory, especially for people. Jax had muscles on his tall frame, not something she'd pictured on a Native. His arms looked as though he could carry a few hundred pounds, yet he'd moved with the speed of a *gazella*, a fast-running plains animal on Ebolia.

From Tam, on the other hand, she'd expected the grace of their race. He possessed the ropey, muscular physique of their people, although he wasn't fully Ebolian. Something about him spoke of mixed heritage. Probably the rugged chin in an otherwise smooth-featured face. He had a delicate bone structure like hers. His long black hair had been pulled back. His hands had been large and rough looking, big for his body. His eyes had shown nothing, unlike Jax's, which would show whatever he emoted. Tam had the expressive face, which would reflect everything inside. They both had windows to their souls in different ways.

They came from different cultures. Ebolians centered around emotion and mysticism. Natives around authority and logic. The unique pairing got them attention as much because of that as because of them being two males.

They both brought up something in her. Something she couldn't put a finger on to identify.

A chance meeting and a brief one at that. That was all. She'd bumped into two men, and they'd talked to her for a minute. Why did she still think about them? They wouldn't be thinking of her. She'd seen their erections, their hard cocks. Yes, she might not be able to have sex, but she surely knew the mechanics of the act. Knew some of the terms from brief lessons. They probably engaged in sex right now.

Hot, steamy bodies melding together. Cocks jamming into orifices wanting to be filled.

She reached her quarters. The dredged-up feelings, or rather, what she couldn't experience, made her feel shitty.

Something sat just out of her reach. It taunted her. A goal she could see, but never quite touch.

Desire. Passion. Arousal.

None of these could be hers until she located her heartstone. Speed needed to be her goal. Marses would be coming for her soon enough. She had to find her stone before he yanked her back with him. She'd never get this chance again. This adventure was a onetime shot. Now that she'd run, when she was recaptured, Marses would ensure the loopholes that had allowed her escape would be patched up tightly. Too tightly for her to ever escape again.

Settler's Mine had to be the answer. She had no time to think about men whom she'd probably never see again.

She tossed her pack with few belongings into a tiny one-person room with few accommodations beyond a bed and willed a vision to come. Something. Anything. A scene in her mind that would tell her how to dig. Where to dig. How to find the thing she must find.

Nothing came.

She clenched her hands together.

The talent never worked when she most needed to see things clearer. Why couldn't the seeing have notified her that her mother was about to die? That her father was about to remate? That her father and stepmother were about to die? No, all these important things had come as surprises. Instead, she had visions of redness, which wasn't even something she could explain. Having the talent sucked, because it never worked on important life events. At least, not for her.

She grabbed up tools and left her room to find her place to dig, after she'd checked out all the found, unclaimed heartstones. Start there and work her way up. Maybe she'd get lucky.

Maybe she'd run into the men again.

But of course, they already had their heartstones and their mate. *Quit being stupid. They aren't here for you.*

Which begged the question, what were they doing on Settler's Mine? They were new arrivals, too. Why come to the biggest heartstone mine in the galaxy if you already had your stone, much less already possessed a mate?

No answers to any questions came to her on the long walk, but the room of unclaimed heartstones soon loomed before her. On a gulp, she entered. The huge room sucked her breath away. There were many shelves of the beautiful stones which lay waiting for their owners to come claim them. She'd never seen so many heartstones in one place.

What if she never came across hers?

Marses would pleased. He wanted to keep her from finding that which everyone hunted. How many times had she begged to be let out and go in search of her heartstone? Too many times.

No. She had to find what she sought.

She wouldn't take failure. Marses would be days behind her. She'd escaped while he'd been away. He wouldn't want to alert anyone what had happened and would take his pursuit slowly. That gave her time to look. Not much, but she'd work with what she had.

The Goddess would shine upon her this time, having shit upon her many times before. The luck of averages had to be with her.

Many milled around the room doing the same thing she did. Looking for their heartstone. They all had lost, furtive looks on their faces.

Did she wear the same look as she made the rounds?

A man with yellow teeth and bad breath stopped in front of her. He wore patched-together clothing. "You having any luck?" He must have spent much to get here.

People probably thought that of her because of the state of her clothes, but she'd dressed that way deliberately. Rags drew less attention than fine clothes. She pushed her hair back as she shook her head. She should have taken the time to braid the mane instead of doing a ponytail. Her hair kept getting in her way. "You?"

"Nothing is glowing for me." He sighed. A sound she'd heard countless times from those without their heartstone.

Many became desperate to find their stone. "I'm sure you will locate yours." Some never did. Usually people were drawn to where to look for their rock, which explained why, when the compulsion hit her to come to Settler's Mine, she hadn't hesitated. Her stone had to be here.

"How many stones you reckon are in here?"

"Hundreds?" She moved around the corner, gaze looking for the slightest glint that a stone might be hers. *Please glow.* If she had to beg on her knees, she would have, but the pleading would have made no difference. The Fates had picked her stone out long ago.

Don't make me wish you in hell, Fates.

A squeal sounded from the other side of the room. A woman grabbed up a glowing stone. "I found it! My stone!"

Her jubilant shrieks echoed through the room, piercing in their intensity to the point Kiann almost covered her sensitive ears.

Cheers sounded as the woman quieted. Tears rolled down her face as she grasped the stone tightly. Activity redoubled in the small room. Everyone regained new purpose with one person being lucky. Everyone walked and moved frantically.

"1,967...1,966 now." The man spoke right over her shoulder.

She jumped, startled by his sudden words. "What?"

"How many stones are in the room. I counted them. All of them." He moved his hand over a cold, dark stone, caressing the edges. The man acted creepy. If only he'd find his stone and leave her alone.

"Oh." She didn't say anything more, not wanting to encourage him to continue to talk to her. That many stones and none of them were hers. Her luck held in the place it always had. The section of no good to bad.

"I'm moving on to look outside of here." His smile became bitter. "You'd better move on, too. Nothing has glowed for you, either."

He had no right to say that. He'd been in there longer than she had, continuing to look.

Her saliva wouldn't move down her throat until she forced it. He was right, but she wasn't ready to move on yet. "I know." She hadn't made the complete rounds yet, or had she? Leaving would mean failure. She had no idea where to go after here. "I'll take one more pass around." If it made her seem pathetic, so be it.

"A red vein opened up recently. This morning, in fact." The man's eyes glowed with something akin to hope. "That's where I'm going next."

Red dots swam as her vision clouded over with them. She almost fell into the table, but managed to hold herself upright, only knocking two stones to the floor. Scrambling, she grabbed for them. Heartstones were tough, but if she broke any, there'd be hell to pay. A broken stone meant someone would die. Too many would look at the rock as theirs whether the heartstone would have belonged to them or not. Mobs had beaten to death unlucky souls who'd been clumsy. Or so the tales said. Scientists said the tough stones were impossible to break, and the tales were only legends.

The man bent to pick one of them up for her. "You okay? You don't look good. A little pale."

Tiredness of people asking her that question filled her. "I'm fine." If only she could control the visions and when they came. The words he'd said before the daydream echoed in her head. "'A red vein?' I thought all the stone was gray." She teetered on her feet, but managed to keep her balance. Had to stay alert and get through this. She'd eat when she reached her room again. Eating had helped before.

"Oh, the mine stone is all gray. But they call a new digging spot a red vein. Because it's a virgin spot." He shrugged. "Not sure exactly why, but that's the method around here. No one has even unearthed a stone there yet, as of an hour ago. That's how new it is." He grinned. "I plan to start there as soon as I leave here. I'm Dred. What's your name?"

"Kiann. Well, maybe we'll be the first to find ours." She tried to calm down her pulsing heart rate. Didn't mean she'd find her stone there. But this might be why the dreams all came in red these days. She forgot her desire to leave the man. In fact, she wanted to kiss him for telling her such a juicy piece of information.

On shaking legs, she headed with Dred down farther into the mine. Would she find her lost hope again? Or maybe even her destiny? Or wind up empty-handed?

Chapter Three

Tam shuddered as Jax's tongue ran across the small of his back. He had many sensitive spots, and his back would rev his motor anytime, anywhere.

They'd reached their quarters after leaving Kiann, planning to go back out and find her again. Somehow they'd stripped each other instead and now were pushing each other's hot buttons.

"You taste better than honey." Jax's voice had developed the throatiness it always did when he became aroused. He sounded as if he purred like a psi-cat.

"That make you a bee?" How he enjoyed teasing and playing with his lover. Jax always indulged him.

Jax chuckled as he nipped Tam's skin between his teeth, sending his eyes rolling back into his head from the delight of the sensations. "Only if I get to be the bee and sting you. With my large stinger."

Tam rolled over onto his back, disengaging Jax. A tease back. Unusual and the response filled Tam with more lust than ever. A little verbal sparring could pump up his libido like nothing else. "Like I'd say no to that." He never said no to Jax. He ran a hand along Jax's side, caressing the muscles of his abdomen, watching them clench and release.

Jax had a flat stomach with lines of muscle like the grill of a shuttle vent. He shifted his weight and moved upward to meet Tam's lips in a punishing kiss. His mouth became frenetic against Tam's. His cock rubbed along Tam's hip. His tongue flicked in and out of Tam's mouth, dueling with his before conquering the pace.

Tam kissed him back with every pent-up emotion inside of him. He wanted his lover to discover the charges building up in him. Charges that would intensify until he could take the sensations no longer and send him over that edge. Wanted Jax to feel every emotion he did. If only he could allow Jax inside of him.

Jax moved his hand down Tam's side, skirting under him. Such a hot touch. Like pouring acid to melt away the skin with heat instead of chemical. He pulled away his mouth, panting.

His hands slipped around Tam's cock without fanfare.

Tam had to appreciate Jax for his no-nonsense attitude.

Tam leaned his head back as his hips thrust against Jax's hand.

Jax pulled at the tip, lightly pinching the end between his fingers. He then lifted those fingers to his mouth and licked Tam's essence from them. "Can't let any drops go to waste."

Tam nodded in agreement and closed his eyes, overcome by his mate tasting his precome. He wanted his lover's mouth on him. Wanted him to do wicked things all over his body with his mouth.

Kiann's face popped into his thoughts. She had had a full set of lips that would do wonderful things over skin. Beautiful eyes that sucked him in. Such strong-looking legs. She'd clench them around a lover tightly. Tight and wet around him. His hips bucked.

The hand didn't return to his cock.

Tam reopened his eyes to see Jax staring at him with a concerned gaze.

His eyes bored deep within Tam's soul. "What were you thinking of?"

Tam wouldn't lie, but that didn't mean he had to reveal everything. He wanted Jax with a need that wouldn't be denied. "Kiss me. My cock. Take me fully in your mouth. Drink me."

Jax cocked his head to the side. "You were thinking of her just now. The woman. The one we are supposed to help find her heartstone."

He didn't remind Jax that they didn't know for sure what his visions meant. They could speculate, but wouldn't know for sure until events became clearer. Jax wouldn't let this go. Best to be honest with him. "Yep. I was thinking of her." He steeled himself for Jax's reaction. He shouldn't be thinking of this stranger during sex with his mate.

Instead of getting mad or even worried, Jax shook his head with an expression of disbelief. "I was, too. The way you leaned back, I thought about her being beside you. Complementing you with her dark features."

They were in sync about something for once. Normally, their rhythms were always off. When one of them was horny, the other wanted… That was a bad example. They both stayed horny for the other. Sex wasn't always fucking for them. There were lots of blowjobs, handjobs, and oral sex. One of them was always up for something sexually.

But a lot of times, one of them wanted to sleep or work when the other wanted to talk. Or one wanted the beach of Galazor, while the other wanted the mountains of Springor for vacation. When one would switch what they wanted to do to the other's side, they'd find the other had switched as well. They never wanted the same things at the same time or even thought of the same things at the same time.

Until now.

The woman had wormed her way into them both. That they both couldn't tear their minds away from her was an interesting sign.

What did all this mean?

Could it be they were supposed to find her heartstone or at least help her look? Or was there more to it than that? It would seem the intense thoughts had to indicate there was more going on than the search for a heartstone. Something Jax wouldn't want to hear.

"Why are we both thinking of her, Jax?" Maybe he had thoughts that would dispel Tam's own.

"I don't know. Maybe because of our task. We don't know where she went or what she's doing now. Maybe we shouldn't…" Jax let out a chuckle. "Scratch that last. Of course, we should have come back here for this. I need you." He looked like an Escar cat who'd discovered a mouse to bat around and play with. They got the same look Jax had now. "I need you now."

Tam's skin prickled with the longing he heard in Jax's voice. They were often both horny at the same time, though Tam's cock had never pulsed as hotly for his mate as it did now or been this hard. "I need you, too." Like eating was his need and want of his mate. The way things were supposed to be even if their mating had been unusual in more ways than one.

Jax ran a large hand across Tam's face, causing him to shiver. The look in Jax's eyes was one of pure possession. He lowered his head to kiss Tam again, but gently, not ferociously. The seductive lips melded to his, seducing in their quest.

And Tam never needed much to be seduced.

Jax pushed away thoughts of the woman, giving himself completely over to the kiss. Nothing to think about right now other than filling Tam with pleasure.

His head swam with the press of Tam's body against his. With the taste of him. Vanilla and spices. The same smell coated his lover. Sometimes Jax wanted to roll in his scent. Roll in Tam. Now was such a time. His admission of wanting made both their souls sing. No one else had ever gotten inside him the way this man had. In many ways that was uncomfortable, but in other ways, it was the most wonderful thing in his life.

Tam murmured against his lips.

His hand slid down Tam's body, exalting in his smooth skin and rippling muscles that moved under his fingers. His skin steamed hot under Jax's hands. He'd never encountered such heat in his life as the one that emanated from Tam.

He reached the edge of Tam's stomach. He wanted to explore something down below, in detail, at his leisure. One of his favorite places to explore on Tam's body.

Tam's breathing changed, and his body stiffened, going straight. He'd anticipated Jax's next move.

Jax didn't give him what'd thought was going to happen, instead asking, "Something you want?"

Of course Tam wanted something.

Jax's own cock laid hard between them. His balls ached for release. His body tingled with the anticipation of coming within his lover's body. He'd never wanted Tam more than that moment. He always thought that when they were about to have sex. Each time rose up above the last.

"Ummm-huh. I want you."

Jax's hand went down to cup Tam's balls in his hand.

Tam's breathing caught in his throat as his hips bucked wildly.

Jax looked for this reaction. The one that made him king of the world. That he could cause such a thing in his mate made his pride surge. He caressed Tam's balls, gently rolling them around. "This?" His other hand came around to flutter down Tam's length. "Or more?"

Tam's voice came unsteadily. "Both."

Greedy. Jax loved that about him. He would give him all he wanted and more. He lived for these moments.

Jax's fingers did more than flutter. He clutched him in tight hands. The touch of Tam's hard cock did things that Jax hadn't anticipated. Tam felt good in his hands. More than good. His own desire tripled in its depth.

Up and down, he moved his hands, over and again, working Tam's length until the man groaned and growled. His hips matched Jax's pace, while Jax couldn't take any more.

He had to be inside Tam right now. No more foreplay. He couldn't even speak, his mind going down one track and unable to form coherent words.

One last kiss and he pulled away from Tam. Flipped him over on the double bed. Wanted to be one with the man who filled his heart.

Tam didn't argue, simply pressed down face first on the mattress.

Jax groped for the lube in the bag on the nightstand where they'd put it when they'd arrived. They'd unpacked their sex tote immediately, as usual. Even that worked to escalate Jax's desire.

Tam looked back coyly as Jax squirted the lube into his hole. Tam sometimes didn't need it, but Jax played it safe. He had no desire to ever hurt his lover. Not to mention the wetter, the better. Tighter, too. As Tam always stayed.

Jax blustered out a breath, trying to calm himself down. Bring himself back into the realm of control. His want, his need, had never been this bad. He was supposed to be in control at all times. But right now, control had been wrestled from him. He couldn't get his swirling emotions and desires back under his iron grip. He counted to ten before moving again because he didn't want to spill or take Tam too roughly.

He'd relaxed again to bring himself away from the wildness inside.

Then, still looking back, Tam licked his lips.

An innocent action, except in the hands of his lover. Tam could turn any move seductive, any action into something more. Now his lover tried to entice him.

Tam wiggled his butt around, still with the tongue licking and the coy look. His eyes sparkled even with their darkness.

Temptation had never been more ready to receive than this.

Jax groaned. Tam loved to tease, but now was not the time. *Get inside him. Take things slowly.* Maybe that would make the unbridled lust better. To be acting instead of anticipating would take off the edge. He moved against Tam's backside, dropping the lube down beside the bed.

Tam moved back against him, pressing himself more against Jax.

Skin slapped against skin.

Jax slipped inside of him and almost roared. Such tightness. *Do not slam down.* He didn't want to hurt Tam, even as experienced as he was, by being too forceful. He needed to give Tam time to adjust.

This wasn't going to work. He'd been too keyed up from the start.

His fingers gripped the sheets as he tried to bring himself around, seeking any control so as not to move. If he moved, he would lose himself instantly. He'd take Tam with a pounding pace whether Tam was ready or not. That couldn't happen.

But Tam wouldn't allow Jax to take things slowly. He moved against Jax ferociously, almost trying to take control of the rhythm away.

Tam had never been this insistent. He wouldn't allow Jax to find his control. He wouldn't back away, and he kept moving against Jax, tempting him to slam himself down inside the man. Take him roughly. Not gently.

He gritted his teeth together. "Stop it." Tam didn't know what he played with, or how close to the edge Jax sat.

"Let loose."

"No."

Tam moved himself backward, slamming himself as much as he could against Jax. "Lose control."

And Jax did. He couldn't help but pound himself into Tam's hole with a viciousness that surprised him. He'd never taken Tam in such a way. He'd never lost complete control, even when he'd orgasmed. But now, he moved wildly. Franticly. Acted almost animalistic in his thrusts.

He tried to slow down, but Tam wouldn't hear of that. He constantly pushed himself back at the same pace that Jax had set for them. Tam wouldn't give him time to collect himself.

His hand reached around to cup Tam's cock, to stroke him up and down. No lube. He cursed himself for tossing the vial down instead of keeping it handy for this. But he didn't let go of Tam's cock. Instead, he worked the member up and down furiously, while continuing his assault on Tam's backside.

Pushing inside Tam to the hilt, Jax felt Tam shudder, felt his body clench. Something warm and wet coated Jax's hand. A second later, a shout of Tam's name took Jax over the edge as he poured his release into his lover.

They both collapsed, covered in sweat and panting.

Jax rolled off of Tam but pulled him close. His hand stroked up Tam's back as they lay there in the quiet.

Tam spoke first to break the spell. "Jax?"

"Yeah."

"You lost control."

The heat moved up Jax's body. "Yeah." Tam had noticed. Usually Jax held himself back. Shame filled him. Had he hurt Tam?

"As much as I've begged you to, you've never done that before." Tam sounded exhausted and awed at the same time.

"Did I hurt you?" Jax wanted to pull away, didn't want to hear the answer. He should have been more careful instead of slamming himself and taking all his pleasures upon Tam. He'd been unlike himself in his actions.

"Nooooooo. Not at all. I..." Tam caught his lip between his teeth. The look on his face showed all. "I enjoyed it, perlin."

Jax pulled Tam closer, rubbing his hand through Tam's silken hair. "Long as I didn't hurt you. Much." How could Tam enjoy such a thing? Such a loss of control? But the evidence was etched there on his face. Jax tried to quiet his breathing.

"At all." Tam reached over a hand to cup Jax's face. His hand warmed Jax's chin. "You didn't hurt me at all." He dropped his hand.

"Good." Tam didn't lie, so he must not have experienced pain.

Jax would have to watch himself more closely in the future. He couldn't lose control this way. He wouldn't be a slave to his lust. He could keep his head during sex and not get lost to the little head. No, his arousal wouldn't dictate to him. Never had. Never would. Each time they'd made love, he'd controlled the act, the act hadn't controlled him. This aberration of behavior wouldn't continue.

"Have you ever been with a woman before?" Tam tapped his chin after the blurted out statement, looking as if he couldn't believe he'd asked the question.

"What?" Jax pulled back to scan Tam's face. Where had that come from? Both he and Tam had had lovers before finding their mate. A smile overtook him as memories surfaced about their meeting, despite the question.

They'd met when a transport ship had delivered henna dyes to Jax's store. He created henna clothing, which he made from the henna plant. Tam had been working the ship. Both of them had been stunned when their stones glowed. Neither of them expected to be mated to another man.

Jax had had a hard time believing the mating at first. But once he'd accepted Tam as his mate, they'd had a good life together. Tam had stopped his wandering and come to live with Jax at the Native settlement on Escar.

"Have you ever been with a woman before?" Tam repeated the question. He didn't look embarrassed, only curious.

"Yeah." Jax didn't give any details as to when and how. Tam wouldn't ask. Didn't matter anyway. The question was irrelevant. "Once." He wouldn't meet Tam's gaze. This moment marked the first time he'd ever lied to his mate. He wasn't even sure why. Curse Tam for asking the questions.

"What was it like?" Tam sat up slightly to make himself higher than Jax.

"Why are you asking this? We are mated to each other." Jax held up his pointer and middle finger. "Two men. That's it."

"But, you never know." Tam placed a hand on his thigh. Usually Jax would exalt in Tam's touch. But not right now. "We could find our third. It happens often enough. We don't know who that will be. Man or woman. I'm only curious. What was it like?"

Jax ignored his last repeated question. "Finding one's third does not happen often enough. Some don't even find a stone much less a third." He had seen poor devils who never located their stones, living a miserable existence. His brother had gone into a religious camp rather than face life without a stone. He'd looked in all the mines. Had no inkling of where the stone could be, as most did. His brother had interned himself in religion rather than face a sexless life or spend more platinum looking.

"But what if we did? And it was a woman?" Tam's face looked as if he thoughtfully considered the possibility.

"Could as likely be a man. Look at Ansel." A big brigand and profiteer, Ansel had made a name for his cruelty and desire to take down the Union Alliance. He also was a part of a trimated all-male pairing.

"You know as well as I do that's rare. Rarer than a bonded male pair like us. Ansel is the exception, not any rule,"

That was probably a good thing, considering what rumor said about Ansel.

Jax let out an impatient snort at the direction of this conversation. So much for basking in the afterglow. Bad enough they had to leave here and find the woman. "Why are you asking this now? What's on your mind?" He put his hand on top of Tam's. Tam never concealed anything from him. "The woman. Kiann is on your mind." Jax had briefly stopped thinking about her, but Tam's period away from thoughts of her must have been even less than his.

"Isn't she on yours?"

"Yeah." If only he could lie and say no. His nature didn't allow him to fib often. He still didn't understand the earlier lie. He pulled his hand away as if Tam had burned him. "Did your vision say anything about her being our mate?"

Tam hummed a second with no answer, which gave Jax all the answer he needed.

"Did it? You mentioned nothing about that."

"No. No, my vision didn't show anything about her being our mate. But..."

"Then, she's not. She's someone we are supposed to help. That's it and all." Jax folded his arms over his chest. He wouldn't accept more until he had the proof, and even then, he'd question things. What would they do with a woman? His lip curled. He knew nothing of females.

"I don't have visions about those not connected to me. Most visions are not concrete in what they say, but the person is always connected to me, Jax."

"Maybe your visions are branching out. Taking a new path. Reaching out to someone who needs help and isn't connected to you." Jax theorized a possibility more probable than the other idea. How ludicrous the two of them could have a woman as their third. The whole idea was laughable.

"Ebolian visions don't do that." Tam's voice lowered. He folded his arms across his chest, too. He looked irritated. "You know that as well as I do."

Jax didn't point out what he knew of the visions was what Tam had told him. Tam only knew from the little his mother had told his father before she died and what he'd investigated, which was secondhand. This contact with Kiann was his first with a member of his race. "You're only half Ebolian. Maybe that's affecting you." Jax sat up straight. "Look, I don't even want to speculate. The woman is not our mate, okay? There's no sense getting all worked up over something that's not possible. Logically, I know it's not possible." Nothing without logic could happen, which was the mantra Jax lived his life by.

"How? How do you know she's not our mate?" Tam's brows drew up across his forehead. "How do you know what's possible and what's not?"

"Because if she were, we wouldn't have stumbled upon each other first. End of story. Drop it." Jax's voice grew sharp at the end. He worked to bring himself back under control.

What was going on with him? He always stayed on an even keel. Being back at this mine had knocked him off balance and that left him flustered. He ignored the piece of himself that asked why he was adamant. Why did the questions even bother him if he was sure? He had no time for illogical questions from his psyche. He got enough of those from Tam.

"What do you mean? Because the woman's stone is supposed to activate her mate's first?"

"Exactly." Jax heard the crow of triumph in his own voice. "If a woman were coming into our mating, we would never have mated. She can't be our mate. She doesn't even have her stone yet. She's still searching."

"But it's not always the woman's stone that activates. Look at Ansel." Tam tossed the example that Jax had used earlier back in his face.

"A rarity that a woman's stone isn't the one that sets off the others." Jax had Tam, and that was enough. Tam was it for him, and he for Tam. Tam had to accept this woman wasn't their mate. Couldn't even be a possibility. Why was Tam being so...Ebolian about this?

"It's rare that two men are mated." Tam glowered back. "We already are an oddity. What's one more thing? Jax..."

He wouldn't let Tam finish. "No. We aren't mated to the woman. We'll help her find her stone and then be on our way."

"You...rigid bastard. You aren't even listening to me." Tam sat all the way up. "You're being illogical not to even consider the possibility."

The hair on Jax's neck set up. How dare his mate accuse him of not being logical? "Because I know…"

"What? What's best? You don't always, Jax. You won't even talk to me about this. Closing yourself off from the possibility doesn't make it any less of one."

"Look." Jax sent out a gust of breath. He didn't want to fight with Tam. He hated when they argued. "Let's go find her. Help her find her stone, which can prove to you she's not our mate. Then, we can move on."

"Fine." Tam moved from the bed to get dressed.

After a moment, Jax did, too. Yeah, he couldn't wait for life to get back to normal and get away from this place. Get away from the woman who'd already turned their lives upside down.

Chapter Four

Kiann walked in from the corridor and instantly forward to a spot, ignoring all others. Her heart danced in her chest, mimicking a ballerina's moves onstage.

She looked around the medium-sized hollowed-out cavern. The walls were the same gray, plain stone that existed everywhere else. Nothing special separated this cavern from any others in the mine.

Yet, this section of it drew her interest.

That had to mean something. Her heart continued to race in her chest as she pulled out her tools. She embarked on the search for something life-changing. Maybe she should say a few words? No, she should start digging. Immediately.

She chipped away slowly at the rock. Heartstones abounded in this new section of mine from the little she'd seen. Someone had been the first to find their heartstone already, and two more had followed. Kiann didn't have to be first. She only wanted to find hers. Didn't matter when.

This has to be the place.

What if she guessed wrong? What if her heartstone existed in another part of the mine? What if it wasn't even here at Settler's Mine?

She forced a swallow down her closed-off throat. *Stop second-guessing.* No, her visions had led her to this place. She'd dreamed of red. This was a red vein. The spot called to her with rightness. Her heartstone *would* be here. She'd find her missing piece of heart.

A disturbing image if you thought about the saying about heartstones.

A hand dropped on her shoulder.

She startled, then cocked her head to the side.

Dred look down sheepishly at her. "Sorry if I scared you."

"Wasn't expecting you, is all." She'd been lost in her own thoughts. Hadn't even heard him approach. Not a good thing when Marses would come after her eventually. She'd have to become more alert.

She didn't see a stone around Dred's neck, nor had she heard any shouts since she'd picked her place. She wisely didn't ask him the question.

He wasn't as wise. "Have you found it yet?"

"No. Not yet." She'd keep saying the "yet" as long as she could. Until Marses dragged her back, the chance remained she could find her stone. She had to keep believing that and keep searching, or she would give up, and then where would she be? Not much of a person or with much of a life.

"Too bad. A few have unearthed theirs." He didn't look too happy about the situation.

"Uh-huh." She didn't want to talk to him while he was in this mood. Despite her bad luck, she was happy for the people finding their stones. They deserved them. Everyone did. Just because she hadn't discovered hers yet, she didn't have to be petty.

"This whole heartstone mine is bogus. Not worth shit." He sank to his knees beside her, sitting. "I think it's a conspiracy by the Union Alliance as to who finds theirs and who doesn't. They keep all the stones in secret. Activating them for who they want. The whole thing is all a big criminal operation."

Kiann didn't respond. She looked at the rock she had to chip away. Red dots captured her vision. She placed her palm on the rock. Warmth. This had to mean something, too. Maybe this particular spot contained her heartstone.

Her throat muscles worked. Could her life be waiting under a couple of centimeters of rock?

Dred droned on some more about the Union Alliance and conspiracy theories.

She tried to listen, but her eyes glazed over. Not to mention she wanted to dig, not talk. Would digging in his presence be rude? She hadn't read up on her manners protocols lately and had only a smattering of lessons on that subject. If only Jax were here. He'd know.

As if he'd heard her, a deep voice made her swing around. "Kiann."

She turned her head to face both Jax and Tam. She couldn't halt her breathing speeding up nor her heart racing from seeing them. She'd never reacted to anyone that way before. The looks on their faces made her warm all over. "Jax and Tam. What are you doing here?" Did she sound too happy to see them? Too joyous? Screw it. She had no time to hide her emotions.

"We came to see if we could help you dig." Tam moved forward. He pointed to the rocks behind her. "Is that where you're digging?"

"Yes. Yes, it is."

Tam hadn't asked her the question that most everyone did like Dred had earlier, "Have you found it yet?" Instead, he'd focused on where she was looking for her stone. He'd realized by reading clues what she hadn't located. She'd never understood why more people didn't pay attention to subtleties. If she'd found her heartstone, she wouldn't still be on her dig site.

Her estimation of the man went up a few notches.

Jax didn't look particularly thrilled to be there. Or maybe he didn't look happy to see Dred with her. His eyes brimmed with warring emotions. "We've come to help you search."

Dred cleared his throat.

"Oh, this is Dred. He…alerted me to the fact this section had opened up." And that they'd termed the new part a red vein, but that would take too much explanation. She'd keep that tidbit to herself.

Dred frowned, his eyes narrowing.

What should she call him? He wasn't a friend. They'd only talked for a few minutes, and that had been the extent of her relationship. She'd known Tam and Jax longer than that, and she didn't call them friends. "This is Jax and Tam. We met earlier."

Dred nodded to them and them to him.

Silence reigned.

Well, this was awkward.

Tam's eyes looked unreadable. "Where were you digging?" His voice sounded clipped as he defiantly reminded Dred that he wasn't actively digging for his stone.

She could tell neither of the men liked Dred on first impression. Wait until he shared a few theories with them as he had her. She'd been ready for him to leave her as soon as they'd arrived at the red vein, despite her tender feelings from earlier at his sharing about the red vein.

Dred pointed to a place across the shaft. "Over there."

"Well, good luck with finding your stone." Jax moved in to pick up a chisel in large hands. "Hope you find it soon."

She echoed Jax's good luck that had been followed by his polite dismissal, which didn't seem Jax-like. Interesting.

Dred nodded as he pushed to his feet. "I'd better set to digging." He moved away with an ambling gait. He didn't wish her luck.

Tam took a seat behind her. "This is the spot you want to dig?" He motioned to the wall of rock.

She nodded and passed her palm over the pulse of rock that beckoned to her. More red spots flashed before her eyes. The visions weren't beating her down, but they were strong. "This is it. Right here." The place that compelled her. Would she find what she sought? Or be disappointed again? Her life didn't seem to run along smooth paths. Just once, couldn't she have a spot of happiness?

Tam put his hand over hers. As if feeling the rock with her.

Again, something situated a few steps out of her reach with Tam's touch. If only she could figure out what stayed out of her reach. Touch the sensation. Yet, whatever it was, it stayed just enough out of her bounds so that the sensation couldn't be reached. Her hand clenched under Tam's.

Another emotion ran along with those confusing ones—one of intimacy. Tam's hand pressed over hers was an intimate action. Something she'd not had with another person in a long time. She didn't want him to pull his hand away.

Jax took up a position with his chisel near to them in a parallel position. "Shame it's low." He tapped the rock with firm hands. His touch would feel as good as Tam's. She would bet on that.

She ached for his hands on her body. The feel of another's hands was what she yearned for right now. Puzzling, to say the least.

"I'll start first. You direct me if I'm going the wrong direction." He nipped away a little rock. "Take a rest."

She'd had enough of one talking to Dred. But she didn't argue, though she wiggled back and forth. Didn't want to wait and watch. She wanted to toss herself in and dig with her hands if she had to. She would do anything to find her heartstone. No wonder people became desperate.

Tam grabbed a small pick. "I'll come at the site from this side."

"I can dig, you know." She frowned as they both carefully chipped away rock where she'd shown them. Digging was slow, intricate work. Too much power caused too much to chip away. Delicacy worked better than brute force.

The shaft had already been cleared enough for them to dig into the walls. The mine crews would inspect each shaft every day to make sure things were safe.

"You will." Tam grinned back at her. "The heartstone is probably a few inches away, embedded in the rock. It will take time to get it out. You'll have your turn."

She looked into his deep, mysterious eyes. They saw enough that they made her shiver, but didn't reveal anything back. Did her eyes look the same way to him? "Do you think my stone's in there?" A swallow hung in her throat as she surveyed them again. What would he tell her? She wanted to hear his opinion. Somehow his thoughts meant something to her, which was stupid. He was still a stranger.

Tam shrugged, going back to digging. "I have no idea. But if something drew you to dig here, there's a good chance that there is one."

No false hopes. Realistic words. Somehow, that meant more to her than anything else.

"There's a good chance that it's yours." Jax picked away a tiny chunk. "No one else can sense another's heartstone. You're the only one who can tell us if we are on the right track. But that doesn't mean it's here."

Not what she'd wanted to hear, but the truth. She wouldn't have believed them if they'd assured her with frothy promises. She'd had way too many of those already. "Why are you helping me?" She rocked back on her knees. "Why help me dig to find my heartstone?" No reason existed for them to have sought her out. Her intrigue grew.

Tam missed the rock at her question. He steeled himself, but before he could answer, Jax spoke. "Because we're going to."

"That's not an answer." They both looked uncomfortable. What was going on? She kept glancing between them both.

"Tam had a vision to come to Settler's Mine. We think we came here to help you find your heartstone." Jax continued his digging, and Tam did, too.

"That's why you are here? Tam had a vision?" Her heart skipped several beats. They didn't share about visions with those outside of their race. The only reason they'd tell her was because she was Ebolian and knew of them already.

"Yeah. He had a vision, so we traveled here to see what needed to be done to fulfill his dreaming. Why else would we be here?" Jax waved a hand dismissively before striking a rock.

Tam nodded. "That's the only reason we came."

"You think you're here to help me?" She fingered her backpack, trying not to think of the repercussion of all this. She of all people knew how visions worked.

"Don't get excited or anything." Jax chipped away another large piece of stone away from the wall.

Did she see a heartstone tail peeking through? No, couldn't be… No glow. Dammit. Which would mean this one didn't belong to her. Any joy faded away. "I'm not. Trust me on that."

Tam stopped again to look at her. "We think my vision led us here to get you your heartstone. And here we are."

"But you and I don't know each other." She swallowed with effort. "At all." Maybe Tam didn't know about the extent of his visions? She hated to be the one to tell him. Probably meant she wasn't who they were there for. The other line of thinking, she wouldn't even contemplate.

She'd exposed the flaw in their logic. Ebolians didn't have visions about anyone they didn't know. All their visions centered on those close to them or on oneself. Not a commonly known fact.

"We think he's branching out." Jax bored out more around the tail end. A heartstone was pocketed there, but no glow emanated. "He's only half Ebolian."

She had been right about his mixed heritage. Tam didn't possess full blood. He probably had a difficult time with their people. Still didn't make sense that he'd been dreaming about her. A half-blood should still center on those closest to them even more than a full-blood. She didn't voice that opinion because she didn't want to insult them.

She'd been wrong about her heartstone being there. This one couldn't be hers. Her stomach churned. "Branching out, huh?" What if she never located her stone?

"Yep." Tam chinked around something of his own. "I guess I am. It's the only thing that makes sense."

"Why don't you let me try?" She couldn't sit there another minute without doing something. Even if it was for nothing.

Tam offered up his tool. "Sure. I could use a break." His finger brushed hers with the passing off. He moved as though she'd burnt him with her fingers.

Hers had been singed by the contact.

As he moved behind her to sit and help her get in front of the wall, their bodies brushed up against each other. His scent filled her nostrils. His hot, smooth skin touched hers.

He let out a strangled grunt.

She wanted to plaster herself all over him, but refrained. Nothing else had ever made her this...affectionate. Yet, something was missing. She again had the sensation that something sat a few centimeters out of reach.

Not that she'd ever experienced attraction. But if she'd had her heartstone, would she have been attracted to Tam? She had no idea what sexual desire awakened inside a Quatarian. Not that she could experience the sensation yet, but maybe this was the start. Books never said exactly what happened.

She moved into place, close enough to feel the press of Jax's leg against hers. Close enough to smell his unique, musky scent.

Would she be attracted to Jax, too, if her heartstone had been in attendance?

She might never know. Not if she didn't hurry up and find the piece of her heart. With renewed vigor, she attacked the wall. If she was going to be sexually attracted to these two, she didn't want to wait any longer.

The heartstone that Jax had started popped out of the crevice in the cavern wall. The inside made no attempt to glow. "There's one."

"Not mine." She could barely swallow, her mouth dried so much, and the dust hadn't been the cause. What if this wasn't the place? What if she'd guessed wrong? Now she'd have two people digging with her in the wrong area. She steadied herself. All signs pointed to here. She chinked away at the shiny underbelly of a heartstone.

With no glow.

They sat in silence a few minutes as Jax checked around for another heartstone, and Kiann picked out the one above her.

She'd almost gotten the heartstone out when she stopped. Tears pricked her eyes.

The stone hadn't shone once. It wasn't hers.

"Need me to take over?"

"No." She tried to cover the fact that she'd teared up. She didn't need their pity. Nor did she want them to know how the loss of something that had never belonged to her to begin with affected her. Someone would claim this stone at some point. And be happy.

But not her.

Jax hadn't come across another stone to dig out.

This one wasn't hers, either.

It was the wrong spot.

The wrongness of the whole situation overwhelmed her. Her chest hurt with the loss. None of the other places had appealed to her. What was she supposed to do now? Marses would come and take her away soon. She'd never get the opportunity to look again, which would mean she'd failed.

Failed in her mission and failed herself, worst of all.

She wanted to curl up in a ball and cry. All the planning, all the trouble she'd taken to escape, all the risks she'd taken to get here. Now, the jeopardy was all for naught. She was too tired to deal with this shit.

A hand pressed on her shoulder. Joined by a second one on her other shoulder.

Tam and Jax patted her skin with careful hands.

She trembled. "I don't…"

"Shhh." Tam knelt down behind her. He pulled her into the curve of his body.

Jax did the same.

She rested effectively between them. Their bodies sandwiched her.

They gave her warmth and comfort. They touched her with bodies and hands. And also with their care.

Something she'd not had since her mother had died many years before. Touch hadn't been something done a lot in their palace once her mom had died. Once her father had died, she'd been lucky to even have someone to talk to. Touching had never been offered by anyone.

She'd forgotten how good it felt to have someone to stroke and caress her back. To have someone's attention.

"Come on. Let's get this stone out." Jax moved forward, chiseling out the rock.

"Yep." Tam picked up another chisel and attacked the other side.

Their loss of touch rattled her so her hands shook a little as she reached forward to make six hands chipping away. "This isn't my stone. Hasn't even started to glow."

"I know." Tam clumsily clipped away a sizeable amount of rock, which fell to the ground in front of him.

"Yeah. We'll get this one out and then find the next one."

They didn't give her false optimism about the next one being hers. But their words filled her with hope. They wouldn't let her give up. They'd keep her trying until she located her stone.

The stone shifted out. She put down her tools and worked it out with her hands. After a little rocking, the stone slipped free.

No glow.

Even knowing that beforehand, she closed her eyes briefly.

Someone poked her. "Kiann."

She opened them, trying to let the tension leave her as she set down the newest unclaimed heartstone. It would be someone else's heart.

And that's when she saw it.

A glow from the rock in front of her.

* * *

Jax scrambled, trying to edge out the rock from the pocket that held tightly to the bottom.

The glowing rock.

Kiann had tried to hide her excitement, but he could see elation bubbling the closer he came to getting the stone out. She stood with Tam behind him, watching him trying to get the heartstone from the place it had been enshrined for centuries. He'd never seen one glow this early in the find.

He tried to hurry the excavation with shaking fingers, wanting her face to continue to grow in happiness and joy. The light in her dark eyes made his stomach tie up in knots. Made him want to see more. He wanted to make her happy. Not a sensation he experienced with anyone but Tam.

This was probably her heartstone. The thing she'd been searching for, and they'd been dispatched to help her find.

Then he and Tam could go home and resume their perfectly ordered lives.

Somehow, that didn't thrill him as much as it should. Their leaving her would mean no more seeing the light in her eyes. No more touching her body.

He shrugged off those thoughts. She was a stranger, nothing more.

Slowly, he slipped the heartstone free of the rock.

Kiann's foot tapped impatiently on the floor.

He took the stone in his hands and pushed to his feet using only his leg muscles. The closer it came to Kiann, the brighter the glow.

A single tear streamed down her cheek.

He wanted to wipe the tear away. Do many things for her. At least these weren't tears of unhappiness, but something about them still captured his heart. She deserved laughter and not tears. "Here you go." He reached out the hand where the stone rested in offering to her.

Her hands shook as she reached for the heartstone. "Oh, my Goddess, it is mine." Her body shivered as though she couldn't believe what she saw. "It's my heartstone." She stopped as she almost reached his hand, drawing back for a second as though she expected the stone to disappear.

Jax closed the distance so that her fingers touched the heartstone.

"Shout it from the rafters." Tam laughed from beside her. "Shout it out." When Kiann didn't take the stone, though she touched it, he pushed her arm. "Pick your heartstone up."

She managed to curl her fingers around the small stone. "I can't believe I found my heart." Her hand clasped the heartstone loosely as she held it up to look. She held it in one hand up to her face, spellbound by the glow. "I can't believe..."

A hand reached over and grabbed the stone from out of her reach. "Give me that." Dred let out a big snarl. He'd approached without them noticing, and he snatched the stone up, even as his face contorted into something mad.

Kiann tried to grab the stone back, but he shoved her away. "Give that back. It's my heartstone." The fear in her voice sounded palpable.

"What are you doing, dammit?" Tam took a defensive stance, pushing Kiann back behind him as though he expected Dred to hit her. Dred looked as if he might consider doing that.

The man looked down at the still-glowing stone. "It's not fair." He clenched his fists around the stone. "It's not fucking fair."

"I don't give a good damn. You give that stone back." Tam raised his voice to the fullest Jax had ever heard him speak, which led to a shouting match.

Tam acted quickly to use words and not his power.

A second into the confrontation, Jax realized no words were adequate to reason with the man. He wouldn't give up. He was beyond reason. Jax would have no alternative but brute force, and he wouldn't dick around with talking. Not his usual method, but he'd do what needed to be done to get the stone back. He'd only get one shot at getting Kiann her heartstone back. Best to form a plan of attack.

"Life's not fair." Jax spoke quietly even as he approached the man, sizing up any weaknesses. "It's never been fair. You need to give that stone back."

"I'm older than she is." The man palmed his useless cock through his pants with his free hand. "I've been looking longer. I can't even have a fucking erection, much less fuck someone. I should've found my stone first." He released his cock as though done displaying that it couldn't work. "It's mine. Mine, I tell you."

Even more evidence that the stone didn't belong to him. As soon as the heartstone chose a man, erections could happen. Jax shrugged even as Tam fussed again. "It's not Kiann's fault. She didn't do anything to you."

Jax moved even closer, assessing how the plan would work. "Not my problem." He held up a hand, causing Tam to stop talking. The man didn't hear anything that Tam said. Might as well not waste the breath.

"No. It's not fair," the man sneered, his lips twisting upward, making him look ghoulish.

"Don't care." Jax grasped the man's meaty paw in his, squeezing the hand before Dred could react. "Do care about this. Release the heartstone." He'd get the stone back for Kiann. The idiot wouldn't be hard for him to subdue. "Kiann, come get your stone from Dred. Tam, help me hold him."

"Let me go." The man tried to twist away, but Jax kept his hand wrapped around Dred's. He wouldn't let go. Wouldn't lose this stone for Kiann.

"Give me the stone." Jax swerved with him as the man did wiggle maneuvers to get free. "Now."

Kiann moved forward to try to unwrap Dred's fingers.

Tam helped hold Dred steady with Jax.

"No. It's not fair. This stone needs to be mine." The man struggled even as they took him to the ground.

Kiann managed to snag the stone from the man's fingers. She darted back away a few steps. Again, she looked at the stone as if she couldn't believe what she'd uncovered.

Had Jax looked that way when he'd finally acquired his stone? Probably.

Her look made this struggle worth any amount of trouble.

"Nooooooo. This stone is mine. It shouldn't be yours."

A baby-faced man approached them with quick paces. He looked serious. "Is there a problem here?" He looked to be an Etruscan. Did that make him who Jax thought? Probably. His timing couldn't be better. If only Jax could have gotten in one punch before this intervention.

Kiann talked at the same time that Dred did. "He took my stone." She held her heartstone to her chest as though she'd never let go again. She hadn't even had time to put the stone on a chain before Dred had tried to steal her heart.

Tam released Dred and kept himself between Kiann and Dred.

Curse him. Jax released the man's arm. If only he could have taken him to the ground in pain, even with a man that Jax suspected was Amory standing there. But the action wouldn't look good. Besides, she had the stone back. That was enough.

Jax took a deep breath and released the man's hand. This wasn't his way to fight, with violence and anger. He straightened his back, folding his arms behind him, and cleared his mind of all his rage. Tam was supposed to be the high-strung one, not him.

"She took my stone." Dred made a grab for the stone, despite Tam being between Dred and Kiann.

She held the heartstone tightly to her.

Jax kept his wary gaze on the crazed man as he joined Tam in front of Kiann.

The man folded his arms about his chest, looking more authoritative than Jax would have expected with such a youthful-looking face. Yeah, this must be Amory. Mate of Bren and Zelda. What good timing. "You both are claiming that stone as your own?"

"Kiann found it first. It glowed for her as soon as the stone came out of the rock. She's the owner. See how the stone glows for her." Tam pointed a finger. "He tried to steal it. Took it right out of her hands."

"It's mine, I tell you!" Dred roared. He tried to get past Tam and Jax.

Amory pulled out a phaser. "Stop. Now."

Dred didn't look happy, but he paused in his snatching. "Who are you to come over here?"

"I'm Amory. We met when you arrived." Jax had been right as to the man's identity. The man now looked at him for confirmation of what Kiann and Tam had told him about Dred. "Did he steal her heartstone from her? It glowed for her first?"

Jax nodded. "He did." He bowed his head. "I swear it upon my life."

Natives' words were considered their bond.

Amory would understand that better than most, being Etruscan. "I should have known." Amory sighed. "You've been causing all kinds of problems, Dred. I think we need to talk. With Bren and Zelda, too." He motioned the man away. "I'm sorry about this. This wasn't his first incident, but it will be his last one. Go help yourself to a free drink at the bar. Tell Clyde I sent you." Amory walked away with Dred screaming at him as he pushed him along beside him.

A litany of "It's not fair" moved out of the cavern.

Kiann ran a hand through her hair. "Thank you both. I don't know what I would have done had he done that, and you weren't here."

Warmth moved up Jax at her praise. *Voila.* The reason for them helping her with her heartstone had been revealed. They'd been there to prevent Dred from doing something stupid, like destroying Kiann's stone. The resolution had been simple as that.

He shot a triumphant grin at Tam as warmth spread across his chest. Tam should listen to him more often. Now, they could get off this infernal rock and go back home. Even though that meant leaving Kiann behind, which bothered him more than it should.

Tam looked thunderstruck. Why should he? Wasn't like they hadn't suspected what they'd come here for.

"Glad we could help you. Looks as if our job…"

Tam interrupted. "Look down."

"Huh?" Jax frowned but looked down at his chest where Tam's gaze rested. His stone burned a vibrant, choppy red. Not unusual. He looked up to ask why this was important. The light burst in time with Tam's as it always did. The glowing hadn't been a reason to interrupt them.

His gaze circled around to find Kiann looking as bothered as Tam did. What was wrong with her? "What the…?" He broke off as he noticed something.

Kiann's heartstone burned in time with both of their stones. A matching crimson bangle lit up her hands. Pulsation flickered in perfect rhythm with theirs.

Jax's arms dropped by his sides.

Kiann was their third mate.

Chapter Five

Tam looked back and forth from Jax's stone to Kiann's. They still glowed, pulsing in time to each other which meant they matched his.

Their mate.

She stood before them. Not anything he'd ever expected to find, especially here of all places. Settler's Mine would forever hold a place in his heart. First, he'd located his stone, now he'd located his second mate.

Kiann's face paled. "To be clear—making sure I understand—this means we're mated, doesn't it?" Her eyes grew wide, exposing more white than he'd seen in her gaze before. Her dark eyes revealed nothing. But her body posture and face told him of her nervousness. Of the shock at finding her mates standing before her right after she'd discovered her heartstone. She had a lot to adjust to, getting two mates at once.

They all did.

"No. This can't be." Jax's hand came up to finger his stone. "There has got to be a mistake."

"Nope. No mistake." Tam rubbed his chin. "Yep, this means you're our third mate." His chest swelled to the point breathing was difficult. He'd never expected to find one mate, much less two. This was overwhelming. Already the desire at finding his mate worked on him. His cock strained against his leather pants, wanting to claim her. He wanted both of his mates to seal the deal between them. That might take a while, though. They had a lot to work out first.

He looked at Kiann. He had no idea how to deal with a woman. He'd have to learn quickly. He wouldn't lose her. Jax would have to educate himself as well. Only this would be hard for Jax to accept. He looked at Jax as he started in. *Please don't say anything to hurt her.*

Jax felt uncomfortable around women, and he didn't deal well with change. This whole situation would make him angry. Tam would have to work to smooth things over with both his mates. Probably for a long time. He had his work cut out for him. For now, he'd work to keep Kiann from walking away, and Jax from alienating her.

"No. You and I are mated. She's something else." Jax placed his arms over his chest, stubbornly. He closed himself off from this possibility. Tam wanted to pry open his arms and his mind. He rubbed his chin as Jax tightened his stance. "If she'd been our true mate, then our stones never would have glowed first to each other's."

With each word, Kiann's face fell a little.

Damn him for his stance of logic. Jax had a point now as he had earlier. The reason why they'd never expected a woman to come into their relationship. "They are all glowing *now*. That's what counts." Tam stared into Jax's disbelieving face, trying to tell him not to say anything more. He didn't want to see Kiann hurt and wanted to comfort Jax. The two warring emotions tore at him. He couldn't breathe as his chest constricted, then his breathing leveled out.

He would handle this situation. Make them both see.

"No. Our stones glowed to each other's. It can't be..."

"Logical?" Tam took a step toward his lover. He had to bring him around. What was the best way to do that? "Not everything in life is, Jax. You know that." An Ebolian and a Native mated were illogical enough for most, not to mention they'd been two males together first. Now they'd have a third irrationality to discuss with those who asked them questions. Logic had no place in mating. Only he couldn't say that to Jax outright. The words would only make him angrier, and Tam had to cool that anger down, not speed his rage up.

"No."

"Yep."

Kiann remained silent through their entire exchange. She took a step toward the exit. She planned to slink away from this confrontation.

Though he didn't blame her, Tam wouldn't let her leave them. Not before finding out how to find her again and asking her to wait for them. He pointed to her and motioned her back to them. "No. Don't you go anywhere." They needed to hash this out. Jax would have no choice but to eventually accept her as his third mate, and for all his bluster, he knew that. Fate didn't go around asking who you wanted as a mate. Nor did it particularly care when the situation wasn't easy to work out. A favorite saying among all Quatarians was that the Fates had a sense of humor. This mating proved that saying. To put them with a woman had seemed laughable. Until they'd met Kiann.

"I think it would be better if I left." She didn't move back toward them but stayed where she stood. Her face pinched and still remained pale.

"No. No, it wouldn't. He's…" How could Tam reassure her? With Jax spouting off and looking murderous? Not to mention anything he said, though true, would wound Jax. He said nothing else.

"Leave." Jax's voice rose to crack apart as he glowered. "Leave us, please. We need to talk. Tam and I."

Wincing at Jax's words, Tam surveyed the cavern. No privacy. They'd already acquired an audience. Maybe Kiann had a point for them all. They needed to get out of here and discuss what had happened. Maybe if he could get Jax alone, he could work out what went on in Jax's head. "I think we all should go somewhere more private."

Jax moved to Tam's side. "Our quarters?"

Tam nodded. That would give them privacy to talk and maybe even cement themselves as mates.

Kiann walked away again.

"Kiann."

Jax glared at him as though he'd spoken to a devil.

Tam's mouth closed together tightly. Jax would have to learn to deal with this. Tam would make him see reason about the small woman they'd been mated to. Jax had to come around, otherwise where would that leave Tam? "What are your quarter numbers?"

"Why do you care?" Her voice sounded defeated. As though she'd been rejected already.

"Because you're our mate. That's what led me here. Why I had visions pertaining to you. We have that connection." The mating explained so much. Jax should be able to see the logic in the situation, but for once Jax acted on his emotions and didn't think.

Tam's jaw set. He'd make Jax see the logic and get past all the emotions he had. He'd make Kiann stay with them until Jax dealt with her coming into their lives. He had no other choice. It wasn't every day that one came across their third mate.

"Give me your quarter numbers. Jax and I do need to talk alone for a few minutes. But after that, we need to talk to you."

Jax muttered something under his breath.

Tam ignored him, instead imploring Kiann with his expression to please listen to him and also to give Jax some time to adjust to this new development.

"You won't come." She swallowed deeply, looking as if the action calmed her. "It's okay, Tam. I understand."

"We will come." Tam reached out to touch his stone and show it to her. "We're mates. No matter what we have to sort out. Give me a few minutes with him." He tapped his chin, looking into eyes so big, they seemed endless. "Please."

She nodded, even though she didn't look thrilled about the situation. "I'm in B51. My room's on the left B corridor."

This wasn't working out the way Tam had thought finding his third mate would. He'd expected happy celebrations, not this arguing and unease from both his mates. The course of mates never ran smooth. They'd find a way to all be mates. He'd see to that. "I…we can find you."

She licked her lips, looking as though she was about to cry. "Okay." Her voice sounded husky, sounding as though she fought back tears.

Tam went over to her and pulled her fully against him, ignoring any reaction from Jax. She smelled heavenly. Something spicy and flowery. Like an aurora lily from Ebolia. The flower suited her.

He stroked a hand along her back. Desire coursed through him as his cock became even harder. He stiffened with the force of his emotions. With the assault of his senses. He wanted to toss her down on the floor and have his way with her. Not a good thing with an audience. And with Jax in an uproar, his desire would have to wait. But like the lily, she'd be worth waiting for.

His mind and heart had converged to say one simple word as he held her: "Mine." She belonged to him, and his psyche knew it. No wonder his desire to come to Settler's Mine had been impossible to ignore.

Her stomach brushed his erection. She jerked back as though the touch had bitten her. "I'd better go."

He'd shown where his mind stayed. A good thing for her to know. Such an innocent to react as she had. Had her first desires been for him? There was a good chance of that as she'd just found her stone. "We'll see you later. In an hour at most." He watched her walk away, hips sashaying along. She was a woman who'd never know how seductive she could be.

How beautiful. Tam would delight in showing her every day how she made him feel.

Jax grabbed his arm. "Come on."

Once Jax came around.

He followed Jax back to their quarters, not even attempting to talk in the crowded corridors. His mind went to Kiann and getting back to her. He would sort Jax out. Tam knew him inside and out. He'd work to ease the emotional upheaval. Then, they'd work on claiming their mate.

They walked inside their quarters, and Jax let go of his hand as they went through the door.

Jax rushed to their bags and tossed them on the bed. He grabbed the little they'd unpacked and shoved things into the bags.

"What are you doing?"

"Packing. Time to go home." Jax's voice sounded clipped. Distant. "Get your stuff together." He'd shut down his emotions. Shut down himself in an attempt to quell his reaction to this situation and the stress, which Tam couldn't allow.

Tam pushed down his irritation at being ordered around. "We need to talk about Kiann."

"There's nothing to talk about."

"She's our mate, Jax." *I won't let you run from this.* He resisted the urge to tackle his mate and hold him down until he admitted the truth. Tam couldn't allow himself to get frustrated. That would only lead to more arguing.

"Nothing to talk about." Jax continued to busily put things into their bags. He wasn't even packing his usual orderly way.

Tam approached him from behind, dropping a hand on Jax's shoulder. Jax stiffened and then relaxed, but didn't turn to face him, letting Tam talk to his rigid back. "There is. She's our mate."

At that, Jax did turn around. His face withered and dropped with anger. "No. There's been a mistake." He tossed another item in the bag, while not even looking behind him to see he'd missed. "You know as well as I do, the Union Alliance doesn't support male mated pairs. They engineered this somehow. Union Alliance did it. I refuse to accept this…"

Tam cocked his head to the side, looking in his mate's eyes. "That sounds about as likely as one of Dred's theories that we overheard while walking up to Kiann. Why are you running from this? What has you scared?" The direct approach. He didn't have time to be coy.

"I'm not scared." Jax bit out the words from clenched teeth. "It's a mistake."

"Something has you in its grip. If not fear, then what? You're not acting logically." Tam held up his hand to stop the protests. "You aren't. Her stone glowed with *ours*. The mating would explain why I had the visions to come here." He placed his hand on Jax's shoulder again, squeezing it tightly. "She mentioned red. Our stones glow red."

"It cannot be."

"The mating feels right inside of me. As it did with you. You can't tell me this doesn't feel the same to you in some way."

Jax didn't deny his feelings. Simply crimped his lips together, which told Tam more than if he'd spoke. "Why? Why won't you accept this?" Tam couldn't accept he might lose both his mates if this did go sour. He wouldn't.

Jax moved away. He walked to the dresser with his back toward Tam again. "Because I've never been with a woman. Never thought about a woman. How did this happen? We were happy, you and I together. The two of us."

Tam stood back a minute digesting what Jax had said, then approached him. Jax wouldn't look at him. He wrapped his arms around Jax's waist in complete acceptance of the man, if not his actions. Jax stayed rigid.

For Jax to lie about being with a woman earlier was a huge reaction. Jax didn't lie often. Tam didn't understand everything going on within Jax, but he thought he understood enough. Either way, he had to influence Jax's stance to see Kiann as their mate. "I've been with only men. And only you have been...well, satisfying. But I know she turns you on. Admit it."

Jax's voice came out low and bothered, making Tam strain to hear him. "Fine. She does."

"Does what?"

"She turns me on."

The hard-won declaration made the blood rush through Tam's veins. Somehow knowing that Kiann turned Jax on as much as she did him, sent Tam's arousal spiraling. "Has a woman ever turned you on before? Especially this much?"

"No. A woman's never turned me on before at all."

Tam kissed Jax's forehead softly. "Me, either. It's because we hadn't met our mate before. No man had turned me on as much as you did before I met you."

"She's going to change everything."

The reason for the outburst. Jax, like many of his race, didn't deal well with change. With the glowing of that stone, everything had changed. "Yep. Yep, she will." Tam wouldn't lie to him. "And we'll deal with the changes, perlin, the way we have with everything since we met: together."

Jax turned suddenly and pulled Tam into his body. His lips sought Tam's with a ferocity. A wildness that made Tam's knees weak. The kisses left him breathless and made his body burn with untapped arousal.

Jax kissed Tam heavily, grinding his pelvis against him. His tongue dominated Tam's, pilfering in every crevice he could find.

Tam moaned, enjoying the rush of all these sensations in his body. Jax had kissed him before, but this was different. Jax didn't usually have this urgency. A need that Jax often didn't let come to the surface. Tam rubbed against him, giving as much back into the kiss as Jax would let him.

Jax pulled away with a moan. His hand went down to yank on Tam's pants. Violently. He popped a button. He pulled them down around Tam's ankles, leaving his butt exposed. The chill of the air caught him off guard. He shivered with that and with the wildness that Jax rarely displayed coming out.

Jax pushed him around to bend him over the nightstand, not even bothering to take off Tam's shirt. He shoved forward, pushing his hard cock against Tam's butt and the hole in the center. He rubbed against him, pressing in enough to be pressure.

Enough to be pleasure. Enough to tell Tam what would come in the next few minutes.

Tam strained forward, aching with need and want. Needing to release. His cock couldn't get any harder. His balls drew up close to his body.

Kiann's face swam in his vision.

One side for him and one for Jax. When they were all ready.

He moaned at what Jax did to him and his own thoughts flittering over his second mate.

Goddess, he was ready now. He'd explode with the arousal if sating didn't happen soon, if Jax didn't take him now. "Hurry."

Jax's hand reached down into the drawer beneath Tam's body. He grabbed a bottle of lube and next thing Tam realized, his hole was coated in the slick liquid. Jax pulled back to part the sides to ensure a good coating of the lube.

Even this out of control, Jax would never do anything to hurt him. He'd take care of his lover's needs before his own. Tam went a spiral further in his desire. Not anything he'd thought possible.

Jax surged against him in a powerful thrust, entering his lubed-up hole without preamble. The move propelled his cock deep inside of Tam.

Tam gasped at being breached. The position exposed him, bent over as he was, while his lover controlled everything. He shuddered in his delight and moved his butt backward as much as he could to encourage Jax to do more.

Jax pulled back, only to dip in even farther inside of him. He grabbed the sides of Tam's hips, holding him down for the penetration.

Tam saw stars bounce back and forth before his vision. The pleasure point that Jax hit next with an even deeper thrust took Tam to the moon and back. His cock spurted come, giving in to the intense pressure to release. Tam's whole body quaked with the force of his release as sweat coated him.

Jax shoved into him again and again, taking him in the manner that Tam preferred. Jax's pace was fast and furious, not measured and gentle like usual, which thrilled Tam to no end.

All of Tam's nerve endings crinkled in response. This was heaven. He'd never seen Jax lose control so fully. He intended to reap all the benefits of the event.

Jax stiffened, calling out Tam's name as his orgasm rocked him down. He pumped for what seemed to be hours, filling Tam full of his come. Several more aftershocks rocked him before he finally stilled the pumping action of his hips.

Breathing heavily, he pulled away from Tam. As Tam turned to face him, Jax puffed out a deep breath. He looked embarrassed by the quick fuck they'd had. His eyes radiated his concern. They didn't do quick sex this way often. For the second time, Jax had had to take him, too, as opposed to only sexual play.

Tam moved to the bed and patted the mattress to invite Jax to lie beside him. Jax spread out, entwining his limbs with Tam's. Tam tried to get his breathing under control.

He moved forward to press a light kiss on Jax's lips. Jax kissed him back sweetly. "I like it when you lose control." He licked his lips, moving in even closer. This had been different. He'd never seen Jax lose control, and now he had, twice in the short time since they'd arrived at Settler's Mine.

No, that wasn't entirely true. The loss of control had been since they'd first met Kiann. "You lost control the first time right after we met Kiann. As you never had before. Now you did that again."

Jax pulled away.

Tam studied him as Jax returned the look with seriousness. He'd gone too far too fast, but he needed to get things in the open.

"Tam..."

"It's the truth, isn't it? More than you want to admit. Didn't you wonder what sex will be like with her? Between us all, even as you took me?" He stroked along Jax's arm. "I know I did. I wondered how tight she'll be. How loving. I thought about her, Jax. The same way you did."

"I..." Jax hesitated, then relented. "Yeah, I thought about her." An admission that spoke volumes. He partially sat up. "She doesn't have to be our mate, though, because of thoughts. What if I'm right? What if the Union Alliance..."

Tam pushed a finger against Jax's lips to shush him. "They didn't. This was Fate acting on us." He reached out a hand to stroke along Jax's strong jawline. Such a strong, proud man. One who needed to accept the truth. "I need you to accept Kiann into our lives."

"Why?" Jax pulled his head away from Tam's touch. He looked as if he wanted to deny everything all over again. Tam's progress dropped out from the cosmos.

Tam made sure to look Jax directly in the eyes. "I need you to accept this because I want her. If you won't take her as a mate for yourself, do it for me." He rushed through the words. "I want you both to be my mates." Tam stood to lose much if they didn't accept their status.

"What if I can't?"

"I don't know." Tam sat up. "All I know is that I need and want you both." He slid from the bed. "Let's go talk to her before she runs from us." They'd been long enough without going to her.

"I…I'm not ready to claim her."

The first act of sex sealed the bond between the mates. Lust came first, and then emotional bonding. The first sex act between mates was a special thing among most races. "I know that. I'm not asking for that yet. I will. Right now, let's spend some time with her. See where it leads."

"Fine." Jax got up from the bed and dressed.

Not much, but it was a start. And the best Tam could hope for right now.

* * *

Kiann's head pounded as she sat on her bed, staring at the walls of her small quarters. Her legs were restless and kept shifting around. She wanted to pace her small room the way a caged animal did, not that pacing would do her any good; so she sat. Wanted to be anywhere but there. Yet, she'd told her mates to find her there, so she couldn't leave yet.

Not that they'd show up.

Her hand came up absently to clutch at the new stone around her neck. She'd placed the stone on the chain her mother had given her long ago.

Her heartstone.

The missing piece of her heart.

She closed her eyes. The cool smoothness of the stone felt slippery under her fingertips. She'd stumbled onto what she'd been lacking in her life up until now.

Desire.

The heartstone had brought with it the ability to be turned on. Brushing against Jax and Tam's bodies had set her aquiver, made her heart flutter on many levels. It had been intense enough to take her breath away.

Her nether regions swelled. Pulsed. Got wet. Ached. Even her breasts had grown heavier.

She'd had some sex education. She'd known what was supposed to happen when arousal could be reality, but it was much different than what she'd been prepared for. She hadn't suspected how delicious, how scrumptious every part of her would grow. Every part of her body seemed to have a reaction.

"What am I supposed to do with two men?" she asked the empty room, which gave her nothing in answer.

Oh, that's right. Fuck them.

She shivered as she pulled her wayward legs up under her. Whether in arousal or fear, she couldn't tell.

The two of them. In bed. Sweaty bodies. Aroused cocks. Mouths that tantalized and teased. Hands that caressed and pinched.

And her in between the two different dominant males.

Not that they wanted her for anything sex-wise, much less being a mate to her. They'd dismissed her. Walked away.

Even her mates didn't want her.

"To hell with the Fates."

Whenever she'd daydreamed about her mates, she'd never pictured a scenario that involved them not wanting her.

A soft sigh broke from her lips. Her eyes teared.

No, she'd have none of that. She rubbed at her eyes forcefully.

Why was she sitting here feeling sorry for herself and being miserable? She unfolded her legs. After all, she had…to do what? What pressing thing did she have to accomplish? Nothing had been on her agenda but finding her stone.

She'd done that.

Now that she had her stone, she could…

What? What could she do? Go home?

Her hand flew to her mouth.

What the hell was she going to do now?

Planning for after she'd located her heartstone hadn't been on her mind. A part of her hadn't truly believed she'd find it before Marses caught up to her, but here she was, heartstone in hand and no Marses breathing down her neck.

Now that she had acquired her stone, Marses wouldn't be happy.

This heartstone made her an even bigger threat to him.

Her gaze darted around the room. How quickly could she pack up? Running might be in her best interest. She could leave the mine and leave her mates behind.

She closed her eyes. *Her mates.*

A rush of longing rolled through her that things could be different, that they'd accepted her without question.

However, finding her mates made her the biggest threat Marses had ever faced. He always faced down his threats with one constant.

Force.

Her eyes flew open. "He's going to kill me."

When he discovered she'd found her heartstone and her mates, she'd be in danger. The only way to take away the threat was to take her out.

Holy shit, her mates would face the same danger. Because the only way to eliminate her as a threat was to take them all out.

* * *

Tam stopped outside the door. His heart accelerated from sensing his second mate on the other side.

Jax almost ran into him.

Their bodies touching had the usual effect on Tam's libido. A skyrocket. He hissed as Jax didn't pull away, but instead kept pressing against him. "Stop that."

"You want me to stop?"

The only reason Jax hadn't pulled away was because there was no one around, and he wanted to stake claims on Tam before they faced Kiann, but even that made Tam want it to continue. "No. Yep. I don't…"

Kiann yanked the door open.

They both stared as Kiann, who looked even paler than before, ranted at them. "Get in here." She motioned for them to come into her room.

Tam stepped through first with Jax close on his heels.

After scanning the corridor, Kiann slammed the door behind them with a resounding bang.

Her room had even less space than theirs did. Bed was smaller. More compact. The furniture wasn't as nice.

Her stuff had been packed into bags that she had on the beds. She planned to leave. To leave them behind.

"Not just no, but hell no." Tam swung back around to face her. He had to gape again at her face.

He'd been right. She did look paler than she had when he'd seen her last. Her face was pinched. Eyes wide and frantic.

Something had happened. His concern shifted from her leaving them to her welfare. "What's wrong? What's happened?" Something had changed for her since she'd been in their company last.

Jax took up a defensive stance with his arms open and ready. He didn't say anything, but his look had shifted to one of concern as well. He saw what Tam did. He might claim to be removed from her and not to care, but his emotions shone through in his eyes and his actions.

"Okay. Look. I don't know of any other way to say this." She swallowed convulsively. "You two are now in danger."

They looked at each other before glancing back at her.

"In danger? From what?" Tam frowned. How could they be in danger from being mated to her? He couldn't see that happening.

Her nose crinkled adorably even though worry caused the wrinkle. "It's a long story. We may not have much time. I don't know where Marses is or how to check without alerting him where I am."

Marses. A familiar name. Where did he know that name from? Tam couldn't decipher where he'd heard it before. He scratched his head, trying to remember. From the shiver in her voice, he was someone she feared. And that she feared someone made him want to act like a jungle cat and attack.

"Why would we be in danger?" Jax positioned himself to be looking at the door and to be between the door and them. The first thing he'd do in a time of danger or threat. No matter what he believed about this mating or her, Jax took her seriously. He'd protect her, too.

At least that moved them a step forward.

"Because you're mated to me."

Tam couldn't help a chuckle. "How in the galaxy could being mated to you cause us any danger?" Jax and he had always been able to handle themselves in any situation. Surely this fragile creature couldn't cause them any danger.

"You take this seriously." She shook her finger at him, reminding him of a schoolteacher he'd once had. She was tiny to be ordering him around. "I'm not kidding around."

"He'll take you seriously, but Tam has a good question. I fail to see how being your mates could put us at risk."

"You don't know much about me." Her tone lowered.

Tam's body chilled. Another good point. They knew next to nothing about her and her of them. The name still niggled at him that she'd mentioned, but he couldn't place why. "Why don't you tell us? Share who you are and why this is a problem."

She frowned and paced by the bed. "We have to get out of here soon. I'm telling you, he's coming. I have no idea how far behind me he is. Finding me, he'd be mad. Me and a heartstone, he'd be angry. Me and mates, he's going to hit the ever loving roof."

"This man didn't want you to find your heartstone?" Jax watched her walk back and forth, his head moving with her. He remained on alert, keeping his eye on the door, too.

She snorted. "No, he didn't. That's what I'm trying to tell you. He's kept me from finding mine for years."

Which was criminal. To keep a person from their heartstone was a heartless thing to do. The missing stone made sex impossible. Deep feelings impossible. Family beyond one's birth impossible. Being a full person was hard to do when one didn't have the missing piece of yourself.

"Why would he do such a thing?" Jax searched for the logic in what would cause someone to do that to someone else. His face also registered his anger. An anger that Tam shared.

"Yep, why?" Better be a damn good reason. Or else when Tam did meet up with this Marses, whoever he was, he would teach him a damn thing or two about etiquette and politeness.

She glanced at the door even as she continued to pace back and forth. She remained full of nervous energy.

Tam couldn't help but notice her breasts doing a bounce, the sway of her hips, and her proximity to the bed. He shifted his weight, his cock lengthening.

He licked his lips as he watched her walk.

Jax looked captivated as well.

Despite the situation, the lust had activated in them both and wanted its satisfaction. No matter what the cause of her agitation.

Kiann looked at them both with a puzzled look on her face. "What are you two thinking about?"

Tam grinned, trying to look innocent, but probably not succeeding based on her look. "Nothing. Nothing at all." He resumed his serious face. "Go on."

Jax echoed him. "Nothing. Go on."

Her eyes remained wary. "Uh-huh. Whatever it was, you both had the exact same expression." She stopped walking. Pinioned them with her gaze as if trying to get them to admit what had been on their minds.

Both of them ignored her, giving away nothing they'd been thinking about.

Jax waved a hand. "Tell us about this danger." His face resumed his seriousness, as well. "Tell us more about the man who kept you from your heartstone. The whys and hows, so we'll understand the risk."

Tam wanted to add the words "bastard" and "asshole" behind Jax's words, but refrained from speaking aloud. He still couldn't figure out how being mated to her could be dangerous.

"He's my stepbrother. My dad was mated to my mom. They had me. Then, she died. He found another mate, a woman. She'd adopted two children before she met him."

She paused as if letting those relationships sink in.

Jax whistled. "That's rare. To meet a mate after one mate dies."

She nodded. "The odds of it happening are low. But my dad…" A wistful smile took over her face. "He was happy. For a while. I was, too, with my new siblings and mother. One of the other children, my stepsister, died of disease."

Sad that Union Alliance hadn't worked harder to eradicate diseases on the outpost Ebolia and others. Instead, they'd been fighting a never-ending war.

"Sorry to hear that." Tam wanted to ease her pain. He moved closer.

Jax moved closer as if he wanted to do the same. "Your father isn't still alive, either, is he?"

She shook her head. Her face cracked as though she might cry, but she caught herself at the last second. "He and his wife were killed in a shuttle accident."

"That left you and the other child?" Jax leaned back against her dresser, still keeping watch on the door.

"Yes. Marses is my other stepsibling. He's mated and…" She hesitated before plunging ahead. "…a strong man. Everyone respects him. He's well-known. A leader." She didn't sound enthused, more like she was reporting facts and nothing more.

Not if they'd known what he'd done to Kiann. If anyone suspected what Marses the mated had done to Kiann, he wouldn't be well regarded. He'd become a pariah. Yep, Marses would become Marses, the Pariah. That would be a good thing for him, to have to pay for what he'd done to Kiann. The catch in her voice told of the bad happenings between the two, which in turn brought out Tam's protectiveness against Marses, the Pariah…

Tam froze as the name clicked. His mind went into a flurry of activity. Bouncing back and forth between the small amounts he knew of Ebolian politics versus the chances of this happening.

"Wait a minute. Marses?" Did his eyes ask more questions than his lips could form coherently? "That's the name of your stepbrother? The one who's after you? Who kept you from your heartstone?" Marses was a common name. There could be more than one. Her Marses didn't have to be the Marses that he was thinking of.

She nodded. Her face fell as though she knew what he'd figured out.

"Surely you aren't talking about Marses the Royal?"

Biting her lip, she moved her head up and down again. She tried to look detached, but mostly she looked worried. "Yes. Yes, I would be."

Tam's stomach sunk low to his knees as he tried to remember everything he could from what he'd followed of his country.

"Who's Marses the Royal?" Jax looked impatient. Probably because they knew something he didn't.

Kiann didn't answer, so Tam supplied, "The ruler of Ebolia."

Chapter Six

Kiann rubbed a hand through her hair. Weariness dragged on her shoulders, pulling her down into the murk. There was still much to do before she could rest. Running away, for instance.

"He's not of royal blood." Jax still looked confused by what he was being told. "If I'm following all this. Marses is your stepbrother? Your father was the king of Ebolia? So how can he rule?"

"Yes. You've got it right." She puffed out a brief swoosh of air. "Technically, I'm the one with royal blood, who is supposed to rule. I'm tied to the blood that dates back a couple hundred years." Had she been schooled in ruling, she probably could have named the exact moment her family had taken power. But she hadn't been. Ebolian royalty started their training in their teenage years. They only had small lessons in childhood. By that time, her father had been dead, and Marses had kept her a prisoner in a wing of the palace. A tiny swell of anger at what she'd been denied pulsed up. She pushed the emotion down. It didn't help anything. "But he has the power. He took over when Dad died and has kept the throne." He'd ruled with an iron hand. Not a bad ruler. Not by any means. But now, he had no desire to give up his crown to her, either, no matter that she'd come of age.

"Why didn't you take the crown when your father passed?" Tam put his hands in his pockets. He looked as though he was trying to digest all this. Even with mixed blood, he knew who Marses was and what this meant, which was not good things for them.

"I was only nine. Marses is a lot older than I am. At first, he was supposed to rule until I could take over, either because of age or having attained my heartstone. But he's never stepped down. And..." Her hand came up to clutch at her stone. "As long as I didn't have my heartstone, I wasn't exactly a threat. Ebolians want a ruler who can give them a future line."

"Which you couldn't."

"Until now. He's kept me in the shadows. I doubt most remember he isn't the true ruler and is not of the line." She'd been overlooked and forgotten about. Marses had seen to that. She'd not attended any royal celebration or functions since her father passed. Kept in seclusion and away from the limelight, she'd gotten used to being in the background.

"You came to find your heartstone and get your kingdom back." Jax looked thoughtful, as though he mulled over all the facts.

She let loose a small laugh. "I came for my heartstone. I was tired of living with muted feelings. Of not knowing what I could have. I escaped. It wasn't about ruling Ebolia. It was for me." She'd needed to find herself. Warmth filled her as she cupped her heartstone. With the discovery of this stone, she'd found the completion of a circle within herself.

"But now, you can take your rightful place on the throne."

Jax pointed out the obvious, but her place had never been in her thoughts. "It wasn't the first thing on my mind." Hard for most to believe, but ruling hadn't been her primary motive for doing what she had. She'd wanted a life apart from what Marses planned for her. He'd stolen much of her destiny.

Her heart throbbed. She'd only considered being free, but Jax was right. She could take her rightful place. Continue her family's legacy. Only surviving interested her more at the moment. "Marses won't see my actions as for myself, but as coveting the throne. He doesn't want to give up his power." Which led to them all being in grave danger.

"He'll think you're trying to take over." Tam shifted his weight. "No matter what your true intent."

"Tam's right. He'll think that you'll depose him."

"Yes. And now, well, I have mates as well as a heartstone. Mates who could give me…the next heir." That would matter much more than the heartstone to Marses.

"Damn. That does make you a danger to him continuing as king." Tam's gaze shot to the door. "He doesn't want to relinquish the power that he's gained, does he?"

"No. He doesn't. He planned to keep me in seclusion until I turned twenty-one. Then give me over to the Sisters of the Mount, a religious shrine for those who don't have their heartstone. No one leaves there once they go in." She should have been glad he hadn't outright killed her. Because he could have with the power he had acquired. But he hadn't wanted to look bad in the eyes of their people. He wanted honor. At least that had kept her alive. But at what price? He'd taken away her childhood. Her teenage years. Much had been stolen from her. Now, he might take her mates. Only she wouldn't allow that. She wouldn't allow him to hurt them.

Determination filled her. No matter what their protection cost her. "He'll kill us before we can…oppose him. Or start a new line. He wants his line to continue on the throne."

"Jax, she's right. We're in danger. I may not know a lot about my culture, but I know this: Marses the Royal is ruthless." He removed his hands from his pockets. "There were rumors that he'd orchestrated the death of the king. Nothing ever came of it that I remember, but…now, I wonder."

Icy tendrils moved through Kiann's veins. She'd been secluded. Maids who didn't talk to her had been all she'd seen, and they changed every six weeks. She'd never heard those rumors. "People said Marses killed my father?" Her voice caught at the final word. She still couldn't believe he was gone. Sometimes when she'd been younger, she'd snuck into his favorite study and sat, pretending he might round the corner at any minute. He'd been a good man and an even better father. Such a bitter loss. If Marses had taken that from her…?

"They were rumors I heard." Tam looked at her, and his gaze became apologetic. He hadn't realized she hadn't heard them. "But I don't know that for sure. I mean, rumors will say anything."

"Did you ever hear rumors of me?" She trembled a little, wanting the answer, but not wanting to hear what he'd say.

"I've lived off Ebolia my whole life. I didn't catch every piece of news. My mother died when I was little. She was the Ebolian."

He didn't give her a straight answer. He didn't have to. "But you heard those about my father." Her lungs deflated. Marses had pushed her from the public's eyes stringently so that no one would remember her. He might have succeeded. The people wouldn't support someone they didn't know anything about. An impossible situation brought on by his quest to drive her from the public's awareness. So much for any hope of reclaiming her life.

"Those were huge. Important rumors." He realized his misstep as soon as the words left his mouth. "Not that you aren't important…" His arms folded in front of him.

Jax shook his head. "Nice. Ignore him."

"No. It's okay. He pushed me to the side for that reason. I wasn't allowed in public. I wasn't allowed freedom in the palace. These things were done so that there wouldn't be talk of me. I wouldn't have support among my people for any push to rule." Still, it didn't cheer her to hear that Marses had exactly what he'd wanted. Any hopes she had of reclaiming her life had been dashed. She'd been talked about so little in public for the last eleven years, no one would know anything about her, even if she did try and take the crown. Marses had armies and people backing him. She had two reluctant mates who'd been thrust into danger. Better to move on and bring together a life outside of Ebolia. "Look, we're the only ones who know about our mating. If we kept quiet about what happened…"

"There were other people in the cavern." Tam moved toward her side. "They saw us. Heard us."

"But we are the only three who know exactly what happened. If you two go on your way, nothing ever happened. No one can say the mating happened but us." Which was what they wanted to do anyway. "Then Marses won't come after you. You won't be the threat. All we have to do is cover the mating up, and you won't be in danger." Her mind ticked off all she'd have to do to make that work. She could pull it off. She refused to let her emotions surface about losing her mates. Marses had won after all. She'd never have a normal life. If he'd been there, she could have shouted her anger. But he wasn't, and these two weren't responsible for the situation.

"But you'd still be in danger." Tam frowned. "He won't be happy you have the potential of the heartstone. You're now an impediment to him staying in power. If the people find out about you… You're of the line. You have your heartstone now." He straightened his back. "We should stick together. That will make it easier to stay safe."

"If this is some misguided sense of protecting me, don't." Something new occurred to her. They hadn't been concerned with her safety when they'd first been mated. Greed had a way of manifesting itself in strange way. She'd knock that illusion from them right now. "If it's because you think you might take a crown one day for yourself, don't. Because I don't need the former, and the latter is stupid. Marses will never let me take over, much less along with my mates. I'll be lucky to keep my life, much less anything else." Her whole existence would be concerned with surviving, not taking over some crown. She tried to tell herself that the crown didn't mean anything. But her father's kind face kept swimming around her mind. Along with her mother's. The stories she'd heard of their ruling lineage echoed in her mind.

No, she couldn't go home and reclaim something of her life. She'd never be allowed. She had no training for the crown, even if she could. Nor did she want to be put back in the prison that the palace had become for her. She'd already escaped being put in the religious shrine. They didn't accept anyone with a heartstone. There went Marses's plans for her. He wouldn't be happy about that, either. She could hear him ranting now. Both of their eyes narrowed, Tam's in particular. "I don't care about taking the kingdom."

"Good. Because my time on the throne won't happen. Your best bet is to pretend you never met me, that our stones never glowed, and to go our separate ways." Her voice didn't catch on the words. Her spine straightened. She'd never known she had such strength. To give up her mates would be one of the hardest things she'd ever done.

Maybe later, she'd regret what she'd done. Now, only purpose drove her.

Tam didn't say anything.

"You two can go. I'm going to book passage…"

"No." The voice was quiet, authoritative, and clear.

Both of them swung their heads around to stare at Jax.

Tam's eyes opened wider, but he didn't comment.

"What did you say?" Kiann tossed things into bags again. She must have heard wrong. After all, Jax had been the one decrying the fact the stones had glowed. He'd been the one protesting their mating.

"No." He didn't add anything or embellish. Nor did he smile, frown, or let emotion creep into his face. But the eyes, oh Goddess, the eyes. They stormed and raged. They dared her to argue with him. They made her shiver with their intensity.

Made her want to fall into his arms, safe and protected, and forget all about their danger. But that was something she couldn't do. *Be practical.*

Tam's grin grew big and super sexy, looking thrilled by this pronouncement.

Kiann was anything but thrilled. Why did men have to be stupidly stubborn? "What do you mean, 'no'?"

"I mean what I say. No." Jax moved toward her with quiet grace. "You will not leave us. We won't let you. Not because of greed or any thought of protecting you, though we do want to. We'll stay as the mates we are meant to be." He caught her face in his hands, twisting her chin up to look him full in the eyes. "Don't like it? Tough."

***

Jax glared down at the woman who stood before him, glaring at him as he held her face in his hands. Such fire glowed from within her. Her eyes glowed up at him as if they were luminous, black storm clouds. Such a beautiful face.

He looked at the stones glowing around all their necks. A moment of intense emotion could always bring about the light.

"I don't like it." She pulled her head away from him. "I don't like it one bit. You would be in danger."

Tam puffed out his chest. "We excel in danger."

No, they didn't. The most dangerous thing they did daily was using a tool. They might get a cut or something. Once a month, they might go out on a shuttle, which could be dangerous. That was all they did as far as risk taking. But Tam's pronouncement sounded good. "Yeah, we're tough."

"I thought you didn't believe I was your mate. That you didn't think the mating could be right." Her voice grew bitter. "You should be happy I'm leaving you."

Jax should have been happy about this scenario. Why wasn't he? He couldn't explain his turnaround. Except that when faced with the knowledge they might lose her for good, his mind had screamed against the possibility. His heart had clenched, making his chest hurt. He wanted to fix things with her, even though he still didn't know what he wanted from her. But he wasn't ready to lose her yet. Not this way. "I... Look, I may have trouble dealing with what the Fates dealt us." He drove out a breath. "But I can't deny what you are to me."

A *tick tick* sounded nearby. It was either a clock or a hammer pounding. Or maybe it was his heart with these admissions.

Her head cocked to the side. "Oh, but you can."

"No, we can't deny what we are to each other." Tam shuffled his feet, a nervous habit. "Ever."

"Sure you can. You two have each other already. You pack your bags. You walk away." She slapped her hands together as if she dusted them off. "Easy peasy."

Such a tough look shone through her face. But even Jax could see she didn't possess the bravado she was trying to display. Her face still had a pinched look. Her eyes were flat. She would walk away from them to protect them. She had that strength. But she wasn't as together as she wanted them to think. "But where does that leave you?" If they walked away, she'd be left without her mates. Mates didn't do well without each other, even those who rejected whoever the Fates had chosen for them. She'd pine for them forever, and they for her. The chances of her having another mate out there were astronomical. Threesomes were more common than twosomes. And foursomes were off the charts rare.

Her father had been one lucky man to find another mate after losing one to death.

Until he'd died.

Jax wasn't going to say anything, but that many deaths around Kiann made him suspect that Marses the Royal had a murdering streak. He'd had no reason to kill Kiann before now and had probably figured he might need her alive one day. He'd been biding his time until things blew over from her father's and his mother's death. Jax had no proof, but thinking logically, well, things made sense, which meant the danger claims weren't exaggerated. Kiann was on the front line of that risk.

"Alone. The way I've been…since my mother died." Her eyes flashed. "I don't need your protection or your misguided sense of honor. I can take care of myself. I've been doing that since Dad died."

Jax clenched his fists. What had Marses done to such a little girl to make her think she had to do things alone? Curse him. Jax wanted to pound Marses for keeping her from her heartstone for too many years, and he wasn't as emotional as Tam. Tam would need to be watched if they ever encountered Marses.

'Course, if she hadn't come to Settler's Mine when she did, they wouldn't have been there. "You don't have to be alone. It's not some misguided chivalry. You are *our* mate."

"Again, a little earlier you couldn't wait to get away from your mate. I do put you in danger. That's a fact." She looked spooked. As if she might dash away at any minute. Her eyes widened. "I don't want to be responsible if anything happens to you."

"Nothing will. We're good." Jax approached her as carefully as he would any wild animal. Who'd have thought the mate the Fates picked for him would be a woman? Such a foreign creature. He'd never dealt with them much in his life. At least Tam had a mother and a sister, albeit he hadn't known them well. Jax had had no women to deal with. His mother had died at his birth. This one would give him a runaround. Maybe he needed that. Maybe he had been too complacent in his life with Tam. His complacency had almost cost him both his mates and still could. "You don't have to be responsible for us."

"Yes, so you say." Her mouth pursed. "Look, you don't have to worry. I'm not going to come after you. I'm not going to stalk you. You two run away, don't tell anyone about me, and you should be safe. Free."

Tam blinked at her. "I don't want to be free."

"Neither do I."

Kiann looked as if she didn't believe them.

Jax couldn't blame her. He'd let his resistance to change get in the way of how he should have acted. Now he longed to reassure her that he knew his butt from a hole in the ground. "How can we prove that to you?"

Tam nodded. "Yep, how can we?"

"You don't." She looked at them as if they'd gone nuts. Her arms came up to fold around her chest. Her ample chest.

The sight hit Jax right in the heart. And in places a little farther below the belt. He wanted to dip himself into her and never let go. He'd only experienced such before with Tam. His mind might not know what it wanted, but his body sure did.

"We could shout it out." Tam moved toward the door. "Announce our mating to the whole mine. Will that make you believe?"

"Tam."

He opened the door and yelled at the top of his lungs. "Kiann is my mate. And Jax's. Thought you should know."

Her mouth curled as she fought the urge to smile. "You are a nutter."

Tam held the door open for Jax. "Your turn." He swiveled to face him.

"You don't have to do this." She didn't expect Jax to.

A moment of proof. A moment of decision. Despite his misgivings, he did need to give this mating a try. He went over to the door and yelled, "Kiann is my mate. And Tam's." He slammed the door to face her. "Satisfied?" He stalked over to her. "That make you believe our intentions?"

She looked him full in the face, biting her lip nervously. The scent of flowers drifted to him. "What changed your mind?"

He moved in close to her. Their bodies almost touched. He lowered his lips to hers. His vision swam as he took her lips in a joining that rocked him to his core. His heart drummed even as his nerve endings pulsed with new awareness. Her scent set him on fire. Her touch made him burn. Nothing had changed. But he'd accepted the inevitable to come. He'd still have his issues, but the Fates were already working on him. They played within his psyche, which was evident in the way his body responded to her, to being with her.

He pulled away to whisper, "This."

***

Kiann's head reeled from the kiss. Not that she knew what kisses were supposed to be, but this one had been intense. She shivered a little, recovering from its onslaught. Nothing had ever tasted better than Jax's lips.

But she couldn't let this one kiss affect her judgment. She was a danger to them and would remain one. Not to mention, when she'd thought of her mates, she'd never thought about them not wanting her, except for the fact of sex, which was what had changed Jax's mind. That wasn't good enough for her. She wanted them to want *her.* Not because of sex. She could use that against them. To make sure she didn't put them at risk.

She pushed away from him farther.

"So what? You changed your mind because you want to fuck me?"

Jax looked as taken aback as Tam. The harsh language made her cringe as well. But it was necessary to make her point. "No. Not hardly."

"That's what you said, isn't it?" She moved away from them both. If they touched her, she might cave. Whose bright idea had it been to give her mates and a heartstone in one fell swoop anyway? Oh yes, the Fates. She never should have gone looking, no matter how compelled she'd been. All this had done was cause her trouble.

"Not exactly."

"You said 'This' right after you kissed me. Didn't you?"

Jax looked uncomfortable. "Yeah. But that…"

"How else am I supposed to take that comment? You want me as a mate because you can have sex with me. Mind-blowing sex. That's not enough for me. I want the full-fledged deal, with emotions." Maybe she'd lost her childhood and her teenage years. But she wouldn't allow herself to lose anything more because of Marses. She wouldn't allow this mating to skate by simply because of Marses and the danger. She wanted the real thing or nothing. No matter what she had to sacrifice.

"Wait a minute." Tam held up a hand. "Time out."

Both she and Jax glared at him.

"What do you mean, 'time out'?" Kiann checked the clock. She needed to get them out of here to figure out where to run. She'd half expected to go back to her home, never figuring she'd have to run away. She should've planned more. Better. She wouldn't make that mistake again. She'd plot out her next move more carefully.

"I mean, you both need a break before this escalates further." Tam's face looked irritated.

"Tam, she needs to..." Jax frowned as Tam waved him quiet.

After they'd both been quiet a minute, Tam asked, "Now, what do you know of mates?"

"Me?" She pointed to herself. What was his game? What could he hope to gain from her with this line of questioning? She didn't have time for small talk and spoke quickly. "I had the same lessons as everyone else." A lie. They wouldn't know that. She hadn't. Marses hadn't permitted her to be educated the way everyone else was. One of the servant's daughters had taught her a few things, including about mates. Only Marses never allowed anyone to serve Kiann for too long, so her schooling hadn't continued after the servant left her service. He hadn't wanted anyone becoming closer to her than to him.

"Your stepbrother, the one who kept you separated from everyone else so that you'd be forgotten about, let you have lessons?" Tam arched a brow.

Busted. Tam was a smart man. He'd seen through her easily. "I...I don't have time..."

"Let me guess." Jax stepped forward. "You learned things informally. From someone else? Am I right?"

"So? They were lessons." She paced back and forth, not looking them in the face. The girl had taught her everything she knew, which wasn't much. She knew enough to know what she wanted and didn't want, though.

"Yep, but you didn't get the full story." Tam followed with his gaze, which took on an appreciative glow.

She pulled out her shirt so that the material didn't outline her breasts as much. Why did that make her uncomfortable? In a different situation, she'd have enjoyed the attention. But right now, she prickled, as if cactus spines outlined her body. Maybe because they knew her too well after so short a time. Or that they wouldn't let her be. She'd been on her own so much, she was used to people going away from her. Now, they wouldn't. Somehow, that made her warm and contentious at the same time. "So? What's that got to do with anything?"

"Mates start out sexually attracted to each other. That's the first thing that happens after the stones glow."

Jax nodded his head. "Yeah, that is partially why I changed my mind. Until you, I've never been sexually attracted...to a woman... It's because you're my mate."

"So?" She ignored the stirrings in her belly that Jax's words evoked. He'd never been attracted to a female before? Now he was to her. Yes, that hit her right in the gut and nether parts. She'd never known words could be titillating.

And hearing him call her his mate? That did things even more unimaginable to her psyche and her arousal.

Maybe they had a point with sexual attraction being the first way of mates. Not that it mattered to her.

Jax continued, "I owe it to Tam and to you to try this. Tam convinced me of that." He shot a soft look at Tam—one that melted her insides and made her envious.

What would it be like to have someone look at her that way? She could still remember her stepmother and father looking at each other. Touching. They'd been loving. She'd kept those memories inside her to give herself hope on nights when she'd been alone. That one day she'd have that in her life, too. Only now, she wasn't sure she ever would.

She shook her head to clear her emotions. Of course, Jax couldn't do anything for her the way he did Tam. He'd known her for two seconds. Yet, she wanted that look, and not from anyone else. She wanted that from Jax. These two men in front of her were the only two beings out there to offer her that chance. No one else could ever mean more to her than them. That was what being mates meant. She'd learned that from the other child. Only she didn't want them to rush into this, nor did she want them in jeopardy. "Why do you owe me anything at all? You just met me."

"Because as your mates, we are the only shot you have at love. Family. True emotional bonding." Jax's words were clinical. Might as well have been a scientist of Union Alliance talking. No emotion reflected in his words.

Her mind shifted back to seeing him and Tam together since they'd met. While Jax was even stiff with Tam, there was emotion there. Yet, there was little yet for her. She swallowed noisily. The reality of those clinical words sunk in, though. She'd heard them before. But the truth was, she'd never thought about their full import.

Her true emotions would be lost without her mates.

Yet those words also honed in on the risk her mates posed to Marses.

Heirs.

Only mates could give each other children. The only shot she had of continuing the line of her family was standing right in front of her.

Marses had no intention of the royal line continuing. Only his line would follow through with the kingdom. That was why he'd done all the things he'd done. To keep her isolated meant no heartstones and no mates. Now that had all been ruined.

She should be happy, both for herself and also that Marses hadn't won. But she couldn't be for one reason alone: the biggest threat to Tam and Jax would always be her.

Could she live with that even with as much as she wanted to have mates? As much as she wanted to feel deep emotions? Wanted to have sex with them? Even now her clit felt sensitive under her leather pants. She wanted touch, wanted their bodies to lie against her. The pants didn't rub at the right angle.

They would.

She didn't want these things, though, if Jax and Tam lost their lives later. She couldn't be responsible for that.

"I can't do this." She grabbed up a bag and snapped the top closed. "I'm a danger to you both, and the longer we sit here and argue, the more jeopardy you two are in. Go home. Pretend you never met your mate." She'd try to forget them. Yes, forgetting would be difficult. Their profiles were burned in her brain. She'd probably think of them forever. At least they had each other, so she wasn't leaving them sexless or loveless. She didn't want to hurt them, so that made this parting bearable.

On the other hand, she would be sexless and loveless. For the rest of her life.

To hell with Marses for doing this to her.

Tam shook his head. "We can't do that."

Jax stepped up behind him. "I won't do that. Neither will Tam."

They made a united front. It would have been awe-inspiring if the situation hadn't been dire.

"You don't get a choice. I'm not some little woman who's going to kowtow because the big strong men want to screw her and order her around." She placed her hands on her hips. "Sex still isn't enough for me. No matter how hot mates' lust starts out." A partial lie. Under different circumstances, sexual attraction could have been enough to start with.

"You don't know enough about mates. Sex comes first. Arousal with mates. Then come the emotions." Another clinical analysis from Jax. "You should give this a chance. The relationship starts out sexually, but emotion comes quickly with mates."

Sounded too predictable, but it could be true. It didn't matter to her. She couldn't risk being with them. "I don't care."

"We do."

"Too bad." She snapped her other bag shut, both of them still resting on the bed. "I've got to get out of here before Marses comes here to find me. You two don't understand the peril you're in."

"We do." Tam walked over and tossed her bag on the floor. "You aren't going anywhere without me!" His words were full of emotion. As was his face. "Nowhere without me."

"I'm not going to be…"

Jax took her other bag and slapped it down on the floor. The flung bag made a thudding noise on the stone, but he hadn't tossed her case the way Tam had. His words were in control, not loud like Tam's had boomed. "You won't leave me, either."

She stared up into their determined faces. "You don't get a say. I'm the only one with say in my life." That hadn't been true for the longest time. She had her freedom and wasn't going back. "I won't be anyone's bitch. Not even yours." Dammit, why didn't they see what she said was true? Why wouldn't they just let her go? Her hands clenched by her sides.

"We're not asking you to be our bitch. We want to be your mates. Leaving us doesn't support that."

"If you don't let us come with you or stay with us, we'll follow you." Tam's voice went low and deadly. She hadn't heard him hit that note in his voice before. "To the ends of the galaxy. We won't rest or stay away from you. We will find you wherever you go."

"We'll search everywhere. Methodically."

An evil grin lit Tam's face. "We'll make sure Marses knows who we are. That we're your mates."

She stilled. She hadn't thought about them doing that. "He'll kill you for that." If they went up and announced themselves, Marses would have them slaughtered. From the determined look on their faces, she could see them doing that.

"You don't save us by leaving us." Jax folded his arms across his chest.

"Don't leave us." Tam's voice took on a pleading note.

"You don't even want me. You're not sure about being with me. Why are you doing this?" She could have stomped her feet in frustration. They had to see reason. But even logical Jax wasn't using his logic.

He leaned in to run a hand down her cheek and neck. Her skin sparked under his hand. Molten iron dripped onto her skin from his touch. Never had she thought touch would be this way. "Honestly, I don't know what I want. I've never felt this way about a woman. I'll make mistakes, but I have to see where being mated to you leads." He sidled up to her. "Won't you see where it leads with me?"

Pretty words, but the road would be hard for them all. Could she subject them to peril? Or would leaving them be more difficult than she'd ever thought? "Mates are a lifetime commitment." A wrong decision could kill them all. But a part of her wanted to be with them beyond measure. They offered her normalcy. They offered her touch, both with their bodies and with their feelings. They offered companionship. Such things she hadn't had in a long time. All the things she'd longed for stood in front of her in these two men. How unfair was that?

"We'll see where this leads for now. Worry about the lifetime later." Tam was suddenly there and leaned in for a light press of his lips to hers. "Take things one step at a time. But we have to take that first step."

Jax still stood beside her. "Together."

Her lips tingled from where Tam had touched them. "You two aren't going to let me go, are you?" No one had ever cared about her. Not since her parents. It made it hard to walk away from them. Why should she leave what she most wanted in the galaxy?

"Not on your life." Tam chuckled. "And we're both pretty stubborn, if you can believe that."

She could. "Are you sure about all this? Because being with me won't be easy. It will be risky."

Nods. From them both.

Their surety helped to drive out her doubt. How could she not believe in them with their eyes honestly brimming in front of her?

"Okay. I guess we're in this together."

Tam laughed and grabbed her around the waist. He swung her around, taking her feet from the floor. "I knew you'd agree." His mouth latched onto hers in a punishing kiss. A kiss that stole her very breath.

She panted as he broke the kiss. She'd had no idea what an embrace could do to her. He tasted so good, felt so good against her body.

Jax came up behind them, pressing his body against her back. His erection stroked her butt, pushing into her. To know, even as unsure as he was, that he still wanted her, stoked her fires despite her words.

She was sandwiched between them. Funny how that kept coming up. Being between them that is. A standard ménage sexual position.

Jax pushed her hair to the side to press kisses along her neck. Her skin tingled with awareness.

Tam guided them all to the bed.

She arched a brow. "What are you doing?"

"Celebrating." He smiled, and she went weak in the knees. "We have to celebrate our mating. Celebrate our togetherness."

She didn't turn, but asked Jax, "Are you ready for this?" She didn't want to push him faster than he wanted to go.

He stiffened against her. And not his hard cock, either. "I… We should celebrate." His voice didn't sound thrilled, but did sound serious.

Not exactly a grand endorsement or an outright yes, but right now, she'd take what she could get.

Jax lay on the bed, taking her with him, followed by Tam. She faced Tam with Jax facing her back. There was no room left over to wiggle. They filled the bed and more. She'd need a bigger bed from now on.

Maybe the two of them would fill her and more tonight. No, that wouldn't happen. Jax was still too unsure. But maybe soon.

Tam pressed his mouth against hers again. His tongue swiped against the seam of her lips, triangulating into her mouth.

Jax's hand ran circles around her back. Giving her a massage while Tam kissed her so deeply, she would have swooned had she been on her feet.

Touch had been missing from her life for so long. The craving gnawed at her with these men caressing her body.

"Relax," Tam murmured against her lips. "We'll take care of it all. Of you." He sounded so sure, so comforting. He might become her lifeline yet.

She wanted time with them more than she'd ever wanted anything in her life. She had never wanted anything else more than this moment. Not even her desire to find her heartstone compared to this.

His tongue subdued hers as it twirled around.

She gave herself over to the onslaught of sensations. How could she not? He tasted so fine, so good. His flavor imbued her senses.

Jax went under her shirt to find her spine and work his way up and down it with his fingertips.

Her whole body relaxed, giving Tam even more access to her nether regions.

Tam's hand pressed against her middle and caressed her skin with nimble fingers. His touch scorched her. "You're so soft." His hand lowered to her belly button, then went even lower to drift under her pants. His other hand came over to unsnap her pants.

"Tam…"

"Shhhh. Just let me give you this, for now."

Jax shivered against her back. "Let us for now." His hand continued to work her back. His hands had such strength. He kneaded her muscles expertly. He didn't cause pain but put pleasure into all her nerve endings. He knew how to do it just hard enough, and his touch relaxed her. What would it hurt?

Did he give Tam massages like this?

He must.

Her pants came fully undone, and Tam's other hand swooped into the breach. He found her sex without any trouble.

She gasped and stiffened at his hand on her. She should have expected it, but it caught her off guard and pulled up so many emotions within her.

He rested it there for a second without moving, letting her adjust to the intimate touch before proceeding any further.

Jax pressed another wet kiss on her neck. He shifted up to find her ear. His teeth gently nipped her earlobe.

Her whole body shivered as if she were in a blizzard. Hardly true. She'd found the most intense heat that ever had existed anywhere in the galaxy. Volcanoes had nothing on the molten warmth rising up in her.

Tam's finger finally dipped into her sex to find the sensitive skin. "So wet." His voice sounded strangled.

Jax's hips bucked against hers. He must like hearing that about her. His tongue slithered into her ear, slipping deliciously in and out, just as Tam found her sensitive nub. Tam plucked it back and forth between his fingers.

Her thighs shot open more. She'd known about the button, but hadn't known how another touching it would affect her after finding her heartstone. It had just felt pleasant to play there before because of how sensitive it was, but this was completely different from merely pleasant. This was explosive.

Jax continued his thrusting into her ear with his tongue even as his hands rubbed her shoulder. Yes, his strong hands would cause pleasure every time they touched her. Anywhere they touched her.

Tam's finger drifted down to find her channel and enter her with one finger, causing moisture to funnel out and coat him. His thumb remained on her nub, keeping a quick pace.

Touch had never been like this. She'd never known sexual desire could be this way. That it could fill her up like this.

With her mates.

Who could have abandoned her and hadn't. They'd stuck around despite the dangers, much to her wonderment.

The climax grabbed her with hot hands and took her into the stratosphere. Least she thought it was a climax. It sure was "the pinnacle of her desires," as the books had said. Nothing had ever felt like this.

As Jax removed his hands from her back, Tam pulled his hands from her pants. He sniffed them, covered with her essence. Then he licked them, one by one. "Your taste…ahhhhh." He offered the last finger to Jax.

Jax leaned over and slipped Tam's finger into his mouth to taste her cream.

Her stomach clenched as a shudder rocked her insides. An aftershock brought on by the view.

Jax suckled the finger before releasing it. He looked more aroused than she'd ever seen him. And sexy as ever.

She looked back and forth between them. The most intense experience of her life had just happened. She'd had her first orgasm, with both her mates as the cause.

Tam pulled on the front of her pants as if he'd take them all the way down.

"What are you doing?" Jax blew out a breath behind her.

"Continuing this."

Jax stiffened. She felt his body tense.

He wasn't ready for more. Not now.

She put a hand on Tam's. "Not yet. We probably should talk more first." She reached down to snap her pants back together. "Before we go further." She didn't say what she'd felt about Jax, but took control.

Jax relaxed behind her.

Her heart warmed, and she wanted to put him at ease. After he'd tried things with her, that was the least she could do. He hadn't had to participate, but he had.

Tam sighed. "I guess." He bounced from the bed as they both shrugged to their feet, too. "What are you planning to do now?" Tam picked up her bag and set it on the bed. "Where were you going anyway?"

"I don't know. I hadn't planned that far. I didn't plan this well. I had an opportunity to escape and took the chance. I didn't think about what I'd do if I acquired my heartstone." She sat down on the bed beside her bag. "I didn't think about what I'd do if I obtained mates. You two were a surprise." Though she hadn't vocalized her willingness to try, it existed as a given between them without saying the words aloud. Was that the way of mates? Unspoken agreements and emotions? And intense encounters like they'd just had?

"No more to you than us."

Jax looked serious as he changed the subject. "How far do you think Marses is behind you?"

"I don't know." If only she had some way to track him. Her lips pursed as she thought about how close or far away he could be. Would he figure out what she was up to? Of course he would. Marses wasn't stupid. He'd know what she was looking for, which made him even more a threat to them.

"We need to find that out." Tam tapped his chin. "Let me go call in a favor or two and see what I can find. I have some friends and relatives on Ebolia. They might be able to pinpoint his location. That would help us figure out our next move."

"That would help us plan a logical destination from here."

Which would leave her and Jax alone. "Okay." She clenched her hands together in nervousness. What would they do while Tam was gone? Jax was still unsure about being mates. Tam would—at least at first—be the glue that cemented them. At least until Jax could get on the same page and she could let go of her fears about him. If he were to eventually reject her, she'd not withstand the onslaught. If they were to pay the price for being with her, she'd not be able to live with herself. No, she shook her head. She'd never let that happen.

Tam shot out a loose grin, not noticing her shiver, though Jax's observant gaze flickered toward her. "You two behave." Tam moved toward the door. "On second thought, don't behave." He left them with laughter following his steps.

As the door whooshed closed, Jax glanced at her. Their eyes met. His fired up, a kiln ready to burn.

Behaving might not be an option.

Chapter Seven

Jax looked toward Kiann, who looked a little nervous. Probably because she wasn't sure where she stood with him. He'd do what he could to put her at ease. Where did she stand with him? He wouldn't be good at faking anything he didn't feel. If she expected that, she'd be disappointed. "What…"

"What…"

They both talked at the same time and stopped as they heard the other.

Kiann laughed nervously. A titter that sounded loud in the quiet room. "Sorry. Go ahead."

"No, you."

"No, you."

This was getting them nowhere fast. Jax smiled to put her at ease and sat down on the bed. The bed where they'd shared an intimacy. It had been a first step, but a small one. And he wasn't ready for the bigger ones. Yet. Might as well get comfortable, though, and make her feel better. He didn't know how long Tam would be gone. "Come sit with me." Would that be an icebreaker? It should be. He wanted her near him. He patted the seat beside him. Would she take his invitation? He'd never been this unsure of himself. His anxiety unnerved him.

Slowly, she ambled over. He released a gulp of air he hadn't realized he'd been holding. Gracefully, she lowered herself and sat beside him. She kept her body from brushing against his, so he scooted over until they were touching. He needed to feel her against him, but understood why she hadn't been sure enough of herself to take the advantage. "What were you going to say?" Her voice grew stronger as if she was becoming less anxious.

"Nothing important." He leaned back so he rested against the wall and tried not to think about how good she felt next to him, or how nice she smelled. He could sniff her for hours, never tiring of her smell. "How exactly did you wind up here? At Settler's Mine." A little small talk might do well to ease them both, and take his mind off of his stiff cock.

"Visions pointed to here. I had this urge to come."

Sounded similar to Tam with his visions and urges. His two mates were alike. Maybe that helped to make him wary. If they were alike, where did that leave him? He shook his head. He hadn't been logical and therefore had been stupid earlier. He'd not make that mistake again. "And you kept seeing red? In the visions?" His hand came up to finger his stone. His heartstone lay cool against his skin.

"Yes. I'd guess now that's because it's the color of the glow of our heartstones. Everything broadcast in red in my head."

"Probably." He turned his head to look at her and got lost in her eyes. They were subtly different than Tam's eyes. Must be that he was only half Ebolian. Her eyes were darker, but Jax couldn't draw away from her gaze. They reminded him of a predator's eyes, as Tam's did. She held him fast, as if he were a game animal in the spotlight or a predator being hunted with light beams. Was she the predator? Hard to fathom with her delicate looks, but she'd find him to be difficult prey. Or maybe things were the other way around. He would hunt her with gusto when the time came.

The curve of her jaw intrigued him with her angular bones. She was beautiful in a way, though most wouldn't have thought so because of her dark eyes and sharp features that screamed her Ebolian heritage. She conveyed fragility, which brought out his protectiveness. 'Course, being his mate brought that out in him. But standing up to the two of them proved she wasn't as delicate as she looked.

Her lush mouth moved as he watched, entranced by her. "What?"

"Huh?" He pulled his gaze up to her eyes. "What did you say?"

"Why are you studying me?"

He blinked. Was she naive to ask that question? Most of the lovers he'd been with were more experienced than he. Even Tam had been. Always before, lovers noticed his staring and liked him being mesmerized by them, especially as he sometimes came across as too collected.

Kiann had less experience than he did. A first for him.

He answered honestly as he always did. "You intrigue me."

"Me? Why?"

"Because you're..." He exhaled. Tam liked compliments. A female must, too. He should have paid more attention in classes on family planning when they'd covered both of the sexes. "Beautiful." He waited to see how she'd react.

A flush lit her face. "I didn't think you liked women." Her eyes widened as though she couldn't believe she'd said what she had. A look he'd seen on Tam's face many times before. The familiar combined with differences in this woman made her all the more alluring, instead of putting him off.

He'd done well with the compliment. Good. Maybe he'd learn quickly about females. He'd have to. "I never said I didn't like women."

"Then, what did you say?" Leaning forward, she placed her hand under her chin to rest on, while looking at him. She was getting more comfortable with him. Relaxing. A good thing.

Getting more cozy, Jax spoke more carefully, as he usually did. Of course, if he'd thought before he'd spoken after their stones had glowed, they wouldn't be having this problem now. "I said I'd never been attracted to a woman before. That's true. I've never been with a woman or even around them. Where I grew up, there were mainly men after my mother passed on. I grew up on the Seaboard. Then I moved to Escar, which doesn't have a lot of women. And that's where I met Tam." He couldn't help but break out in a smile. Best thing that had ever happened to him.

"The only reason you're attracted to me is that I'm your mate." Her voice lowered to a muffled whisper. "If I weren't, you wouldn't be."

Was that a spate of bitterness he detected in her quiet voice? She still had problems with that issue. "What if it is?" What was the problem with that? "Doesn't change the fact I do desire you." This was how relations worked for mates. It had for thousands of years—ever since Quatarians had come to need heartstones. Why was she bothered by that? Maybe her reaction had to do with her being secluded and abandoned in death by her parents.

"I don't want to be with someone who only likes me for being their mate." She folded her arms across her chest.

"I never said I liked you."

She gulped down a breath of air.

He'd shocked her. Had he shocked himself? No, he'd always been forthright with what he thought. "I don't know if I like you or not. We just met. I think I'm going to like you as I get to know you. What I've said all along was that I'm attracted to you. Lust isn't like, by any means."

"But that's still the only reason you feel anything for me, even lust." Her cheeks pinkened more with the last word.

He shook his head to disagree. "I have a twinge of lust as you're my mate. That comes first. But do you know the only thing that can sustain lust—even lust caused by a mating?" He met her eyes and wouldn't drop his gaze. She had to understand the complexities of mating. Something she'd never been taught. His fist clenched and unclenched about the reasons why she'd never had a decent education about the stones that drove their destiny.

"What?"

"Like and love. You can have lust without those two things. But the stone doesn't cause instant like or love. Those things you have to work out on your own." He reached out to stroke her hand. The soft skin under his fingertips eased him in way he'd never dreamed. He could spend hours touching her, centimeter by centimeter. "Like and love are the only things that can sustain lust."

"How do you work those things out?" She trembled beneath his fingers.

He steadied her fingers by holding them. "Intimacy."

"Intimacy?"

"Getting to know each other. Knowing that your mate doesn't like *caledonia* root. Or *melong* hair makes him itch. Or that you like the smell of the henna we use to make clothing. Or that he likes..." He licked his lips. What he'd been about to reveal was too soon. If she stayed with them, she'd find out soon enough. Both of them would want him to lose control. She would be similar to Tam in that. Jax would never make his way out of the bedroom. He shifted his weight, relieving pressure on his cock. He'd never complain about it, either. "You get the idea."

Her breathing spasmed. "I suppose I do."

"We'll find out all these things about you. That's what will make the lust last. Not the stone." Though the stone was the kick start, things moved past what the stone caused. Or at least, that was how he saw the world.

"Suppose you don't like me? Or...love me?" Her eyes shone bright in the dim light of the room.

He caressed her knuckles. Such long, delicate fingers. He separated them out one by one to run his fingertips down them.

She shivered.

"I don't know what will happen. But I think I'm going to like you." Only time would tell. Right now, for the first time since Tam had pushed them to come here, he was looking forward to the future. And whatever it held.

They sat in silence for a moment. He held up her hands in contrast to his. "You're small compared to me. Or Tam." He hadn't meant to say the words, but they came out of him anyway, and it wasn't exactly a compliment.

She didn't take offense. "Females are generally the smaller of the species."

There were a few notable exceptions to that rule. But for the most part, women were smaller than men. He'd been taught that in education classes. Funny, the stuff he remembered as opposed to things he couldn't recall. If only he remembered more of how to deal with women than their sizes.

Their smallness was a reason for him not to lose control.

He'd thought Tam too delicate for his carnal desires. This one would be even more so. "I know that. I just didn't expect the reality of the statement." He hadn't expected the reality of anything about her.

She cocked her head, watching him still running his hands over hers. "I think we're going to be saying that a lot—about each other and things as mates."

He grinned at her, and she smiled back. He liked her smile, which made her whole face light up. Somehow that he'd brought the expression on warmed him. "Yeah, I think we will be."

The door whooshed open, and Tam came in, putting his keycard in his pocket. "You two doing okay?"

She looked at Jax, and her face smoothed out in relaxation. "Yes. Yes, I think we are. What'd you find out?"

"Good. I'm glad you two are doing well together because Marses is almost here. We've got to get off the mine."

* * *

Tam watched carefully as they waited to board the transport ship. He kept scanning the new shuttles and ships coming onboard for any sign of the person he sought. The Prince of Ebolia would come in with much fanfare. Or at least he always had before. Tam had seen his arrivals on other places broadcast over the computers. They included lots of trumpets, red carpets, and entourages.

It should make him easy to spot.

The bastard. Tam would be hard-pressed not to make a scene.

Kiann tapped her foot impatiently. "When are they going to let us on?" Her whisper carried through the air.

Most would have taken a smaller shuttle instead of the transport. But neither Jax nor Tam knew how to fly, which made flying themselves impossible. Tam had always wanted to learn piloting, but had never gotten around to lessons. Jax had no desire to learn anything at all about flying, content to let a pilot do the work. Where they lived, hardly anyone flew themselves. Transports were common. Other places had made learning how to fly a priority. Etruscans, for instance, were taught from birth. Most had their own shuttles, even those who weren't wealthy. Renting a vehicle there was cheap compared to other places.

"Takes a while to board." The shuttle had had its passengers disembark a few minutes before. Now the vehicle took on fuel. Then, they would board more passengers and take off. Tam knew the routine by heart.

She humphed. "We don't have a while."

"Not used to flying domestic, are you?" Jax shifted his weight under their bags, which had to be heavy, but he'd insisted on carrying them all.

Whatever had happened between them while he'd been gone had left both of them looking content. Not as nervous as psi-cats as they had been looking.

One day, they'd have only their bag for all three of them. That thought sent spirals running down into Tam's stomach.

If only Kiann and Jax had messed around with each other. A shame they hadn't taken advantage of their time together. Had Tam been the one left alone with Kiann, he'd have been all over her. He couldn't keep his thoughts from going there, even now with the danger surrounding them.

"To tell you the truth, I never flew much at all. I'm an impatient person."

"Was coming here your first interplanetary trip?" Maybe some small talk would distract her from her hurry.

"The first one in a long time. I'd traveled before with my father and mother, but I don't remember a lot about the trip."

That had to have been a long time ago. Tam took a survey through the crowds again.

Out of the corner of his eye, he saw the crew open the gangplank doors. They'd be checking tickets and letting people onboard. Their trip was ready to begin and not a moment too soon. His chest heaved with relief.

"About time." Kiann shuffled forward as the crowd swept that way. She bumped the man in front of her.

The man glared back at her. "Watch it."

Tam pulled her back against them. "You watch it."

The man grunted at them.

Jax crept up, letting the man know that he was with them. Another point in favor of two men ménages and pairings in Tam's eyes. Two men together could make another man back off from a fight.

The man glared but turned back around to mutter something derogatory to his female companion.

Tam grabbed Jax's shoulder to squeeze. To remind him they shouldn't incur notice right now. No matter what someone else said about Kiann's parentage or habits. Jax took insults seriously. Words were only words, though.

Jax glowered but didn't say anything, taking the hint from Tam.

People slowly milled up the incline to the shuttle. They would soon be onboard and away from here.

Willing everyone to hurry, Tam tilted his head to the side, staring out down the large corridor.

A tall man with hair so dark black it almost looked blue strode down the corridor. He wore power like a mantle on his shoulders, giving him even more height and presence. Throngs of people parted out of his way.

Tam inhaled; he moved his body around Kiann.

So much for rockets and fanfare.

Marses must not have wanted to announce his presence on Settler's Mine. No, he couldn't advertise the fact he'd come there to nab someone he'd kept out of the public eye for so long.

"What is it?" Kiann's voice carried much louder than it seemed it should have, resonating above the crowds.

Or maybe the blood pounding in his own ears caused the effect. Tam moved even closer to flank her side. To block her from view as much he could. He had to protect her. "Shhh." He willed her to listen and not question him further. Had the tall man heard her? Would Marses sense her presence and stop?

Marses didn't stop, but kept moving at a measured pace like a jungle cat loping across the rainforest floor. If only Marses would speed up, get on by them. His departure would let Tam breathe easier.

Kiann swallowed, her throat moving convulsively against him. She knew what had gotten Tam intent and close to her. Did he see her foe approaching?

Jax had moved in beside her on the other side, dropping the bags at his feet. He grasped her arm and pushed her behind him. Now both Tam and Jax stood between her and the man who sought her for his own gain.

The people boarding had stopped again. No one would notice their huddle.

Marses continued to move past them, followed by a man Tam hadn't noticed at first. He must have one bodyguard with him.

Tam tried not to be too obvious about his scrutinizing Marses. But he couldn't draw away his gaze for long. Marses had done a lot to Kiann to keep her from being who she was meant to be. The only saving grace was that Marses hadn't had her killed or attempted anything on her life.

A shudder racked him. Had Marses done that, they never would've met her. Never would've known their other mate. It would've been a crime. That was all Tam had to be grateful for to Marses. Everything else, he could hate him for doing.

He kept himself in check. A part of him wanted to attack Marses and make him pay for doing what he'd done. But that would alert everyone to their presence. Best to keep silent. Lie low.

"What's wrong?" Jax had felt him shudder, so close were their bodies. Kiann had probably felt him, too. "Does Marses suspect? Did he see her?"

"Nothing. It's fine." He would have to control himself better so as not to worry his two mates.

Marses moved on with determined strides to the next set of corridors. He'd probably go to see Zelda. Put out a bulletin on Kiann without identifying who she actually was.

How would he explain his search for his stepsister? A crazy cousin? A runaway slave? He wouldn't tell anyone the truth. He couldn't, or he'd bring attention to the fact he wasn't of the line, and Kiann was.

Marses disappeared from sight.

"He's gone."

Jax grabbed the bags as they regrouped. They were almost to the door to board the shuttle. They'd be onboard and away in a few minutes. Marses would be able to track them, but only so far. Tam intended to disguise their tracks as much as he could.

Then what?

Tam frowned. He had no idea what came next. He and Jax weren't spies or super agents. They made henna clothing. Marses had access to technology and assets unseen. How would they keep Kiann safe from his long reach?

Seeing Marses made the situation all the more real.

Somehow they'd have to find a way to keep Kiann safe. But how?

* * *

"Where was this shuttle going again?" Kiann settled down into the small seat between the two big men.

Jax stretched by the window.

Tam blocked her on the aisle side.

Her knees shook despite her best efforts to calm herself. Marses had been at the mine. He'd been close to her. Within stone-throwing distance. If he'd found her with Jax and Tam, he'd have had them all killed. They would've been easy targets for him to take out.

No, he wouldn't have done the deed himself, even if he'd caught them. He was too slick for that. He'd pay someone. Although his hands would never be bloody with his acts, they'd still stain him with their tarnish.

Hers would be outright bloody with the death of her mates. Mates she hadn't even consummated with. They'd had a brief moment, but hadn't gone all the way.

Her lower muscles clenched. Low-spun desire ripped through her. Yes, adrenaline could do some strange things. Her hip burned on the side where Jax's body touched hers. Her thigh tingled from contact along Tam's. She was sandwiched in the middle again.

She'd be there permanently if they ever achieved their place as a threesome. She'd never understood how that worked, even after the short sex education talks she'd gotten. It didn't seem natural. But now her treacherous body flamed up at the thought of a more intimate type of sandwiching they could do. This wasn't the time or place. Would it ever be?

"To the outposts at Dareleck." Jax kept his voice low.

"Dareleck is an outpost moon where no one cares about who you are and where you come from." Tam waved a hand. "Refugees flee there all the time. Identities change quickly."

"You're going to change our IDs there, aren't you?" She pushed down her libido. The danger hadn't passed them by. The energy would be channeled somewhere else, but the act couldn't happen. Yet.

Tam nodded. "Among other things. We have to come up with a plan." His face turned thoughtful. The dimple in his chin winked at her, fascinating her. The way his hair stretched to his shoulders in a dark cloud beckoned to her interest. Jax's went to his waist in a golden rope. They made quite a striking pair. They must get a lot of attention. Light and dark, emotional and staid.

Now, they were hers.

Something occurred to her for the first time, which made her pause. "We left together." It was stupid of her not to realize what that had done.

"Yep, we did." Tam leaned back.

Her voice lowered. "Marses will figure out you two were with me. He'll ask around, won't he?" The stunning pair who got a lot of attention had left with a woman on the run. How could she have been so stupid? They should have left in shifts.

"Probably."

There would be records. And people had seen them together. They hadn't hidden themselves. Had anyone seen them enough to figure out they were mated? Plenty knew about her heartstone. It wouldn't take much speculation to figure out she'd been with her mates when she'd left. Marses would methodically recreate what had happened. He was good at that. "I've completely disrupted your lives, haven't I?"

"Yeah." Jax leaned back in his place against the window.

Tam glared at him, but Jax didn't seem to notice, or perhaps he noticed but didn't respond. After all, he'd been honest. She could count on that from him. "You have, but we needed shaking up."

Honesty, but with a purpose to her coming into their lives. Had they needed some excitement? She clenched her hands together. Had they needed a third coming into their relationship? Probably not. All she'd done thus far was make them have to leave in a hurry and be unable to go back to their own lives on Escar.

A hand clutched hers and tightened around her wrist. Fingers slid into hers as his hand moved up hers. A rough hand. A hand that gleamed against her pale skin, tanned against cream. A warm hand that made her hand tingle with a wantonness that she'd never had stirred in her before.

"Don't worry. We'll find a way."

A way to what? Survive? Exist? Because that's all she would be doing. They'd be running forever. Unless she somehow found a way to take her life back. How could she? She'd have to find a way. She had no desire to take her role as ruler back because of what it would cost her, but she wanted to live. She wanted to protect the two men around her. Even if they didn't stay together, she wanted them safe.

Her eyes closed. Goddess, how things had changed. She'd never thought concretely about her mates, but she'd never expected them to not be thrilled at being mated to her. There had been the romantic ideal of falling into each other's arms and having sex in the way of Ebolian bunnies. It didn't happen that way for her. Nothing in life had ever happened the way it should.

Fingers stroked her hand, reminding her of who sat beside her.

She opened her eyes to stare into calm, dark eyes.

"It'll be okay."

If only he could promise her that and mean it.

* * *

Their arrival at Dareleck was uneventful. They got new identity cards for a pretty price of platinum. No one cared there about who they were as long as they had money. Everything was going well. Except that Jax checked them into two rooms, which set off Tam.

"Why two?" Tam looked frustrated.

Jax had rejoined Kiann and Tam to tell them about checking in. "Is she planning on sleeping with us tonight?" Jax fingered the key. Two or one had been his question, and he'd come up with the wrong answer. This showed him he couldn't make Tam happy right now. A rarity. Everything had increased the strain between the two of them, which had begun when Kiann became their mate. He probably couldn't have made the right choice.

"I can answer that. No." Kiann came over to snatch the key from Jax. "It's better that we have two."

"But..." Tam frowned, still looking agitated. "We shouldn't leave you alone. What if Marses comes to take you? He could get in a room where you are by yourself, and we wouldn't know until it's too late. We could protect you better in the same room."

She shrugged. "You'd hear me. I'd make sure of that." Her soft gaze shifted to Jax. "He made the right decision. I know we aren't ready for one bed." Slinging her bag over her shoulder, she moved on to find the rooms in the small area of guest suites. They had to walk down a long hallway that passed by a lounge to get to their rooms. The aged carpet looked as though a few bodily fluids had stained its fibers.

Tam fell in behind her with a frustrated step.

They probably wouldn't have room for three in one room anyway. Or the bed. From the looks of things here, Settler's Mine's lodgings had been spacious. Luxurious, even. From the looks of the clientele, things at Settler's Mine had also been safer.

Jax had kept moving in between the people's stares and Tam while they'd been getting new IDs. And Kiann. They both evoked a lot of interest. Ebolians were a secretive race.

"Yet." Tam's voice was low enough that Kiann hadn't heard him.

After picking up their bag, Jax moved to follow behind his mates. He couldn't help but train his gaze on his lover's succulent body as he stalked in front him. He walked on, his lickably curved rear encased in black leather pants. Jax's cock flew to attention. Not the best timing for that kind of arousal, especially with Tam's irritation with him. That didn't mean he couldn't enjoy looking, though.

Tam stopped short behind Kiann, and Jax ran into him, pushing Tam into Kiann. A train wreck of people.

"Sorry," Jax and Tam echoed each other.

Did Tam notice his arousal? If he did, he didn't comment.

"Why are we stopping?" Tam slid back a little, but Jax didn't move away from him. He kept their bodies in contact, letting himself stick around longer to enjoy. Then, he moved away quickly from Tam, even while cursing himself for caring about being in public. Tam wouldn't have, but he wasn't Tam.

"Because I know that woman." Kiann's voice sounded hollow, shocked. She cleared her throat.

Jax tried to follow her gaze and see who she talked about. The tone of her voice made him pause and worry. Who could she have seen here?

Tam moved in front of her to block her from the view of the tables in the small neon-lit lounge she pointed to. "What woman?"

She pointed a shaking finger in a direction. "That one. I've met her before." Her voice was as shaky as her hands.

Jax surveyed the full-chested woman sitting on a rustic chair. An Amador. She was huge for a woman, and her hair was the color of swamp slime. She made both him and Tam look small. The clothes she wore barely contained her assets. "Where did you see her before?" The woman didn't look to be the type to run around in royal circles. Especially not in the circles that Kiann would have been allowed to attend. Her contact with others had been minimal. Why had this woman been allowed near the princess?

The anger was tangible in her face and voice. The shock had ebbed. But who was she mad at? "Remember I told you Marses wanted me to join a place where those without heartstones devote themselves? I may not have mentioned where, but it was Sisters of the Mount."

"Yep." Tam nodded solemnly. "You had mentioned Marses planned on you joining."

Jax stared at Kiann. He didn't see what this woman had to do with Sisters of the Mount. A sinking sensation dragged down his stomach.

"*She* came to talk to me about the order. She was supposed to be the head abbess of the order of the Sisters of the Mount." Her face flushed with small, high spots on her cheekbones.

Jax's head shifted as he peered around Tam for another good look at the woman talking animatedly in front of them. "Her? Are you sure?" That woman didn't look as if she was an abbess. She looked as if she was someone who fucked for money. This didn't bode well.

"Yes. Her name was Bettsini. She wore different clothes, though." To pull off a role as a woman of service, they would have had to be. "She talked about devoting my life to service of the Goddess, not coveting a heartstone or giving in to the sins of the flesh. That's her. I'm sure of it."

"There's only one way to find out for sure." Tam took off for the woman. "Bettsini?" He walked around her as he called her name before stopping directly in front of her table.

She stared down into an empty cup as though she could fill the glass up with her eyes. "Yes, sugar. Bettsini is about to get off—not the way you'd have to pay for, but off work. I'll be back on tomorrow, though, sugar. You can pay for me then." The woman curled her head around to look over Tam for the first time. "'Course, maybe I can work after hours tonight." She licked her lips, her eyes firing up at the sight of Tam as she stood up.

Jax shook his head. It figured his lover would evoke that reaction. The dumb woman had used her real name to fool

Kiann. 'Course, Marses had never expected Kiann to encounter Bettsini again, especially in this place. Bettsini wouldn't have thought she'd see Kiann again, either. How ironic.

Tam grasped her arm. "I have some friends who want to see you."

"Oh, no, sugar. I don't do more than one. No couples. Or more. Bettsini…" She froze as Kiann walked in front of Jax. The woman's ample bosom heaved. She recognized Kiann, confirming what Kiann had told them. "I have to go. I'm off work." Gone was the playful lilt to her speech.

That was all the answer they needed. This woman was no woman of service. She was a prostitute.

Marses had perpetrated the fiction that she was a woman of service or order. Sisters of the Mount, Jax's butt.

Either Marses had been duped, or he'd tried to dupe Kiann.

Jax would bet it was the latter, which would mean only one thing.

Marses had wanted Kiann dead.

The most logical conclusion Jax could draw from the evidence. His entire body tightened as he digested what had happened. His gaze flew to Kiann. She was a smart woman. She'd figure out the score. It would hurt her. Curse Marses.

"Did he know?" Kiann's voice came out tight as she placed her hands on her hips. She almost panted with the force of the words.

Jax had never seen her this animated. She was beautiful, even in the face of danger or confrontation. Her anger brought color to her skin. Even with this hard situation, she was an intriguing woman to watch.

"I don't know what you're talking about. What's this? 'He'? Who you talking about?" Bettsini talked fast but wouldn't meet Kiann's eyes. A factor indicating her guilt. She didn't lie convincingly enough. This time.

"You know full well who I'm talking about. Did he know what you were?" The words spat out of Kiann's mouth.

Tam's gaze was on her, too.

A sigh rolled through beefy shoulders. Bettsini knew she'd been caught. "Yes." She twisted around. Her face blanched in her admission. "I did it for the money. He offered me seven reams of platinum for that job. All I had to do was talk to you about sanctuary. I didn't even have to spread my legs."

Marses had been about to trick Kiann into thinking she was going into a sanctuary when there wasn't going to be one. His plans for her had been bad ones. Somehow, Jax would make sure that he paid the full price for his duplicity.

His hands clenched. He would have gladly beaten Marses for deceiving Kiann. Her fallen face raised emotions in him he didn't understand.

"Look, I never expected to see you here. Don't tell him I told you anything." The large woman shivered. "He told me that if I let slip what I'd done to anyone, he'd have my head." She licked her lips. "He had me beaten after I talked to you." Another shudder rocked her as she rubbed up and down her arms. Her fear was evident.

Kiann turned away from her. "I won't tell anyone what you told me. Don't you tell a soul that you saw me." Her eyes looked lifeless.

Dismissed, Bettsini scurried away.

Kiann looked as if the worst thing that could have happened, had. She faced Jax and Tam. "He never intended to send me away to an order."

Tam nodded. "Doesn't sound like it."

"Why deceive me? Why lie? Why the charade?"

Jax moved to her side as they walked on. The questions were rhetorical, but he answered them anyway. "Because of who you are. You're the true ruler, and he knows that."

"But he's spent *years* making sure no one knew who I was. Why does he have to resort to trickery now?"

"Yeah, he's spent years keeping you hidden." Which was a shame because this vibrant creature never should have been squirreled away. "But there are those who still know you, right?"

Tam moved around to the other side of her. "Yep. There'd have to be."

"Of course. My nurse. Certain servants."

"And..." Jax paused. How far should he take this? She knew the answers already, but maybe hearing them might make them more real. They all had to understand the risks they were taking. "It's a matter of record that you exist?"

"My birth was recorded." She sounded as if she were humoring him.

"He couldn't eliminate everyone who knew you, to blatantly take you out of existence. That would reveal too much. He had to devise a way to get you out of the picture so he could eliminate you behind the scenes. Those who go into those orders don't come back out. They don't talk to outside people. Everyone would have believed you were in seclusion." Marses had been setting her up to kill her in a way so no one would catch him. Anger boiled hot and heavy in Jax's gut. He would have gotten away with it, too. If Kiann hadn't run, she would have died.

Her face went stark white.

"Jax." Tam's voice sounded disgusted.

"What? That's what he was planning…"

"But you didn't have to blurt it out like that. Say things blatantly and matter-of-factly. This is her *life* we're talking about."

Which was exactly why Jax had said what he had the way he had. She had to understand her predicament. This was her life; she had to know the complex danger she was in. He glared at Tam. Could he do anything right today?

"No. No." Kiann waved a hand. "I'm fine. Jax is right in what he said. I like your honesty." The latter was directed to Jax.

He had no other way to be. He didn't usually tell lies or couch things in pretty words. He told people how things were. It never occurred to him to put things in gentler terms when she needed to hear things out loud.

"So now we know"—Kiann moved into their rooms through the swishing doors—"what Marses had planned for me all along."

"Yep." Tam pushed through the door behind her. "Jax, why don't you see about finding us some food? I'm hungry." He looked at Kiann. "How about you?"

She nodded. "I am."

Jax's eyes narrowed. Tam wanted to be alone with Kiann. He probably wanted to comfort her after Jax had made her realize how twisted her stepbrother was.

How did he feel about that?

In ways, the two of them together bothered him. Yet in other ways, the thought of the two of them together made his libido charge forward full force. They were alike, Tam and Kiann. Yet there were differences. He'd have fun finding those differences. Maybe. One day. If he could bring himself to find out what intimacy could be like with a woman. "Do you both enjoy the same dishes?"

Kiann grinned. "I will eat anything. I'm not picky."

"I don't know if I can find Ebolian fare."

Tam put a hand on the door. "Anything is fine, Jax. We'll see you in a while." He shut the doors between him and Jax.

Jax stood there a moment, staring at the sliding doors. If he didn't find a way to conquer his misgivings about their mating with Kiann, he might lose Tam as well as their third mate. A sobering thought, but a true one.

A life without Tam would be a life not worth living.

He turned away and walked to find a restaurant with a determined spring in his stride. No, he wouldn't let that happen. He would find a way to accept both of his mates. He had to trust the Fates. Even if he thought they were cracked for putting a woman in their lives.

Chapter Eight

Tam looked at the doors closing in front of him. Jax had watched him until the last minute. The jackass.

No, that wasn't fair to his lover. Jax was dealing with the situation about as well as could be expected. But he needed to deal better. Use a little tact. Again, not fair to Jax. He'd never had tact. He wouldn't change overnight because they had a new mate. Tam needed to stop expecting that of him.

Tam turned to face Kiann, taking in her beauty. He was now alone with her. His blood pumped through his body at a fast pace. Mostly down to his cock, which didn't seem to understand danger, only arousal. Her face looked sad, which didn't bode well for anything of an amorous nature. He tapped his chin to calm himself. He needed to be there for her. "I'm sorry about Jax."

She looked at him as if puzzled. "What?"

"His...lack of...tact." Tam closed the space between them to a few meters. "He tends to be..."

"Brutally honest?"

He nodded. "Yep."

"I like that in him. It makes him different." Her voice lowered as she turned her face away. "From people who don't deal straight so they can get their way." Bitterness drenched her words like salt in the sea.

He approached her and put his arms around her. After a moment of indecision, she relaxed in his arms. They stood that way for several seconds. He listened to her breathe and internalized her soft, delicate scent, which suited her. Each movement of the intake and outflow of her breathing tickled him. The actions were rhythmic. He leaned down to kiss her head. He could get used to this. Only one thing was missing. Jax. Jax would complete the embrace, either holding her on the other side or in back of him. He needed to hurry back with the food, to take part in what they needed to do to bond as mates.

His stomach growled in anticipation of eating. Maybe he was hungrier than he'd thought.

"He was going to kill me."

He stroked up her arm, ignoring all else but her. "More than likely that was his plan."

She cuddled into his body like she was a small psi-cat. "He would tell people I'd gone into that order, meanwhile doing whatever he wanted to me." Her body shook with the force of her emotions. "I never thought he'd do that to me. I knew I'd be a danger to him if I found my heartstone or mates. But I never thought he'd try to eliminate me before then."

"I know."

"I was stupid. I should have known. I should have seen that coming. I should have known…"

He leaned back to hold a finger to her lips. "Shh. You couldn't know anything about what he planned to do. You couldn't see what he had hidden from you. Nothing is your fault." Her sadness and her anger filled him. He wanted to take those emotions from her and take away the source of her angst. He wanted to make life all better for her, even though he couldn't. Nothing would take away the knowledge of what Marses had done and had planned for her. The only thing he could do was ease her pain.

Tears brimmed in her eyes, stopping on her lashes. "I won't be duped again by him. Not ever."

"No. You won't. Jax and I won't let him lie to you again." He'd die before he let her go back to Marses.

Her black-as-night eyes looked up into his, searching them. Her mouth trembled. "You can't always protect me."

"We can try, Jax and I." He took the moment and leaned over to kiss her. Her soft lips opening under his made him groan with ecstasy. Her scrumptious taste tantalized his taste buds. Her hot feel sent an inferno raging inside of him. Her lips parted more under his to let him explore. They felt different from any mouth he'd kissed before. He wanted to melt into her like a candle to the flame.

She met him kiss for kiss as he ran his hands up and down her back. She moved in close to him and rubbed her body against his.

Like sandpaper to metal, the friction created made heat boil up along all his nerve endings.

Her lips wouldn't let his go and kept meeting him in a frenzied mating of mouths. Her hands came up to stroke his sides, and one tangled in his hair.

Still he wanted more of her touch. Wanted more of her body.

No, he held himself in check. This wasn't the time. He needed to get to know her more before he took her. This woman deserved perfection for her first time. She deserved everything and more.

She rubbed her pelvis against his cock, and he thrust back and forth against her, unable to resist the temptation. But he'd let this go no further. He couldn't. Not for her sake. She'd laid her protection in his lap. He wouldn't fail her.

When she finally pulled away from the kiss, she was winded. "Wow." Her lips parted, giving him an invitation to dip back in.

He didn't take the invitation. "Yep." He watched her lick swollen lips. Other things on her would be swollen as well. Like nipples that would bulge in front of his eyes. And lips down in her pussy that would drip for him. He straightened his back. Good thing he'd paid attention in all his classes on mating, especially those about females.

She tugged on his shirt, pulling him back against her. "Hold me. Hold me for right now."

He raked his teeth over his lip. He didn't have to be told twice. He wrapped his arms around her, holding her tightly. He leaned into her.

"I don't know who I am anymore. Or who anyone else is." She leaned into his body as if trying to burrow into him, away from all the bad things in her life.

He'd let her hide in him if only he could. "I know who you are."

She looked up at him with wide eyes. "Who am I?"

"You're my mate." He stroked along her back, dipping into each knob of her spine. "You're the one who completes Jax and me. That's who you are." She'd become important to him in such a short time. He wanted to give that back to her and more.

"Am I? I seem to have brought you nothing but…"

"You are our mate. Don't ever forget that. You'll bring happiness to us. I know things are tough now, but they'll get better." That was something else he'd see to. She'd been denied so much of her life. The time had come for her to live to the fullest. Somehow, he'd hand her that.

"When? When do they get better?"

"I don't know. Maybe as soon as I kick Marses's ass." He leaned back to wink and let her see his teasing.

A chuckle broke free from her. "Stand in line. I'm first."

"Point taken." The doors swished open. "Jax can be after me."

"After you for what?"

* * *

Kiann had to laugh again at Jax's expression. He looked as if he had an idea what they were talking about but didn't want to know.

"Kicking Marses's ass."

He set down a few bags of food. "Oh." He nodded to them both. "I'll gladly do that. If I ever get a hold of him…"

Icy tendrils moved through the words. He didn't finish the thought, but the ending was obvious.

A tremble moved through her. He sounded tough and evil. Not that she'd known him long, but she'd never heard such vehemence in his voice toward someone else.

For her.

Whatever else Jax thought of her, he was angry for her sake. So was Tam. A large ball rolled up in her stomach.

No one had ever been angry on her behalf before.

She'd spent too much time isolated. Never getting to know anyone. Seeing them move on after a few weeks or months. The only constant in her life since her father had died had been Marses.

Who wanted to kill her.

"You look pensive." Tam unloaded the food from the bags. "You okay?" His gaze burned through her reverie.

"Yes, I am." She sat down in one of the chairs in the small room. The seat creaked alarmingly under her weight. All of the furniture in the small room had seen better days. Maybe even better years.

Tam filled a plate with recognizable meats, fruits, and vegetables. "Is there anything here you don't want?"

She shook her head and then saw how much he'd heaped on top. "Good grief. That's too much food."

"Nah. It's enough." He handed her the plate and commenced filling another one, which he handed to Jax. He'd given them both about the same amount of food.

She eyed Jax. Big man and her small self, and Tam gave them equal amounts of food. He did like to take care of his mates. A smile crept out. Tam was balm to her shattered soul.

She still couldn't believe Marses had been out to kill her all along. What had happened to the young boy who'd played with her when their parents first married? Was the crown that important?

Not to her. Family legacy be damned. She didn't want to kill anyone over ruling. Not even Marses.

Jax let out a tight smile. "Thank you." He approached the bed and sat on the mattress. It made similar creaky sounds, which made him eye the bed suspiciously.

"There's another chair." Kiann took a bite of food and realized how hungry she was. On the run, meals had been hit or miss. Wherever this had come from, the food tasted delicious.

He made a face. "After the noise that one made when you sat down, I'm not trusting them."

"Like the bed's much better?" She wiggled, making the chair make noises again, but the seat held.

Jax shrugged.

Tam sat on the bed by him. "Me either. If you made it creak, we might make it break." His eyelids lowered. "Though might be fun to try."

She nodded, trying not to shovel food in her mouth, and ignored the innuendo. Nothing, not even palace food, had tasted this good, which showed how hungry she'd been. Jax and Tam had tasted more wonderful when they'd kissed her. She'd now embraced them both. She shifted her legs. What kisses they'd been. Her thighs clenched. The center of her body ached deliciously. Another try of their mouths on her would be a good end to the day. Any day.

They all ate in silence, and before long, she'd cleaned her plate.

"Little hungry?" Tam smiled as she got to her feet and tossed the plate on the table.

"More than I thought."

"Did you like it?" Jax stirred around something in gravy. Must be the meat.

She'd barely noticed what she ate. Probably best with food from a questionable kitchen. "I did."

He didn't smile, but looked pleased that she'd enjoyed what he'd brought.

"So what now? We have our new identities." Now they'd be on the run. What a life she led. Her breath exhaled in a whisper. She'd brought them into a hell of a mating.

Tam set down his plate and stretched. "We figure out a destination. I think we're safe here for a while. The hooker was scared of Marses; she won't call him."

"And that destination would be?" Kiann sat back down and yawned.

"Wherever we want to go."

Jax set down his plate as well. "Yeah, we'll look at cities and where we can best blend in."

As Ebolians, she and Tam would never blend so well. Ebolians stuck with their own. She yawned again. A full belly made her tired. "But that doesn't do anything to take Marses off our backs." Nothing would. Her brain hurt from thinking about that fact. Somehow, she had to find a way to freedom for all of them.

"No." Jax fingered the bedspread. "It doesn't."

At least the linens on the bed looked clean. The room might be small and well used, but someone had tidied up. She wouldn't let herself think about what might happen when Marses found them, instead focusing on the present, on the small details of the room she'd spend some time living in.

With these two men.

"We'll deal with that later." Tam leaned back on the pillow. "Right now, I think we should get some rest. We can leave here in the morning and book passage on a transport. Once we are away from here, it becomes harder for Marses to track us."

"Good idea." Jax collected his and Tam's plates to put with hers. He closed up the food with a snap.

"Okay." She grabbed her bag and went to the door that separated their rooms. "See you two later."

Tam frowned. "You could sleep here. With us."

"I don't think that would be a good idea." They had much to get used to. She didn't want to rush anything between them. Could she stay in here and not have things advance? Hardly likely. She enjoyed what they did to her too much. And going too fast wouldn't help any of them.

"Why not?" Tam's whole face frowned. He was expressive. Emotional.

"I just don't."

"But what if something happens while you are separated from us?" He looked as if he would argue with her for some time.

She wouldn't cede to him. Couldn't. "You said you thought Marses was far enough behind us." They'd be safe here a while. How long, she didn't know. Marses would trail them, but he would take a while to work out all the details. They could use that to their advantage.

"Well, yep." His voice lowered. "But I don't like the idea of you being separate from us."

"She needs time, Tam. We all do." Jax walked to the door. He opened it and walked through the room.

Under his breath, Tam muttered, "No, you do."

The undercurrents came back between the two men. Not anything she'd ever wanted to cause.

She shook her head. "Don't." She hated being the cause of trouble. "He's right. We all need time to adjust."

Jax came back in the room. "It's all clear. The door to the outside is locked. We can leave this door open, and she'll be safe."

"How much time?" Tam asked. When they both looked at him curiously, he continued, "How much time do we need? Before things grow between us?" He still had that impatient look on his face.

"There's no time limit. It's when we *all* feel comfortable enough. But we *all* have to feel that way." She didn't add they might never feel comfortable enough with this arrangement. He didn't want to hear that. He wanted them to succeed, which made her warm and gooey inside. She moved by Jax. "Thanks for checking out my room." She'd never had anyone looking out for her. It was oddly comforting to have someone doing that.

"No problem."

She started to shut the door behind her.

"No." Jax caught it with a hand. "Leave the door open."

"But…"

"I don't expect anything to happen. But I don't want you cut off from us." Jax's mouth set in a firm line. "The door stays open."

Her hackles bristled under his commanding tone. As quickly as they reared, they settled back down. He was concerned for her welfare. He wanted to protect her. Other than her parents, no one had ever done that for her. Not to mention an open door would give Tam and Jax no privacy. Something that would deny them any intimate talks or sex. They were doing this for her. She couldn't argue with any of that. "All right."

She moved into the room and dropped her bag on the floor. The room looked identical to theirs, complete with old-looking furniture and the same amount of cleanness. She needed to wipe the long day from her body and mind—another yawn broke out—and get some sleep.

After a shower, she lay down in the bed. Exhausted, she didn't stay awake long. She heard murmurings from the other room, but was asleep before she could decipher what had been said.

* * *

"You're mad at me." Jax stated the obvious as he looked at Tam. The evidence was there in the man's face and body position. They'd had their share of arguments in the past, and he'd learned to read his mate well. Not that Tam was hard to read. While he could be diplomatic, with Jax he wore his emotions like a banner.

Slight snores sounded from the other room. While Kiann had gotten ready to sleep, so had they. The routine all had been normal and usual.

Only everything had changed.

Tam was angry with him. Jax wasn't sure how to fix anything. Only that he had to try and make everything right again.

"I'm not mad."

"Bullshit."

Tam reeled, eyes widening at Jax's use of an expletive. He didn't use them often. Tam scratched his chin and then shook his head to deny what Jax had said. "I'm not mad. I'm frustrated. I'm as prickly as a psi-cat."

Tam loved the little creatures for some reason. He spoke of them often. "At me." Jax climbed into bed. Would Tam follow him? They'd never gone to bed upset with each other. He didn't want to start now, but he couldn't pretend everything was going well. That wasn't him.

"At the situation." Tam's hand clenched tightly. "I...I want her. Badly, Jax." His hand continued to ball and release. A quick check revealed a thick cock under his leather pants.

Under different circumstances, Tam's erection could have been used for fun. Jax sighed. "I know." His own need for the woman superseded most anything else, even with his need for contemplation. He'd never known longing could intensify like this. He hadn't known it could grow uncontrollable.

Tam's desires had to be tenfold worse. He'd already become sure of his feelings. That would increase the arousal and desire. And the need.

To the boiling point without a climax.

"You want her, too, Jax. Despite everything that you question about our mating." The challenge for Jax to deny the words existed in Tam's clipped words and the upthrust of his chin.

As if Jax would lie. That was what had him in trouble in the first place, that he wouldn't tell an untruth, and when he had lied, it'd gotten him in deeper. That Tam was challenging him to lie proved how far gone Tam was. "Yeah, I do want her. But, do you know what will happen if we tackle this before we're ready? If we take her before the time comes?"

"What?"

"We'll lose her. She's serious when she says she wants us to care for her. You know as well as I do I won't lie. Not to you or her. Not about this. We take her now, we lose. She'll bolt, no matter that we are her mates." Her running would affect them both in ways Jax couldn't comprehend. At least, they'd have each other, unlike her, who'd be alone, but nothing would ever be the same between them. He'd realized that not long after the mating. No matter what happened, everything had changed. And so he'd started to deal with the changes.

"I have to wait, too?" Tam lowered himself to the bed with a bounce of his body on the springy mattress. A grumble rumbled in his voice.

At least Tam would sleep with Jax. He might be irritated with him, but that he wasn't seeking another place to rest was a good sign. Jax hadn't thought of a solution, but with Tam's words, he jumped on a logical way to sort this out. "No. You don't." He hadn't considered this before. But why should Tam wait? There was no reason for him to. Logic said Tam could move forward with or without Jax, and then Jax could catch up when he was ready.

Tam's hand moved up to stroke his chin as though that were the last thing he'd expected Jax to say. "You mean that?"

"If you are sure of your feelings toward her, go for it." The thought of his mate with the woman in the other room wasn't one that made Jax queasy. Instead, the images inspired all kinds of thoughts roaming within him. His cock reminded him they'd been longer without sex than any other time in their relationship.

"I'm sure of what I want with her and you." Tam rolled over to face him. "I thought you'd be…disagreeable." His grin was sexy. Huge. He looked more at ease than he'd been for a while.

Jax shrugged, his cock lengthening more. He'd made his mate happy, something he always longed to do. "Why not? She is our mate. I know that I'm unsure, and until I get sure, she won't have me. But that has nothing to do with you two." Eventually, he'd have to deal with his reluctance and figure out the future. But that was between him and Kiann.

"What about...I'd be her first."

Kiann was a virgin. The first man to take her would be her first lover. "I'm not concerned with that." He wasn't. "I didn't care that you weren't a virgin. There will be plenty of firsts for all of us to deal with." Jax had never taken pride in being first because it was only being last that counted.

Tam reached a hand to stroke down Jax's face. The featherlight touch made Jax lean into Tam. "You're practical."

"Always." It was part of his nature. Jax wanted to give himself up to Tam's touch, but first they had to talk out some things. They needed a plan. Not some trumped-up, half-assed plot, but a real idea of where they were going next. "What are we going to do about Marses? She's right. He won't stop coming. Fake IDs are only good for a while." They needed to use the time they'd bought for themselves to its fullest.

"We'll come up with something. We have to." Tam's confidence was catching. "You know if she takes her place as ruler, she'll take us with her as co-rulers." Tam shifted close enough that Jax burned in the heat from his body surrounding him. "That would be something."

Two men who'd been unaccepted by society taking on a throne with their third would be impressive. "Yeah. It would be." Having Kiann at their side would be even more impressive. If only she wasn't a woman. He could have dealt more easily with another man coming into their lives.

Tam ran his hand down to Jax's chest and pushed inside his shirt to tweak a nipple. They'd both put on clothes, despite usually sleeping naked. Neither of them had known what would happen until they'd talked. Now, all they needed was a more concrete plan. "I guess since I can sleep with Kiann, I can with you, too?"

"Anytime you want." Jax closed his eyes, giving in to Tam's hand on his body. Such slowness and gentleness, he would go wild after a while. Tam's touch always did that.

Lips met his and gently explored and thrust a tongue inside.

That ended their talking about the future and about the woman for the rest of the night.

* * *

The visions whirled around Kiann, drawing them into their murky depths. Emotions swirled under her consciousness.

Red surrounded her and enveloped her in its softness. Its protection. Softness and warmth invigorated her. She'd never been this alive. So taken in by something. So safe. She stretched within the confines of its cloud.

She turned over on the mattress.

Icy blue tendrils infiltrated the red. Coldness swamped her. An ache moved through her chest. The blue ripped her away from the red, though red kept up a fight to keep her.

The sheet twisted around her, a snake threading through her legs. She frantically turned this way and that to get away from the tangles. It reminded her of the blue that wouldn't release her despite the knocks of red.

Red smote blue. Blue fought back. All around her, they warred.

Their struggles pushed her, pulled her, and she turned this way and that in the bed. Half aware of the real world, she was still in the grip of the dreamscape.

Clouds of both colors covered her mind, refusing to let her wake all the way. She remained partially in both realms.

As the smoke of the colors cleared, she caught a vision of a woman. What was she doing? *Walking up steps. Her face turned to face Kiann's watching eyes.* The woman was her.

She climbed onto a throne. The throne of her people. The green jewels running up the side winked at her from their settings amongst intricate gold carvings. The throne looked jubilant. A dark man placed on a crown even as he smiled at her. Two red hazes took seats on each side of her.

People cheered, milled around her, and clapped. Their faces looked happy to see her on the throne, even as they pointed and watched.

She twisted again on the mattress, almost falling out of bed.

Where had the blue gone? Surely it would come back. Menace them with its chill. Take her again.

A redness covered her with mist. With whispers in her mind. It's okay, you know. Time for you to live now.

Arms wrapped around her. "Are you okay?"

Strong arms.

For a minute, she fought them. They might be blue. They might hurt her as things always did. Despite the assurances of the red, she'd seen too many things come back to haunt her. The arms wouldn't release her, and the voice continued to croon to her.

Her eyes opened to reveal Tam's concerned eyes. She relaxed in his grasp.

"Are you okay?" Jax's voice sounded as worried behind her. He stepped into her line of sight as she sat up, placing her back against the headboard.

"I'm fine. I...uhhh...I'm fine." How would she explain the vision she'd had? Her seeing was never straightforward. It was always subject to interpretation. Heck, the nightmares might have been from the strong foods she'd had for dinner, instead of any vision of the future.

Tam released her to sit at her feet on the bed. "What happened?" He pushed blankets back up on her pants-covered legs.

Jax sat down beside him, causing the bed to dip.

Two concerned faces kept their gaze on her from the foot of her bed. Neither of them wore shirts. Hard pecs breathed in front of her eyes. Tam's pants weren't tied at the top. They'd been thrown on. Did they sleep in the nude? Now that was a picture for her to contemplate. Much better than red and blue hues.

The force of the vision drove out her notice of her mates' state of undress, drove away all but thinking of what she'd seen in her dream.

She didn't answer as her thoughts raced. Closing her eyes against the beauty sitting before her so she could assemble her thoughts, she caught her breath. The dream had been intense. She'd never experienced anything similar to this vision, even those beckoning her to come to Settler's Mine. The visions had been so real, even with the haze of the colors swirling around her dream.

What did the colors signify? And the throne? How could she be climbing into the huge chair that the ruler of her people ceremonially ruled from?

"You had a vision, didn't you?"

She opened her eyes to find Tam staring at her with a speculative look even as he tied his pants. "Yes. Yes, I did."

"Was it about a throne? You stepping onto it? A crown being put on your head? A crowd watching?" He rubbed his weary face with a hand.

Her eyes went wide. "What? How could you know that?" There was no reason he should be able to call up her vision. No reason for him to know what she'd been dreaming about.

"Because I had the same one a few minutes ago. Until Jax woke me up." His lashes lowered to hide his eyes from view.

That was impossible. Ebolians didn't have similar visions or the same ones. They didn't dream in tandem. "That can't be." She pressed a hand to her mouth as she sat up straighter. Her back left the headboard. "You couldn't have had the same dream I did."

"The throne was gold with green jewels up the side."

"You could have seen photos." The Ebolian throne had been well-documented in the media, unlike most things in their culture. "Not in your dreams." There wasn't anything unique about that part of her dream. Nothing to show he'd had the same one.

"You ducked your head as the dark man put on the crown. He smiled at you and looked happy. The whole damn crowd looked happy."

She gasped in air. That was how it had happened in her vision. The joy on the people's faces still gave her pause. Their expressions had made the vision unique. Tam somehow had seen what she'd envisioned.

That was impossible.

"You saw those things in your thoughts, too, didn't you?" Tam's voice lowered to a mere whisper.

"Yes."

Jax reached out to stroke her leg under the blanket. A surprise. He reached to comfort her before Tam did. Not anything she'd expected. "I woke Tam up. He was restless and grumbling. As you were."

"How could we have had the same vision?" Those things didn't happen. She shivered under Jax's touch, even though the blanket still covered her skin. As unexpected as the caress was, it wasn't unwelcome. She savored his caress, as Jax had come to her without being asked. No one had shown her affection for so long. She leaned into his touch as if she were a starved Ebolian puppy, unable to help herself.

"I don't know." Tam shook his head, his gaze trained on Jax's hand on her leg. He looked mesmerized by the touch of one mate to the other. His hand moved as if he would touch her, but instead he lowered it to beside Jax. It wasn't touching, but it was close enough it could have been. He didn't want to break Jax's moment with her. She realized he probably worried if he did, Jax would pull away. "Was there more to your vision?"

She nodded. "Colors. Red and blue. They were fighting over me." She hesitated, but then swallowed heavily. "Blue took me from red. By force."

"I didn't see any colors." Tam scratched his chin with the hand not resting by Jax. "What could that mean?"

"Does Marses wear a particular color a lot?" Jax continued to offer his touch, grounding her. Making her better. It made her insides much better than the light touch should have. Probably because of his unexpected reaching out to her. "Maybe blue?"

"The royal robes are blue. He wears them a lot." Even to unofficial functions. He lived in them. Her head came up with her own interpretation. "Blue could be Marses. I do think of blue when I think of him." The blue had ripped her away from the safety net of red. Her heart hammered in her chest.

Tam leaned forward, and his stone ignited both of theirs. A red beam pulsed from all three stones. "Red's obvious."

Jax nodded. He looked as if things made sense to him. "I think that vision shows us what we need to do. We'll need to be careful, so that the first part doesn't come true." He turned his head to study the door. He'd be on alert from now on.

They couldn't stop what was to come. Could they? Had an Ebolian vision ever been altered from not coming to pass?

She almost couldn't say her next words, but she had to get them out. Surely this couldn't be what the vision suggested? But the logical conclusion reached from that dream went one way, not in any other direction. "You think I'm going to take over the throne?" Nausea rolled around her stomach.

Chapter Nine

Tam nodded. "I agree. I think that's what the vision showed, in great detail to both of us." Unsteadiness saturated him about having the same dream she'd had. That was unheard of from what he knew about Ebolians.

Why? Why would they share a vision? Even as mates, sharing didn't happen. Unless the situation was so intense that it called for this type of psychic energy between them.

No, nothing about that made sense.

Unless she was a stronger psychic than he.

Which could make all the difference in the world. He was only half Ebolian. Perhaps she was broadcasting her energy to him to influence his own gifts? Maybe his visions weren't his own, but were hers? It would take one damn strong seer to do that. A seer like Ebolia hadn't had in an age. Or ever.

Though he'd studied Ebolian history, he'd never encountered anything that mentioned these acts in real time. Some theorized the scenario could happen with a strong psychic and a half-breed, but it had never been proven.

Still, his skin jazzed from everything that had transpired. His erection pushed out from his body like a poker. He'd never desired anyone as much as he did Kiann. He needed to make her his. He needed to make love to her.

He wanted to take her with Jax and make her theirs at this moment. He didn't want to wait.

One look into Jax's thoughtful face told him that wasn't going to happen yet. At least Jax had started being honest. He wasn't trying to pretend something that wasn't there. Jax had no airs to put on, and when things finally did happen with him and Kiann, Tam could be sure those things would be real.

"How…I mean, I don't want the throne. I've never wanted to take the throne away from Marses. I only want to live my life as a person, not a prisoner." She twisted her hands together.

"You are the true ruler." Jax shifted away from Tam. "The last of your line, until you procreate."

"He's right. Destiny says you should rule." Tam watched a shudder run along her skin. Goose pimples swept under his fingertips. "Does ruling scare you that much?" He'd never make her do anything she didn't want to do.

Her voice lowered. "No."

He almost asked, "Then why the reaction?" Then he realized the touches had caused her reactions. Both he and Jax had their hands and gazes on her. He dipped his own hand into the molten lava, otherwise known as her skin, with each pass of his fingers. Did Jax feel the same way?

"Even if I wanted to rule, how would I go about taking over? I can't exactly waltz back to the kingdom and say, 'Hi. Remember me? I'm here to take over.'"

Jax puffed out a heavy breath. "That's exactly what you do." His eyes caught the fire. Such passion evoked things in Tam he couldn't explain.

Tam stared at him. What was getting into Jax? Then, he saw Jax's eyes drawn by the woman's cleavage. Yep, he might say he wasn't ready for intimacy, but his body and physical signs spoke otherwise. His mind and heart wouldn't be far behind the physical. Tam would be there when they caught up.

Kiann's words came with hesitation. "How do you mean?"

Jax tore his eyes away from Kiann's chest only with effort. "I mean Marses is away, right? He's not on Ebolia."

She nodded. "Yes. He's on Settler's Mine, or was. He's trying to find me."

"We throw a few false trails for him to follow, head back to Ebolia ourselves, and stir up your people. One look at your bloodline, and they will be begging to support the true ruler of their planet."

"To do that, we'd have to get hold of the media." Tam leaned forward, his eyes on Kiann.

"Exactly."

Plans were Jax's forte, as was carrying them out. Tam had never been more proud of his lover. This one was brilliant. Getting the people on their side would work. It would have to.

"Yes. That'd be the easiest way." Her throat moved with her halting speech. "We'd have to bolster support to my…side. They don't know me." Her lip trembled. "At all. He hid me away well."

"You're of the line." Tam clasped her foot in his hand, giving her any comfort he could through his touch. She'd been used to being in the shadows. It had to be hard thinking about coming out into the limelight. She'd have a lot to adjust to. They all would. "I may not be fully Ebolian, but I do know what that means to people of our heritage."

Jax blew out a breath. "He's right. Your lineage will mean a lot to the people in your kingdom. Those of any kingdom, for that matter. Natives would eat it up. I'm going to get us started. Book passages to scatter our identities to the four quadrants of the galaxy. By the time Marses finds the real us, we'll be on Ebolia getting the people on our side." He pushed to his feet and then looked back to Kiann. His face softened more than Tam had ever seen. "That is what you want to do?"

They'd do what they had to do to save her and themselves. Choices had to be made to secure their future. Kiann had to decide a big part of what would happen next, though.

Tam watched Kiann work through being put on the spot by Jax's question. And how gallant of Jax to ask. He could have plowed ahead without getting any of her input, although it was her decision to make. His lover continually surprised him, even with the situation at hand.

"Yes. I think that's our best bet." She bit her lip. "I want to keep both of you safe from harm. Right now, you aren't." She nodded while her throat moved up and down in a swallow. "Yes, I think this is our best option."

Jax lowered his head as if in a slight bow to her. Not a full-blown bow, but impressive in itself. His elegant muscles contracted and unrolled before them in his stomach and pectorals. "I will do my best to make what you want happen, Kiann. I promise you that. I'll get this started." He stalked to their room to finish getting dressed.

He was back in a moment, looking fully armed and sexy. How many weapons had he strapped on? Tam had been stunned to find out the quiet, Native henna-clothing maker had an extensive weapons collection. His face had that purposeful drive that Tam couldn't resist.

Too bad there was work to be done.

"What should we do? While you're gone and doing stuff to throw Marses off the trail." Kiann looked poised to get out of bed and get busy. What she intended to do, Tam had no idea. The decision to return home and take back her rightful place had given her purpose, as it had Jax.

"Stay here in our rooms. Wait for me to come back. Easier that way." He hesitated at the door, but didn't look back. His back went rigid as his shoulders straightened. "Tam?"

"Yep?"

"What we talked about earlier. You remember the conversation." Without saying any more words, Jax shoved a finger to the button to open the doors and stepped through them.

Tam's head raised as he stared at the closing doors.

Jax had given him permission to have sex with Kiann.

Not that he needed it, but better than doing it against Jax's wishes or behind his back. His whole body tightened. This was a great gift that Jax had given him.

"What did he mean?" Kiann looked to Tam and back to the door as his gaze settled on the beautiful banquet before him. A banquet he was dying to partake of. "What did you talk about earlier?"

"Nothing for you to worry about. It was only Jax's way of reminding me about something."

"What would that be?"

For once he didn't mince words. Maybe he was learning something from his Jax. "How much I want you."

Her quick swallow told him more about her state of mind than anything else.

* * *

Kiann looked into dark eyes that reached to her soul, beautiful eyes that saw inside of her. Desire rippled across her skin with shivers that rocked her to her core. "You do?"

"Of course. I've wanted you since I first saw you."

The words filled her with surprise. She hadn't known, with the way things had happened, how he considered her. Not exactly. She'd hoped, but she hadn't known. She watched as he moved forward on the bed, coming up to lie alongside of her.

His hand reached out to caress her cheek gently.

She leaned into that light touch for a brief moment before pulling away. Truth was she wanted him as much he wanted her. There was only one issue. "What about Jax?" She didn't want to come between the two lovers any more than she already had. She wouldn't, either. She couldn't fathom Jax reminding Tam about wanting her.

"He's fine with us moving forward."

"Without him?" Her voice rose.

"Yep. We talked about it."

Must have been an interesting conversation. If only she'd witnessed the dialogue. "Is he sure?"

"Jax never says anything without being sure." He touched her cheek again. "He'll come around, you know. He needs time. He doesn't want to do anything until he's sure, but he doesn't want to hold us back, either."

She didn't pull away from his hand this time. She couldn't help but lean into his touch. "But what if he can't deal with this? And if you and I are…already intimate, that will cause problems."

Tam frowned, his face tensing up before relaxing as if he hadn't contemplated that outcome. "No. Jax will come around."

"He might not." The way her luck went, she had her doubts. Her throat dried too much to swallow. She wanted this, but didn't want to cause any more problems. What should she do? Who should she deny? Herself or her desires?

"He will. I know him. You're our mate."

If only she could share in Tam's certainty. "I won't cause problems between you two." A vow she'd keep above all others.

"You won't." He leaned down to press a soft kiss against her lips. "We will work this through."

Therein came the moment of choice. She could deny Tam what he wanted—what she wanted—with some notion of protecting Jax by not taking further intimacies until he could join in. But what would that do for them in the grand scheme of things? Nothing that she could think of. By furthering her intimacies with Tam, she increased her chances of Jax coming around. Of viewing her as more than a sexual object, as Tam already did.

Her eyes closed. She was selfish enough to want this with Tam. To want Jax to come around. To try any means of convincing him that this mating was what he needed. "You think he'll come around? That he'll accept me as his mate? As your mate?"

"He will."

Her eyes opened as Tam pressed another slow kiss along her lips. Her body lit with fire. An old starter to a shuttle had nothing on her. She kissed him back for all she was worth, making him moan against her lips.

She needed this. Needed to be with someone who cared about her. It had been a long time since she'd had a caring person in her life. She'd never been intimate with anyone like this. Tam did care for her. Even though they'd only known each other a short time, he did. She could sense his internal emotions. He wanted her.

The time had come to press on with her life and claim her mates. One at a time if need be.

The kiss filled her with promises.

She had some say over Jax. Some say over his reactions. Right then and there, her heart thundered for her to make Jax hers. Take Tam now and make Jax realize their full potential as mates.

The only way. The best way to handle this situation.

With renewed vigor, she gave herself over to the kiss, letting Tam know with her responses to him how much she wanted this, how much she wanted him.

She ran her hands over the spirals of the tattoo on his neck before running down to the planes of his hard chest. His muscles flexed under her hands. They flowed in a tantalizing manner with innate strength.

His hand tangled in her hair as the kisses grew more intense, more real.

She was going through with this.

Her first time having sex. Making love.

Her heart hammered in her chest, speeding up her breathing.

The reality of what she was about to do grew overwhelming, and she shuddered. Nothing had ever been so real.

He pulled back. "You okay?"

"Yes." She looked up into his beautiful face. She could tell him anything, and he'd listen. He gave that sense to her, and she took the bait. "I'm a little nervous." She couldn't meet his eyes with her confession.

His eyes smoldered with long-overdue passion. "Me, too."

"You?" He didn't seem to be nervous at all. Her gaze scanned his serious face. "Why are you?" She couldn't imagine why he'd be anxious. They'd take a big step for her because of her lack of prior intimacy. Not to mention, while she understood the clinical makeup of sex, she wasn't sure she understood everything about the act. *Well, you're about to find out.* Thrills and chills raced across her.

"I've never been with a woman before."

Oh. She swallowed. "Oh." She hadn't known that about Tam, though she had about Jax. Interesting the one who hadn't opened up to her had mentioned that tidbit of information, while Tam hadn't told her this before. This wasn't only a first for her, but for him as well.

"I do know what to do, I assure you." His face lit up with a grin as he winked. "And I look forward to doing it with you."

Her breathing eased at his reassurances. Tam would help her with this. He'd be gentle and loving. She relaxed. Trust in him filled her.

"You do know what happens, don't you?" Now, he did look nervous. "During sex?"

"Of course I do." She renewed her exploration of his chest under her hands, causing his lungs to suck in again. This power she had over his reactions made her try harder for a demonstration she was in charge. She'd never had such responsibility before. "I'm not that sheltered." Somewhat sheltered, but she did know what would happen.

His cock would enter her vagina. He'd have an orgasm and fill her with his seed.

Such a clinical recitation of what would happen.

Would the reality be pleasurable? Or would there be pain? Would it fulfill every romantic expectation she had and more?

He didn't give her much time to ponder what would happen next. Keeping his eyes locked with hers, he reached down to untie his pants.

She slid her hand down over the planes of his stomach to above his waistband. Her hand traveled into the open space that had now been exposed by the spreading of his pants. The hair crinkled under her hands. She couldn't believe her bravado. Of course, with Tam it was easy to be brave. He invited her to be.

"Eager, are you?" He sucked in his stomach.

The muscles banded under her hands. "Uh-huh." She undid the zipper on his pants herself, then reached inside his pants to take his engorged flesh in her hands.

Her first touch of a cock.

Her head threw back from Tam's member inching into her hands. Never had she imagined such a thing, not even in her most vivid fantasies.

He leaned back with a groan. "Good."

He throbbed in her hands, his hard cock. It felt like a rod ran through the length. Yet soft skin covered the rigidness. Her hands went from the bottom where she ran into his body to his rounded tip. A slight drop of wetness met her hands.

She played with the liquid in her fingertips.

"It's precome." He smiled at her.

She shuddered at the knowledge. He was that turned on, and she'd done that to him. She'd never known such power existed in sex.

She dabbled her fingers in the drop while encircling the head of his cock. With each touch, she grew drunker from the mastery of her hands over his flesh.

His hips thrust forward, as he enjoyed her learning of his body.

She moved her hand away to pull down his pants.

Where had she found her boldness? Perhaps she'd found her stride in making love to her mate. Never had she been this forward. With little exposure to people, she'd leaned toward being shy. Not so with Tam. He didn't seem to mind.

It felt good.

He helped her shrug down his pants and then reached to the bottom of her shirt. He hesitated until she nodded at him to continue.

Over her head her shirt went, exposing her breasts for Tam's enjoyment.

His jaw went slack as he stared.

She had to giggle at the expression on his face. He had reverence and longing contained in one look. There was even power in disrobing. Yes, this was an act that could be addictive. They hadn't even gotten too far in yet.

He shook his head. "Goddess, you're gorgeous."

She'd never thought to hear anyone say that about her. The words filled her with more sureness that this was right. This was her mate. She was meant to be with him.

He reached out a hand to touch her breast. His hand slipped underneath to cup her.

Warmth spread across her as he moved his hand up to run his palm across her nipple.

Her nipple swelled and ached. It needed something. His touch shot sensations into the pit of her stomach and down below.

He brought up his other hand to stroke her other breast and kept fondling her with master touches.

Each one sent her further along the brink of desire.

Then, he lowered his mouth.

He took a nipple into his warm wetness, closed his lips around her, and suckled her. He kept the suction up as intense as a fire shower.

Her entire being burned in his wake. Her hips bucked wildly back and forth as he continued to draw her in and out of his mouth.

Touching herself had never frayed her soul like this. She lost herself in the sensations. She'd never realized how sensitive her breasts were. Or maybe it was because Tam was touching her.

He lifted his head. "You're sensitive." He sounded amazed by his discovery. Not as amazed as she was.

She cried out when his head went back down, and his mouth latched onto her other breast. Nothing she'd read, seen, or done to herself had prepared her for the reality of sex. Never had this many sensations raced around her at one time. This was only the foreplay. There was more to come.

She shivered. Her nipple had been embroiled in a furnace. Heat and wet surrounded it with careful consideration.

Her head arched back into the pillow.

His hand moved down her stomach with his roughened skin tickling her. He stopped at the top of her pants briefly, then slid his hand down into the front of them.

Her breathing hitched. He was close to another place that felt empty. One that craved his touch.

He continued his pleasuring of her nipple even as his hand found her center and petted her in earnest.

One finger slipped into her wetness to find her clit. A little bundle of nerves she'd already discovered brought a lot of pleasurable sensation before she'd even had the sexual satisfaction to go along with it.

But now it was Tam's finger on her button. Just like the first time, that knowledge was enough to send her spiraling up into the stratosphere. It was his turn to hold the power to turn her inside out.

The instant he strummed her clit, her whole body arched up. Electric currents shot from the one contact, bringing her back off the bed. That one touch ignited fires she didn't even know she had. She almost came from the intensity. The first time had been wonderful. This was something akin to splendor. The first time, she hadn't known what would come next with her mates. Now, she was sure of Tam at least.

She'd been pent up with emotion, wondering what her mates would do. Now she had her answer with Tam. She could release some of that frustration. And would with him making love to her. A moan escaped from her lips. His finger tortured her.

He kept his digit there. One finger was joined by the rest of his hand. Another finger dipped down into her channel and set up a rhythm going in and out.

Her legs spread wide as the climax hit her and ran with her over the edge of a mountain. She dropped off, floating in space as pleasure spasms rocked her.

Her second orgasm with her mate, the shored-up beginnings of a possible life—she'd never forget this moment.

After the sensations had eased, he pulled away his mouth from her breast to look at her. "Beautiful."

"No. You are."

He was.

Looking down at her, hair askew about his head, he was a lovely vision in the slight light of the room. His dark eyes gleamed with passion's hues. He'd never looked wilder or more desirable than he had at that moment, and he'd been fairly desirable before.

He lowered his lips to hers to take in her in a soul-searching kiss. His hands withdrew from her pussy. His tongue wrapped around hers lovingly. He tasted of spice and some toothpaste that she half recognized.

He pulled away to gaze down at her. Then slowly, deliberately, he lowered himself. He pressed kisses along her collarbone, light and the barest wisps of them. He moved between her breasts to press kisses along there. His tongue and mouth teased, quite different from the intense feelings of a moment ago.

Then, he moved farther down to lave his tongue along her belly.

She gulped down a spasmed swallow. Could he be going where she thought he was? Where his hands had been twice before?

Talk about never being kissed. He was about to kiss her in a place that no one had been before. A place he'd touched and brought her enough pleasure she thought she'd die.

She didn't know if she could handle that warm, wet mouth suckling her. Moisture slicked her already slick folds.

He pushed farther down along the bed so his head now rested above the center of pleasure.

Her pussy. That was the term she'd seen used in books.

Her clit pulsed in time to her heartbeat.

He would do something she'd never experienced—kiss her pussy, lick her clit.

Her stomach filled with wonderful butterflies of anticipation. She'd never wanted something this badly before, never wanted another human to do something this much before. People usually disappointed her, but not this time.

He looked up to grin and wink at her. Then, he pushed her pants down along her legs and off her ankles. The pants were tossed on the floor.

She didn't care.

He lowered his head to blow warm air along her skin. Her hairs pricked up. He sucked in to create cold air along the same spot.

She shivered. The need to release was bursting inside her, even so soon after her last climax. What would his mouth feel like? Impatience had her gripping her hands. She willed him to get on with the kissing if he was headed down there.

His mouth lowered to lick along her slit.

Heaven lived in his mouth, and he brought nirvana to her. Her whole body raised along the bed.

His tongue delved into her most private parts, the parts that only she had ever seen or touched before.

Her pelvis arched up and down as her fingers burrowed into the sheet.

He flicked her clit up and down before moving down to penetrate her hole with the tip of his tongue. In and out, he moved, as quick and deep as he could. He moved back up to her clit and drew his tongue over her again and again.

When he sucked her into his mouth, she almost bolted off the bed.

Too much. This was too much for her to take.

The climax rained down on her, covering her in its bliss.

She panted, trying to keep up with the needs for breath in her body.

He lifted his head. His mouth was wet with her essence, which shouldn't thrill her, but did. "My first taste of you from your source."

She shivered. Never would she have expected such a thrill to run through her with those words.

Moving slowly, he stalked up her body to plant a kiss on her parted mouth. He tasted of her cream.

Somehow that wowed her, too. She'd never thought she'd enjoy tasting herself on the lips of another.

He rolled onto his back and urged her up on top of him.

She remained puzzled for a second, even as she climbed aboard. What did he want her to do? She'd never read about women mounting men.

"You're in control, Kiann. Take me as you want to." His voice sounded huskier than she'd ever heard. His cock poked out, showing her how much he wanted her.

He'd given over the reins of their lovemaking to her, for her to control the act.

He didn't want to hurt her. She'd sensed that from the start. This was his way of ensuring whatever happened was what she wanted and all she desired.

She'd lost control of much in her life. To be put in control of this moment… Her whole body quivered with the power.

She'd make this something to remember—for them both.

Where should she start? She'd never done this before.

He still had his hands on her hips.

She maneuvered herself over his cock. Gobbling down a swallow, she lowered herself onto him. Rooting around, his cock tip brushed her entrance.

They both groaned.

Her body slipped against his.

She slid down a little more so that he rested against her. Then he popped inside her opening. Not fully in, barely fitting, she slowed to adjust herself to the sensation of his penetration.

"Oh, Goddess, you're tight."

Yes, she was. Almost too tight around his length. She moved up a little, then back down a little farther. More stretching to accommodate his cock. Her wetness seeped onto him, aiding in the struggle to take him inside.

She'd wanted his mouth on her. That was nothing compared to this deep-seated ache for him to be inside her. She swallowed, trying to take this slow so she was prepared.

Another two passes and she'd seated him deeply within her.

The way he'd seated himself in her life since the stones had glowed.

Oh, how she welcomed his intrusion into her life and opening, even though nothing had prepared her for this moment.

Penetration hadn't hurt. The books had been wrong when they said sex hurt the first time for women. Instead, it created all sorts of glorious sensations. There was pressure and lots of it, but his penetration didn't cause her pain.

But she felt exposed and open to him. The way her life would have to become to her mates.

And there was something more, something to come. The urge to move barreled up inside her.

She moved on him, lifting up again and settling back down. Even more wonderful impressions swept through her.

The veins in his neck popped out, moving the tattoo up and down. Funny how they matched with their black tattoos.

His hands tightened around her hips.

He was losing control and giving himself over to the sensations, just as she was.

Her body caused him to lose control. Her and her alone.

"That's it." Tightening her walls around him, she went up again, then lowered again. She clamped her thighs together as much as she could, clenching around him. He craved tightness, so she'd give him that.

A moan was her reward. She savored that little noise and gave him more.

Another pass of her body across his and his hips bucked.

The next pass was faster. The next, faster still.

A whirlwind of sensations took her by storm as she quickened the pace. Up and down, rolling her hips and tightening around him.

She needed to come, needed to ride that flurry of bliss again. She had to make it there, or lose herself in the attempt.

Her whole body tingled. Her breathing increased to match her pounding heart rate, which in turn matched her actions.

The orgasm ripped through her. She became a piece of paper torn in half. The climax sucked everything she had out to the surface. Air couldn't get into her quick enough. She saw blinding redness in her vision that blanked out everything else.

As her climax neared its end, Tam gave a shout and clutched at her hips with wild hands. His hips bucked frenetically as he spilled his seed into her willing depths.

She collapsed upon him in a mass of jiggling goo. She couldn't move or talk. All she could do was lie on top of the man who'd done this to her.

No wonder people killed to get their heartstones. To get the chance to do this. She finally understood the draw of heartstones, the gateway to sex.

His hand came up to stroke her back.

The quiet near-darkness of the room was inviting and comfortable.

Similar in nature to the man lying with her.

He'd given her so much in the lovemaking. He'd thrilled her. Yet, she could tell him anything. This was what being mated was all about.

Thank you, Goddess, for him.

After a moment of lying there, she heard the rumbles start in his chest. "Are you hurting?"

"When I can feel my innards again, I'll let you know."

He chuckled.

The sound made her want to cause him to laugh again. He sounded sated. She moved experimentally to find things were starting to work again. There was a slight soreness down in her pussy. Nothing major, though. The pressure had been intense while she'd been adjusting. She hadn't done the things they'd done before, so it made sense she'd be a little sore. "It didn't hurt. I'm only a little stiff now." In fact, she felt delicious, decadent. All those things she never had before. "Nothing to worry about."

"Good."

She moved her head across his chest.

He snuggled her close. "I'm sorry that you're stiff."

"Not too bad." She had enjoyed herself too thoroughly to be sorry. She'd have risked that much bliss for almost anything.

"Did you see any colors when you climaxed?"

Redness swamped her vision again. "Why?" She blinked and rolled from him to look up into his face.

He put a protective arm around her, which she snuggled more against under the pretense that she was cold. At least, that's what she told herself. "Because I saw red fireworks when I came. I've never had that happen that vividly." He snuggled closer. "I think you might be projecting your psyche onto me like before."

She stiffened. "That can't happen." One Ebolian couldn't push their vision onto another.

"It can."

"How do you know?" She said the words more stringently than she'd intended. The intimation was there that he was only a half-breed, so how could he know? She cringed, but he didn't seem to notice. She'd been too long without talking to other people; sometimes she forgot how things could be taken.

He continued on as if nothing had happened. "I read about Ebolia. I've...well, I've tried to find out as much about my heritage as I can. There's not much information out there, but I've read it all." He continued to stroke her back with gentle hands. "My mother died when I was small. I was raised by my father. He didn't know much about Ebolians. What I learned, I had to pick up myself. I read a lot of books on the history of Ebolia."

Tam knew more about her own race than she did. She sent Marses to hell in her mind for his interference in her life. What little she knew wasn't enough. Her entire preteen and teenage years had been spent in isolation. The little schooling she'd had before she was denied hadn't informed her about any of these things. Royal matters weren't taught until the royal was old enough.

She swallowed again, keeping her irritation in check. Marses was who she was mad at. She needed to keep that close at hand so she didn't take anything out on Jax and Tam. "Losing your mother must have been hard on you and your father both." The loss had nearly killed her father until he'd found his second mate. She'd been a shy girl, and losing her mother had made her even quieter.

"It wasn't easy on either of us." After a quick frown, Tam's face lit in a soft smile. "Dad did what he could to teach me both heritages." Definite affection there for his father. They must be close. "But I carry much more of my Ebolian heritage than I do my Tarsiduan. Even in looks."

She'd looked like her mother, too. Her father had often commented on the resemblance. Had Tam's father felt the same as her father had? Sometimes she'd sensed her father's pain in seeing her, especially before he'd remarried. Probably. Yet another thing they had in common. "Tell me about psyches. I must not know everything." Her schooling had been too interrupted. She wouldn't get upset with Tam for what she didn't know.

"It's all theory, but a strong psychic can broadcast her visions to other psychics. This is especially true with those who are part Ebolian. That's what I think is happening with you when you have visions. I think I'm picking up on your signal." His eyebrow went up. "Your powers would have to be phenomenal for that. Few are born with that kind of strong power."

Her mind flickered back to a teacher telling her she had a strong mind for a young one, and she needed to develop her psyche. She had been around six at the time. How many times had she heard that before Marses had secluded her? A lot. Had she been in school when she was older, they would have developed her talents instead of leaving them to simmer. "You think I've been projecting my mind onto yours."

Tam nodded. "I do. I think that's why I had the vision to come to Settler's Mine. And why they continue along the same vein as yours."

"Are there any dangers to me doing this to you?" She wanted to hide her face in his chest. She didn't want to hear the answer, but she had to know. She wouldn't hurt him ever if she could avoid the action. Of course, how she'd stop broadcasting she didn't know. She hadn't been aware she'd been doing that.

"No. No danger."

"I guess we should dress soon." She sighed, snuggling more into his body. "Jax should be back soon with our definite plans."

"I know."

"You think he'll come around to being with me?" She'd asked it before, but she needed to hear the answer again. She needed Tam's certainty to fill her well. Jax was an unknown. She wouldn't let him walk away, though. She'd fight him to keep him if she had to.

"I do. Probably soon."

She'd do what she could to make that happen. Her chance happened sooner than she'd expected, because Jax walked in with a proud look on his face.

Chapter Ten

Jax stared at his naked mates, entwined on the bed. He couldn't find words for a second or two. He'd known what they were doing; curse him, he'd given them permission. But the irrefutable evidence of what they'd been up to created a reality in him he'd never expected.

They'd been making love to each other.

His cock hardened as he couldn't block the thought, *If only I'd been a few minutes earlier.*

He would have seen them. Seen one mate's cock go into his other mate's pussy. Seen their reactions, their pleasure. His back straightened at the images that flashed across his mind.

"Are you okay?" Kiann asked, pulling up the blanket around herself to make sure her breasts were covered. Her dark tattoo stood out against her creamy skin much as Tam's always did.

Tam had a knowing smile on his swollen lips. He knew Jax way too well. He'd understand what was on Jax's mind.

The scent of sex hung in the air, too. Jax could smell her musk. His nose could detect a hint of Tam's come, only because he was familiar with the scent.

Yeah, if only he'd been a few minutes earlier. What sights he might have seen.

Kiann cleared her throat.

He'd been standing there for several seconds without saying anything. Gawking. He shook off his reactions. "Yeah. Yeah. I'm fine. I'm back. We leave in about nine hours. Our triplets will be leaving for the next twelve hours and going all over the galaxy. By the time Marses figures out where we are, we should be entrenched on Ebolia. Our real destination is the only one I fully covered. The others are only half attempts to disguise our movements."

The half attempts would convince Marses that any one of them was the right destination. That they were trying to cover tracks but had been unsuccessful at doing so. Some had been done better than others to invoke his interest. And one was particularly well done. Not as good as the real destination, but close. That would throw Marses off their scent. By the time he found the well-hidden destination, they'd already be there.

His chest puffed out with his hopeful success at evading Marses.

Next would come the plan to gear up the Ebolian people, which would take finesse.

"We probably should try and get some rest before we ship out." Tam yawned. "Get up in a few hours and get ready to go."

Sex always made his mate tired. Jax's mouth dried. If only he'd been involved in making his mate tired. "Good plan." He moved toward the other room to find his bed. He'd not slept well earlier with Tam restless in the bed.

"Where are you going?" Kiann's voice sharpened.

He turned to face the two of them. She'd sat up a little farther, but kept the sheet on all the private parts of her. Curse him for being disappointed in that. He might not be sure he could love a woman, but his body was telling him that he could be attracted to one. He'd considered jerking off by himself when he got a moment. He needed to do something to relieve the pressure in his cock. "I'm going to bed to get some sleep."

"In there?" Kiann stated the obvious with a pained look on her face.

"Oh, no." Tam sat up and didn't worry about the sheet. "You're not going in there to sleep while we're in here."

"Well, what do you propose I do, then?" Despite his gaze being captivated by the small expanse of bared skin, testiness came out in his voice. Jax's weariness weighed him down. He didn't want to play games about who slept where. He just wanted to get some rest.

Tam patted the small stretch of bed beside him. "Come sleep with us. Your mates."

The blood roared in Jax's head loudly enough he could barely hear. His heartbeat pounded a rhythm he could barely keep up with. "I don't think that's a good idea." Yet, the idea wasn't a bad one, either. Talk about increasing intimacy. Nothing was more intimate than sleeping together. Waking up with morning breath and tousled hair. But could he stand being near his mates and not giving in to his libido?

"Why not?"

"Because..." Jax waved a hand, not inclined to explain. "It isn't." He would not be ready to take Kiann as a mate until he'd accepted the situation. His mind still raged a big protest over accepting her as a mate. He wasn't sure how he'd reconcile his mind and body. What a dumb soul he was, too, for having all these issues. If only honor wasn't such a big part of him. Then, he could take what they offered and have no remorse about the lack of emotion behind the sex. But he couldn't separate out his emotion from sex.

He had before his heartstone, but he'd been a different person back then, too. The stone changed you. To have sex now would be wrong and lead to hurt feelings. That wasn't anything he would willingly do to Kiann. Her emotional state mattered to him.

Kiann's eyelashes fluttered down to cover her eyes. "We're not talking sex, only sleep." Her eyes reopened with a pleading look in them.

One that Jax couldn't resist for long. The look made his feet take a step toward her as it was. He stopped after only a step. Could he keep his hands to himself?

At his hesitation, Tam motioned with his hand.

Kiann continued, "I'm serious. Look, not to be too graphic here, but this was my first time. Sex didn't hurt per se. But I'm not ready for another round yet. 'Kay?"

Jax had to chuckle at her blunt honesty, so much like what he'd been told he did. He'd heard it hurt for women. One reason he'd been in no hurry to take her virginity. He'd hurt her enough with words. He had no desire to do it with his body. Besides there were other places on her where she was still a virgin. Those he knew how to handle. When the time was right, he'd make her his in many ways and positions. If only he could push himself ahead to settle this sooner rather than later. "You two want me to sleep in here? With you?"

They both nodded.

"I'm still…"

"Shut up, Jax." Kiann let out a big yawn. "I'm tired. Get into bed."

Tam let out a full-out laugh. "I think our mate is bossy."

"Me, too." Jax's hands trembled as he took off his shoes, despite the teasing they were doing to Kiann. This was a big step, but it was one that felt right to him. If it hadn't, he wouldn't have agreed, no matter what his mate insisted.

Instead of creeping on the bed by Tam, he circled it and went to the other side, the side by Kiann.

She flashed him a beautiful smile.

Which made doing this even more worth it to him. Made it even more real. Who'd think a smile could have such an effect on him? The pleasure ran all the way to his toes. From only a smile.

When had her reactions become important to him?

He didn't dwell on that subject but slipped into bed beside her without another word. Even through his clothes, the heat of her skin slid alongside him. The touch burned as if a fire raged under the blankets. He hissed at the evocative sensations pulsing through him and tried to pull back by rolling up on his back. He needed to gain a measure of control.

Maybe this hadn't been a good idea.

Then, she turned her naked body into him and snuggled against him with her head against his chest. One arm went around him, and her hand stroked his other side.

Tam snuggled up behind her, stretching out one arm around her so that it touched Jax, too.

Jax propelled out a breath. Not quite enveloped by his mates, but close enough. Their skin taunted him with warmth and closeness. A kinship.

"'Night, Jax." Kiann closed her eyes and buried her face into him.

Tam's hand squeezed his skin.

Maybe this had been a good idea after all.

* * *

Tam woke to warmth and a body snuggled up to his. He pushed into it to snuggle closer.

He loved mornings waking up to Jax's body against his. He loved his scent; even his kisses tasted wonderful in the morning. At least to Tam they did. Touching from his lover always made such a good way to start out the day. They'd have breakfast together. Maybe even use each other as plates.

In a few moments. Right now, he was enjoying the bridge between slumber and waking. He'd stay there all day if he could.

His cock pushed out from his body, letting him know the early morning erection signaled.

A soft sigh met his ears.

Too soft for Jax.

His hand brushed against something on the other side of the body next to him. Something that fit nicely into his palm. A breast. He released it as quickly as his hand had settled there.

That's when the reality hit him.

He rolled up against the body with his front as the memories of the last few days assailed him.

He was on an outpost with Kiann and Jax. This was Kiann snuggled up to him. Soon, they'd be making a run for their lives back to Ebolia, a place he'd never been, only read about.

But one he had always longed to see.

How often had he dreamed of going to his home planet? The place where his mother had come from. The place of half his heritage. While excited, he worried because of that fact. And of course, the idea that they had one shot to save Kiann's and possibly all their lives filled him with a lot of tension. They wouldn't get another shot. They had to make this work the first time.

He opened his eyes to find Kiann sound asleep beside him. The soft rises and falls of her chest enchanted him. The pattern of her breaths drew his attention. When you could watch a person breathe and be fascinated with that was when you knew you had it bad for them.

How had she become important to him so fast?

He watched her slumber for several seconds, enjoying the curve of her shoulder and the peek-a-boo that her skin played underneath the covers.

He reached out a hand to stroke along her bare shoulder. He had to touch her skin and cradle her warmth against him.

Lazily, his gaze shifted to the person on the other side of Kiann. The third to their matched set. He was surprised to find purple eyes staring back at him.

Jax was awake and probably had been studying him the whole time he'd studied Kiann. Now his eyes appraised Tam with a look that nearly sent his blood boiling.

Jax held a finger to his lips. Then he lowered his hand and stroked it across Kiann's cheek, before bringing it up to caress Tam's.

The gesture made Tam's heart race inside his chest. Such tenderness. Jax might deny he was falling for the little minx, but Tam could see the beginnings of something flaring between the two. Tam's feelings had always been quick to fire, and he'd been quick to jump in right behind them. Jax was doing what he always did, taking his time.

Hope swelled Tam's breast. Maybe they would get there after all. "Like?"

"Her skin is soft. Her bones are delicate." Jax spoke in a hushed whisper as though he didn't want to wake Kiann up. "She's beautiful."

Tam looked down at the woman lying between them. She was a beauty, of that there was no doubt. "Yep."

Jax continued to stroke even as Kiann fluttered away from his questing hand.

She made a face as though the touch tickled.

Jax dropped his hand away from her face, attentive as always to his partner's reactions.

"What time do we need to wake her?"

"In a few more minutes." Jax looked at the clock across the way. "We do need to start getting ready." His voice threaded through a note of regret.

"Yes, a few more minutes." Kiann breathed the words in a huffy breath. Her chest still rose and fell with the same pattern, and she snuggled into both of them as much as she could.

Tam moved closer her. Her fluid heat against him made him burn. "Not that awake yet?"

"No." Her voice sounded heavy with sleep and muffled as her face hid in him. He'd never seen anything cuter than her tousle-haired head trying to hide. "I'm asleep."

"How are you talking, then?" Jax sounded amused as he lowered his head to peer at her.

"Sleep talking."

"Oh." Tam ran his hand down her side. This would get her up. "Then you won't mind if I tickle."

"Cut that out." She yeeped and moved quickly away from his roving fingers.

If only they were roaming to other parts of her. Wet, warm parts. Last night had been one of the best times of his life. His first time with a woman, with her, and it outshone a few stars he'd visited. But their time left here was nil. He'd rather have her safe than diddle with her.

He moved his pointer finger, eliciting another yelp from her. "But I'm sleep tickling."

Jax's hand met his to join him. "Me, too."

Tam couldn't help the thrill pulsing through him at Jax joining him in teasing. They rarely engaged in such teasing of each other. But Kiann brought this out of Jax in ways Tam never could. She brought so much into their relationship. Jax would have to see that eventually.

"Sure you are." She giggled and didn't stop until she'd managed to push their hands away.

'Course, they'd let her push them away, sure the time for tickling was over. Tam didn't want to push his luck, and probably, neither did Jax. Getting to know how far he could push her would be a fun discovery.

"We were."

She rolled onto her back, looking between both of them. "You two are so full of shit, it's not funny."

Jax busted out in a laugh. "No one's ever told me that before. Except maybe him." He jerked his thumb at Tam.

"I know no one's ever said it before about me." Tam waggled his brows. "Except you." More truthful teasing. Jax was the only one beyond his family who would tell him to his face how he felt. Now Kiann would move into that category. A smile broke out on his face. This was working out well.

"Well, maybe someone should. It would keep you two from getting too arrogant." She folded her arms in front of her chest. "Keep you in line."

"Who? Us? Arrogant?" Tam puffed out his own chest in mocking affrontedness. "Not a chance."

"Uh-huh." She reached up to run a hand through her mussed hair. "Oh, my Goddess. I must look a mess." Her hand continued to fiddle with her hair.

"You look wonderful." Jax lifted up on his arm so he rested on his elbow. He had on his honest, sincere face. Somehow, even that moved Tam. He shot Jax a smile to let him know that he'd noticed he was trying with Kiann, which meant more to him than he could express. Things were working out better than he'd expected. "Marvelous, even." Jax returned the smile, making Tam's libido shoot upward again.

She snorted. "Uh-huh."

"You do. You look pretty." Tam nodded in agreement as fast as his head would go. "Hair and all." She'd be a beauty any time of day. She could make him hard with a look. What magic did she possess? The magic of Kiann.

"You two are good liars." She leaned up to press a kiss on Tam's cheek, then leaned over to press a kiss on Jax's. "And thank you for that."

Tam raised up beside her so he could see.

Jax's hand moved quicker than she could move back. He stopped her head and leaned over to give her a kiss. A deep, gentle exploration.

A kiss that had Tam wanting to be more than the one on the sidelines. But he didn't want to move in and break the spell that had centered around his mates.

She pulled back to look up into Jax's face.

The look that Jax gave back was one of intenseness and longing. His eyes blazed his passion for the woman in front of him. That gaze had burned Tam on more than one occasion. He lowered his head again, taking her mouth in a melding that had her breathing picking up considerably.

Tam reached out to stroke along her back, unable to stay apart from the two in front of him. He had to share in some small part what they were experiencing or go crazy from the wanting. He wouldn't intrude to break the moment, but he'd not sit back and stay apart.

Jax's hand reached for his and grasped it tightly against the warmth that was Kiann's skin.

Taking that as acceptance into their embrace, Tam scooted so that he was up against Kiann. The moment her hips thrust in reaction to the kiss she shared with Jax, a moan escaped her lips, sounding like music to his ears.

It would be easy to press into her, to take her from this angle.

And then, Jax pulled away. He dropped his hand from Tam's.

He'd done more than physically pull away. He'd closed himself off emotionally. Tam could see the mask had gone into place.

Dammit. Why had Jax separated himself now?

"What's wrong?" Kiann's voice came hoarse, straining against her intense breathing. "Why did you stop?" When Jax didn't answer, she looked back at Tam as if he'd know.

He had an idea. "Jax?" He wanted confirmation.

"I stopped while I still could." He tumbled from the bed in one graceful push of his body like a psi-cat rising to their feet after a long sleep. "I need to shower. We need to get ready to go." He stalked off without a backward glance in their direction.

Kiann worried her bottom lip with her teeth as she watched him. "I messed that up." She swallowed heavily before looking at Tam. If only she'd let go of her guilt about the problems with Jax. Her face carried shadows.

"No. He's taking his time is all. He doesn't want to give over to emotion too quickly."

Jax was thinking too damn much. If he'd give over to his emotion the way Tam was prone to do, everything would progress much faster. Instead, he had to get mired in his mind, in his thinking about problems. He'd started to feel too much during the kiss, so he'd run from himself. Tam didn't know for sure, but he'd wager that had caused Jax to break apart.

"Whatever." She lowered the sheet to move off the bed. Her skin exposed with each inch of the sheet that fell away.

Even while captivated by her body, he saw the slight wince when she moved off the bed. "Sore today?"

She opened her mouth to deny it, but as if she'd thought better of her answer, she said, "Only a little bit. I'll be fine, though." A smile chased away the shadows on her face. "Maybe later we can find some time to…get rid of my soreness." Her shy overture tugged at Tam's heart.

The shower turned on. "I'd like that." If only they could right now. But she needed some time for recovery. Tam had no desire to have Jax walk in on them because he wasn't sure at the moment what Jax's reactions would be.

What would the next day bring? A trip back to the place that held his origins and the key to their future. He'd visit past and present all in one swoop. Whatever happened, it was sure to be a wild ride.

* * *

Jax watched from his position by the window on the transport as Tam settled in by Kiann. He touched her arm, bringing a smile to her face as they got strapped in.

This newfound intimacy between Kiann and Tam made Jax feel left out. He was logical enough to know that made no sense, yet it was how he felt. He'd been the one to deny himself physical intimacy with Kiann. He'd been the one to stop things before they got started this morning. Yet he found himself on the outside looking in at his mates.

Logic was good, except where others were concerned. Few other beings behaved logically, which knocked all assumptions out of the window.

He blew out a breath. How was he going to decide what to do next? Things had moved fast. They would continue to move faster still. He wouldn't have a moment to himself to catch up.

He'd have to figure out how to adjust with little time to do so.

"You okay?"

He turned his head to see Kiann staring up at him with concerned eyes. She'd noticed his quietness. The concern in her eyes comforted him in ways he couldn't fathom. "Yeah. I'm fine."

The thing that was the most puzzling of all to him was that he liked Kiann. There was something between them. But was it developing into love? He wanted to be sure before he moved forward. He didn't want to hurt either of them with a false positive. That wouldn't be fair to them or him. With Tam, things had been almost instant. With this, he couldn't be sure. Curse his uncertainty.

The transport ship took off with its engines revving and a gravity pull on all the passengers. Nothing was out of the ordinary about takeoff.

Jax developed the sensation that someone watched him. The back of his neck prickled up.

He turned, and a woman's head ducked down. Probably marveling over the race mix they made up and now embarrassed for being caught staring. He'd have to get used to people gawking because of who his mates were. They were now a much more conventional pairing than he and Tam had been, but people would still notice them.

"You sure you're okay?" Tam's arm snaked around Kiann so he was touching both her and Jax.

The warm hand made him tingle as usual. His cock jutted out to attention. "Yeah." Both of them had checked on his well-being.

Jax had been used to being the quiet one before and after he'd met Tam. But Tam never let him be content to rest in the shadows and stew. No, Tam brought him out in the light every single time he tried to hide himself. It looked as if Kiann had the compulsion to do the same as Tam. His gaze turned to the window before inching back to the mates who consumed his thoughts.

Time for a change of subject. "What are our plans when we get to Ebolia?"

"Hit the ground running." Tam's fingers stroked Jax's shoulder, filling him with sensations that made him shiver. "We don't miss a beat. We start hitting media and broadcast who you are."

Kiann's breath quickened. "Are you sure that's best?" Kiann didn't fancy being in the spotlight any more than Jax did, which was displayed on her face in great detail. She needed to get used to being in the limelight. For them to make it out of this, they would have to use the media and become their darlings. She would need her star to shine brighter than any in the galaxy. Lucky thing she had it in her, though she didn't know it yet. Jax saw it in her.

"Yeah, I am." Jax turned a little toward her so her body touched his. "This will put you in the public's eye. Marses won't be able to attack you without getting in the public eye himself." The attention might be the only shot they had at keeping Kiann safe. Marses wouldn't be able to take her into custody without some explanations if her existence had been plastered all over media outfits everywhere. Despite his reservations about the mating, he didn't want to lose her.

More prickles slid up Jax's neck. Someone watched them. He turned. The woman's head ducked down again.

Jax furtively glanced at her, trying to ascertain her motives in observing them. He would need to keep an eye on this one. It was probably nothing. It was no crime to watch someone. Still, it made him uneasy. He kept glancing backward.

"He's right." Tam nodded in agreement with Jax. "I know who to see to do it, too."

"Who?" Kiann brought her hands together in a melding of fingers. Her foot tapped nervously on the floor.

Jax ached to ease her discomfort. "You can do this." She might not be used to being in the forefront, but she had the strength in her. Look at what she'd already been through, and it hadn't broken her. "I know you can."

He reached over and squeezed her hand before releasing her. The smile she shot him made his whole body sit up on edge. You'd have thought he'd given her a sack full of platinum, instead of a touch.

Tam said, "Butler. The Ebolian media mogul. We hit him and his stations. His media delivery systems. Offer him an exclusive. He has the most widespread news system. Even data linkage beyond Ebolia. He's the one to target."

Tam had done his homework, probably from things he'd already known. Jax had ascertained as much while booking their passages. Also, Butler wouldn't let Marses dictate what he showed. Marses had left him on the air, but only because Butler wouldn't hesitate to reveal the government's interference. That made Butler more likely to air them without buckling under to pressure. "I agree."

Tam looked pleased about their selection of the same mogul to target. Disagreements weren't his favorite thing to deal with. This whole situation had to have been hard on him.

Jax wound out a breath. His mate deserved so much better. He'd have to work to make it up to Tam.

Tam's hand squeezed Jax's shoulder.

"Do you think people will believe who I am?" Kiann's feet continued to dance under her seat. "I mean, it's been a long time since anyone had contact with me. They've all forgotten me."

Not hardly. She was a difficult one to forget. Look how much she'd garnered Jax's attention. He wasn't even sure he'd enjoyed most of the women he'd met. "At first, they probably will not believe." People tended to be skeptics. A preponderance of the evidence would be needed to convince them. Jax would keep on the public until they believed. Anything to save Kiann.

Kiann looked more worried than before.

Jax cringed. Had he been too honest again? He always screwed up in that area, though most times she appeared to appreciate that trait in him.

Tam wasn't glaring, nor did he seem angry, so Jax must have been on target with that comment. "He's right. We can plant enough doubt the media will start looking around on its own. They'll find more evidence for us. Marses can't have covered all your tracks."

Jax didn't comment to contradict Tam's hopeful scenario. The possibility was there that Marses had done exactly that. There was a real chance everyone who had known her true identity was gone. Hearsay or secondhand knowledge wouldn't do them any good. If the paper trail of Kiann's existence was gone, it would leave them screwed. Her travel papers to Settler's Mine hadn't shown anything of her true identity.

But if one person or document could validate Kiann's existence, that would work to create enough doubt. They'd keep plugging away at who she was. Keep telling people what had happened and what would have happened if she hadn't escaped.

Jax knew how close they'd come to losing their third mate. His gaze centered on her face. He'd never have known her then, and that would have been a shame.

Kiann's lips pursed.

That's when he noticed her again. The woman blatantly watched them this time.

Jax took more notice of her.

Brown eyes shone under brown hair. She looked similar to a Coronian, a race of calm, peaceful people.

She watched them a little too intently for his liking.

She leaned her head down and spoke into something.

A communicator, perhaps?

He didn't stare back at her but instead took a few furtive glances from the corner of his eye. Why would she be watching them?

His hand clutched the armrest tightly.

Unless…

Marses wasn't the only one pursuing Kiann.

Jax's heart beat faster, as if it were a shuttle flying too high in space.

In all their talks, it had never come up that Marses wasn't the only one after Kiann. They'd assumed he would be.

Marses's desire to keep things quiet had made them complacent, thinking he wouldn't hire anyone else to do his searching for him.

Complacency got one killed. Assumptions weren't logical. Only evidence was.

He cursed under his breath.

"What?" Kiann's trusting gaze impacted him more than he could say as he met her gaze.

Eyes that had trusted him to keep her safe. Now, all that might be in jeopardy. Who could the woman watching them be? He didn't buy it was mere coincidence that she observed them so intently. He'd caught her one too many times. He had no way to tell Kiann and Tam about her without raising her suspicions.

Best to let her think she hadn't been noticed and subtly keep an eye her way. If she suspected someone had noticed her, she might stop her surveillance. Then, he'd not find out anything further.

Who had she been talking to?

"Jax, what's wrong?" Her voice came more sharply.

He lowered his head. Willed Kiann to be quiet. "Nothing." He'd screwed up, but now he'd make it right. He'd figure out what this woman was up to. His hands continued to clutch the seat.

At that moment, all hell broke loose.

The transport shuddered in a sharp motion. The wacky side-to-side twist took Jax's stomach away. What was the pilot doing? Flying wasn't his favorite thing to do. This wacky stuff needed to end. He almost retched.

Tam said as much as he faced the aisle, curving his body. "What the hell is the pilot doing?"

That's when the loud boom and crash came from the front. People screamed and yelled.

Someone had fired upon the transport.

"Oh, my Goddess, is it…?"

Jax stopped her before she could say Marses's name out loud. He didn't want the woman behind them to hear. "No. He would never…" Not unless he wanted an intergalactic incident and the Union Alliance breathing down his neck. Marses was too smart for that.

But who was firing on the transport ship? They carried only people, so it wouldn't be pirates of any kind.

A chill raced down Jax's spine. It couldn't be good, whatever was going on.

"Escape pods!" several of the others yelled as some flung off their seatbelts and flooded the aisles in a panic. "Escape pods!"

Kiann grasped her heartstone as she stared at Tam's back. Suddenly, she began to fade before his eyes. Jax grabbed her even as she faded out of sight. One second she was there, and the next, she was gone.

Jax grabbed through the air even as he registered she wasn't there. This couldn't be happening. His hands pawed nothing. People didn't disappear. Logic said people couldn't disappear, but she was gone.

Tam turned back to look from the melee in front of him to say something and gaped at the empty space where Kiann had been. No words formed for several seconds. "What the…?"

Jax shook his head, telling Tam he didn't know what had happened to her. She'd floated right out of his hands. He gripped his fists tightly. He should have been able to hold onto her. Been strong enough to somehow pull her back from whatever had nabbed her. He'd failed her. Again. His hands clenched into fists. If only he could use them, but there was nothing to pound.

The firing stopped. An eerie silence came with the ceasing of the booms and crashes. The transport hadn't been damaged, or they'd be out of air. Whoever had been shooting hadn't intended to take it down.

Only cause a diversion. Stop them. So they could get Kiann.

Jax's throat closed up.

The pilot's voice sounded. "The attack we've experienced is over. The ship has flown away from us. Please retake your seats and calm yourselves. No escape pods, please."

Many holding their heartstones remained in the aisles, making noises of fear even as the pilot repeated his message. One tried to head for an escape pod anyway, but was blocked by a member of the crew.

Tam slammed a hand against the seat making a thwap noise that echoed in Jax's mind as his heart gathered speed. "Where the fuck did she go?"

"I don't know." Jax touched where she'd been sitting. The seat was still warm, and her scent pervaded the air. But nothing told him where Kiann had gone.

Tam grabbed his shoulders with a tight, clamping grip and stared into his eyes. "Did you do this to her? Or allow it to happen? Why didn't you stop her?"

Jax froze, looking in Tam's desperate eyes. He couldn't seem to force out a breath. "What?"

"You didn't want to be with her." Tam shook him.

"Tam..." He did want to, but he couldn't be with her until he was sure about his feelings. He'd never wanted anything to happen to her. Not this or anything else.

Her loss rolled through him with acute effects.

"You didn't want her. Now, she's gone. Did you do it?" Tam's voice rose in his agony and anger. "Did you have anything to do with her disappearing?" His hands shook on Jax's shoulders.

Tam spoke in emotional outbursts without thinking. Jax counted to a high number before he answered. He would not escalate this thing between them. His voice sounded controlled despite the fact he wanted to yell back. "No. I did nothing, except try and hold onto her before she disappeared." His heart clenched. He should have grabbed her quicker and held onto her. Logic told him it wouldn't have helped, but the rising anger told him he should have done more.

Where could she be? Who had her?

The answers weren't good ones.

He didn't want her to suffer or die. That kick-started his pulse. There were worse things than death. Did Marses have her? Jax had hidden their trail well enough, hadn't he?

In the relentless tide of what he wanted and didn't want, Jax finally accepted what he'd lost.

His mate.

He'd lost his mate. One that he loved.

Yes, he should have recognized the signs of his falling for her, but some people had to lose before they realized what they had. That was him. This loss, this love, was why his chest hurt. Why his stomach had packed up and gone to his knees. An ache had started inside of him from the first moment of her disappearance.

Because he loved Kiann. He loved everything about her, from her pert nose to her slightly crooked toes.

With Tam, his emotions had spiraled instantly. That was why he hadn't recognized this building of the blocks inside of him.

Until it was too late. He'd never told her. Now he might never get the chance.

No, he would find her. His hands tightened. Somehow.

A couple looked over and said, "Oh my God. That woman who was there is gone."

In the chaos that had followed, no one had noticed Kiann's disappearance. Now, everyone did. They pointed, and the decibel meter on the shuttle went up a few notches.

Everyone *except* the woman who'd been watching them earlier.

She looked down at her feet and didn't even try to see who was missing.

Jax's head rose. He saw red flashes from Tam's heartstone, which had probably glowed during their argument. His had the match.

There should be a third one, curse the Fates.

She knew something.

Why else wouldn't she look to see who was gone? Her mouth moved. Who did she talk to? She'd had a possible communicator just before Kiann had disappeared.

He needed to find out. His blood boiled as his hands balled into fists.

He unsnapped his seatbelt and climbed over the seats in back of him. His heart slammed up in his chest.

He loved Kiann, and she was gone before he'd ever gotten to experience the emotion with her. He wasn't letting her go. Not yet.

Especially when someone else might hold a clue to where she'd gone.

"Jax, what are you…?" Tam's panicked voice sounded behind him.

He didn't even look as he grabbed the person sitting next to her and flung him into another row of seats. He slammed his body down beside her on the bench on one knee. Drew his torso up to his full height. "Where is she?"

She straightened up, and he stood to block her way out of the seats. "Who?" Almond-colored eyes met his. Calm, almost a sea of brown. They wouldn't be calm in a few minutes. Not unless he acquired what he needed to know.

"You know who," he growled at the woman.

"I do?"

He grabbed her by the throat and pushed her up against the wall of the shuttle. "You do. You will tell me what you know, or you will be sorry."

Chapter Eleven

One minute Kiann was sitting by Tam and Jax, looking over him to try to figure out what was going on. The next, she started to dissolve. She'd grabbed desperately for Tam's arm, but her fingers went through him. Jax grabbed for her, but he could do nothing except watch her spirited away.

His eyes had shone with a fierce helplessness as she'd drifted out of his sight.

As her particles shifted back together, she shook her head to clear the dust lodging in her synapses.

She popped onboard a small shuttle craft.

It must be geared up with some type of transporter for beings. Union Alliance had outlawed them eons before, but they cropped up every now and then. They'd been deemed too dangerous. Sometimes all the particles didn't make it from the starting point to the destination.

Shaking her head, grateful she hadn't ended up with parts spread across space between here and there, she looked around the seemingly empty shuttle she'd been downloaded into.

Where was she? Worse yet, who had her?

Button snapping sounds buzzed from the front of the shuttle as it took a hard bank to the right. The motion tossed her against a bulkhead.

She pushed her hands against the cold metal to keep herself upright. Her hands shook. She ticked off what she knew.

Someone was onboard. Someone was flying. Someone had kidnapped her.

Her whole body joined her hands in shaking. Should she go look at who had done this? They weren't concerned with her right now, or they would've identified themselves. That left a hollowness in the pit of her stomach. They didn't even think she was important enough to tell her who they were or where she was.

She had to know who had her. What comfort that would give her, who knew? But she couldn't sit here in hiding.

She tiptoed the two steps to the front and peeked around a large cargo container that separated the cockpit from the rest of the shuttle.

Her body came in contact with a force field.

An electric current pulsed down her skin and left pain in its wake.

She jumped back with a startled yelp. Her knees almost buckled, but she managed to stay upright.

A shield separated the two parts of the ship. A force field with a surprise.

Her body stopped shaking as heat ran up her neck. What a shitty thing to do to a person. They'd known she would look around to see who had her, especially when they didn't even try to talk to her. There'd been no warning about the force field.

More button clacking.

Now that she knew where the shield was, she kept a safe distance from the field. She rubbed her stomach, which had taken the brunt of the shock. No sense getting hurt again. What kind of a sadist put a charge in a blocking field?

The answer came quickly as a man pushed back from the controls and into her line of vision.

A man wearing black. All black leathers from his shirt to his boots. Spiky whitish blond hair stuck up from his head. "That ought to do it."

Do what? What did he mean?

She'd half expected to see Marses. She thought somehow he must have found her. She hadn't expected this man she didn't recognize. She didn't speak to him but centered her gaze on her captor.

He turned to face her. His mouth quirked up in a semblance of a smile.

Only a fool would term it an actual smile. Not only did the expression not temper the icy blue eyes, but there was nothing reassuring about those feral whites he displayed between thin lips. "You can't get to me to try anything, Kiann. My suggestion to you would be to sit back and relax." An even more troubling expression dawned on his face. "'Course, I'd like you to try something." He drew a weapon, almost lovingly, and propped it up in his lap. "Anything."

"Who are you?" She wanted to scream in frustration, but refrained. It wouldn't do any good. She'd been close to having her future won with Jax and Tam. What would they think? Would they think she'd abandoned them after all? Or would they realize why she'd disappeared? The latter would be more logical. But the biggest question of all burned her throat. Would they be able to find her?

Her blood ran like ice water through her veins. They had no way to track her. There was nothing on her that would tell them where she was.

While on the transport, they had no way to follow her, either. Once the attack broke off, it would continue on its way without her. Nothing Tam or Jax could do would make them turn around.

There was no way in hell her mates could rescue her. There was nothing they could do for her, which meant she'd have to help herself. Her mind raced over possibilities.

He tapped on the controls behind his back at a beep. "I'm Merc."

Merc? Who was he?

Her face must have displayed her thoughts, because he offered, "I was sent to retrieve you."

He was a bounty hunter, then. She'd heard tales of them from servants, but hadn't suspected they were real.

To hell with Marses. There was no doubt in her mind that Marses had hired the man to seek her out. She wouldn't even ask who'd paid him to look for her.

"Merc…" She broke off. What did one say to one's captor? She had no platinum to offer. No great plans or power to put him into. She had little to reward him with. Goddess, she was screwed.

"Save it." He popped another control with a hard fist. "I don't want to hear your story. If you're not going to challenge me, then go sleep." He turned his back on her in dismissal.

She swallowed deeply, getting tired of the games people played. "I know who hired you."

"Bully for you."

There was only one thing she had to barter, and the time had come to offer it up to him. "I could make helping me worth your while." She dropped her voice several octaves, trying for seductive. No money or power, that left only her body. Her skin crawled with the thought. So unlike her times with Tam and Jax, who made her hot. A coldness pervaded her.

"Could you?" He didn't even turn back toward her. "Have to be a real sweet pot to turn me off this job."

"I think we could work something out." Goddess, they had to work something out. She'd been too close to freedom to give up now. She couldn't, nor would she let herself. "Something to benefit you and me."

"Is your pussy made of gold?"

She blinked at the question. "Huh?"

"Your beaver. Is it made of platinum? Gold? Silver?" He did turn back to face her as he spoke.

Those lifeless eyes of his creeped her out, making her stomach roll. What kind of a question was that? "No."

"Then, it's of no interest to me. Whatsoever." His eyes raked up and down her body. "I can use what I'm going to rake in and buy me some pussy that's…nicer than anything you got."

Hard to swallow being told that. "Oh."

He switched a switch. "Field's off."

"Why?" She didn't move forward for a second. Why would he turn that off? Didn't seem logical to her.

He motioned her forward.

Maybe he was accepting her deal after all, despite his words. Maybe there was hope she'd get out of this without going back to Marses.

She took a huge step. Then, another one. She hit the force field with full impact.

Only he'd increased the charge.

Her body shook with the remnants of the currents floating around her skin. She couldn't control the twitching. How she'd moved out of the beam, she didn't have any recollection. Must have been her body's self-preservation reflex.

Before, she'd not expected the field to be there. She'd walked right into the thing. This time was similar.

Stupid. She'd been stupid to move forward. Only doing something was better than doing nothing. Even if she did get shocked.

She rubbed up and down her front. "The field was still on. Shit." She glared at him. Looked for anything she could use against him. There was nothing on her side of the field. Nothing she could toss over would have any effect on the man because of the field. Nothing could penetrate the shield he'd put in place. Every time she'd try to breach it, she'd get shocked. Not something she planned to do again.

"Was it?" Merc feigned surprise. "Must have hit a wrong button." He moved to push near the same place he'd pushed before. "Come on across."

She shook her head. Twice shocked had been enough.

"Come on." He motioned with his hand again much the way he had the first time. "Come on into my cockpit. It's off. You can show me what that beaver's made of."

He made her sex sound distasteful. Unlike with Tam and Jax, who treated her and everything about her with reverence.

She hated this man.

She eyed him warily before turning and picking up a small nut from somewhere behind her. She tossed it, and the metal bounced back from the force field.

The piece of shit hadn't turned it off.

He truly was a sadist.

He laughed, a hefty tone that sent shivers up and down her spine. Everything this man did sent alarms racing in every sense she had. He'd hurt her if he could. Badly.

"You're smarter than Marses said you'd be." He looked as if that impressed him. Maybe even pleased him. "He said you knew nothing of the ways of the world." He leaned back in his chair, making it squeak under his weight. "You must be learning something."

"Where is Marses?" She could say a few other names she wanted to call him, but wouldn't. That would give Merc satisfaction, and that wasn't anything she wanted to do. He'd already had the satisfaction of her walking into the field twice. She wanted to wipe the smirk from his face.

"He's around."

"Waiting for you to deliver me, I bet." Then, what did Marses intend to do to her? Another shiver rocked her. He would kill her. Unless she could convince this madman not to deliver her. "Merc…"

He held up a hand. "Don't."

"You don't even know what I'm going to say." She glanced around, still looking for anything that might help her. Anything big she could throw at his head. Things over here weren't big enough to support any kind of revolt. The field would do well to protect him from any onslaught from her.

There had to be way out, but she wasn't seeing anything. Her foot tapped in frustration.

"Of course, I do." His face mocked her with seriousness. "You're going to plead your case. You could have the Saints of Yorick within you. Or the Devils of Natives. I don't care. Don't waste your breath." He licked his lips. "All I care about is the platinum. Or about watching you do some general hurt to yourself without my help." He looked suddenly pained.

She tilted her head. "You can't hurt me, can you?"

He hesitated a moment before grumbling, confirming the truth of what she suspected. Marses had told him he couldn't harm her. That was why he'd used the field to hurt her and not his hands. Technically he could say he hadn't been the one to hurt her.

From what she'd seen of the man, it would be the only thing which had kept her safe and would continue to keep her safe. She'd seen too much of what he really wanted to do in his eyes. Making her walk into a charged force field was mild compared to the things lurking in his depths. He wanted to make her bleed, make her hurt, and everything in between.

Why couldn't he hurt her? Why would Marses put down that edict on her safety? After all, he didn't intend for her to make it past him alive.

Because Marses wanted to make sure the deed was done, and done right. He always had been an efficient leader. It made sense he'd want to eliminate her danger to him in one fell swoop.

He wanted to take care of her himself.

She'd get to confront the man who'd stolen her life.

She cast her gaze around the shuttle again. Nothing remained that would help her get out of this. There was no way to let her mates know where she was.

Her mates.

Her breathing quickened. How much did they know about her mates? If they didn't know anything, then maybe at least Tam and Jax would be safe. How did she find out what was known and what wasn't?

"What do you know about me?" She'd ask directly. Pump Merc for information. Take her lessons from Jax. Goddess, how she missed him already. And Tam. She'd only had one night with Tam. It would have to be enough.

He looked at her as if she'd grown a horn in the middle of her forehead. "What?"

"You say nothing I say will matter. That it won't sway you. Well, what do you know about me, then? How do you know I won't sway you? I could have mates..." She stumbled over the words. She did have mates. Danger had them all in its grip with no way to recover without loss. Only she could prevent others from being crushed. She'd save them if she could and take the hit herself.

With her dying breath, she would make sure Jax and Tam were safe even if she had to deny what they were to her.

He shook his head. "I don't care, Kiann, about any mates you may have had or will have. It doesn't matter to me. The Fates are nothing but a bunch of bitches."

His speech was not an indication he didn't know about her mates. But if he had known, surely he'd mention them now. She'd given him the perfect opportunity.

He would have picked them up, too, along with her, if he'd known of their existence. He must not know about them.

The pounding in her chest eased. Her pulse returned to normal levels. Yes, this man would have taken them if he'd known. The edict from Marses to Merc to protect applied to her and her alone, not either of her mates. If he'd known about her mates, he'd have taken them for the mere sport of torturing them. If Marses had known about them, he would have ordered Merc to take them, too.

She'd have thought about that earlier if she was thinking straight. Her head felt like it had been encased in wrap. She'd gotten too hopeful about her future. Now, she'd been called out on it to pay the price.

She swallowed, trying to get her mind back into the game she played. She'd need her wits for what was to come.

Marses wasn't some pain-junkie bounty hunter. It would take finesse for her to make sure he never knew about her being mated.

What happened to her was incidental.

She turned to walk away and go sit down on the bench she'd materialized on. She was done playing with Merc.

"Sure you don't want to come in here?" His voice echoed off the bulkheads. "I'll cut off the force field."

"Cut it out. Like hell you will." She flopped on the bench. "I'm done with you. Take me to Marses."

"You have wised up."

She heard him get up and walk toward her outside the force field. She held her breath, not daring to look up. He couldn't hurt her.

"Look up."

She slowly lifted her head.

He stared back at her from over the container. "You won't play my way. There goes the fun." He pulled a weapon and yanked back the safety. Before she could jump down below the container to try and evade the shot, he fired at her with whatever he had. Hit her, too. "Fucking bitch. Time to sleep."

She tried to pull out the tag he'd shot her with, but she couldn't get it out. Her fingers numbed and felt far away.

He'd drugged her. When she wouldn't play his sadistic games, he'd lost interest in keeping her awake. Now, he was making sure she'd not revolt against him. She wanted to protest that she wouldn't have fought him. That this was unnecessary.

Maybe she should've run into the force field a few more times for his amusement. No, he would have done this anyway. Once she ceased to provide the sadistic bastard with entertainment.

She pitched forward on the ground. The numbness spread along her limbs. Her consciousness ebbed away with a coming darkness taking its place.

Steps echoed through the metal under her ear.

Red swirls of colors flashed before her eyes.

Merc stood above her with a leer. "Sweet dreams, bitch."

* * *

Tam watched with his mouth hanging open at his normally reserved lover, who had his hands around a woman's throat. "Jax." He'd never seen him out of control. If it weren't for his fingers around this woman's neck in a death grip, he'd find the new attitude sexy, but instead, he feared Jax might hurt her.

"She knows something." His attention focused on Tam for the briefest of moments. That was enough to take his mind from what he was doing, and the woman saw her opportunity and seized the moment.

The woman's foot sought purchase and came flying out, connecting with Jax's face, making a thudding sound. Her flexibility was astounding. No one else could have made the kick.

Tam cringed at the noise, and at Jax's head flying back. For a short woman, she packed quite a kick by the sound of the impact.

Jax dropped her as he shook his head, trying to clear the bells that she had rung. He muttered something unintelligible. His eyes widened before almost closing.

Tam grabbed for him. Was he okay? Was he hurt?

The woman came up in a fighting stance that screamed, "Don't mess with me." Her eyes blazed with untempered anger. "I know nothing about what happened to your friend."

Tam glanced back and forth between the two. What had Jax noticed that made him suspect this woman? Tam hadn't even noticed her until Jax had picked her out. Tam had seen nothing. One second, his mate had been there, the next she'd been gone. His heart hung heavy, along with his stomach. Where could she be? What was happening to her?

He'd not rest until she'd been recovered, until she was back in his arms again. Yet Jax was the one doing all the blustering right now.

What a reversal they'd had.

"I saw you watching us, communicating on some object. I saw you." Jax shook his head, as if experimenting to see how far the pain lasted. He would have a bruise. "And you kicked me, in the face."

"You had me by the throat. And it was on the chin." She lowered her hands, but only slightly, seeming to still view them as a threat. Her gaze remained steady. "What was I supposed to do?"

"Tell me what I want to know." Jax's voice went down to the deepest regions of a growl. The thick timbre reverberated in the small ship.

They had drawn an audience. Tam didn't blame them for stepping up to watch. He'd watch this event with an awed reaction, too, if he wasn't supposed to play a part. "Jax, what's going on?"

Yep, this new side of his mate intrigued him. But what in the galaxy could this gentle woman know?

Gentle race...

Coronians...didn't have kickboxing moves. He blinked as he studied her. Nor did they defend themselves in any way whatsoever. They were a peaceful lot.

He frowned.

"I don't know where your friend is. That's the truth."

"But you know *something*."

She didn't deny it, merely shrugged her shoulders one after the other. She was a small woman. Something wasn't quite right about her face. It should be plumper, instead of angular.

The rest of the passengers milled around to their seats, even those watching the situation unfold. They looked confused, as if they didn't know whether to intervene or not. Or which side to come in on if they did intervene. This many people could be bad if they came in on the side of a helpless Coronian against two men beating up on her.

Tam waved a hand, trying to put on his most diplomatic face, to reassure the onlookers. "It was a misunderstanding. We'll work it out." If they'd go back to their seats, everything would be okay. They'd have to keep the rest of this discussion quiet.

Not that she'd want to keep the conversation quiet. She kept glancing around as if she wanted to escape somewhere.

"It's not a misunderstanding. She knows something. And she's going to tell me what she knows, instead of this bullshit." Now, the determined Jax Tam had met before. But he didn't come out often. Once Jax got his mind wrapped around something, there was no changing the course. The woman would spill all before Jax would ever rest.

"I don't know where your friend is. I'm not saying that again to you." She glanced around the shuttle again, as if looking for a way off. "I don't know who took her. For sure."

Tam's head came up at the small amendment. Maybe Jax was on to something. His fingers curled.

"But you have suspicions. I know you do." Jax moved in closer. He took her personal space and claimed it for his own. He was trying to intimidate her. "Don't think I haven't noticed how you evade telling the whole truth. You may not know for sure who took her, but you have notions, and you know something that you're not saying."

The woman didn't look like the type to be intimidated. She put her hands on her hips and stood her ground before Jax. Considering how petite she was, it was impressive.

Before the woman could speak, Tam motioned to them to go farther back in the transport.

Eyes were still prying. If they kept this up, the pilot might end up intervening. Pilots could eject you into space. You'd have to wait in life support for another transport. Or die waiting.

Or another passenger might decide to play hero to the little woman. They didn't need that. Not right now. They needed answers from this woman who was more than she seemed.

"I'm not going back there." She nodded her head toward the back.

So much for getting away from prying eyes. "Before you deny what he said, you aren't Coronian. I know that."

She blinked at him. If he hadn't been watching, he wouldn't have seen the action. The woman was an expert at remaining stoic. "How do you figure that?"

"They don't defend themselves like you did." Hitting another would be out of the question for a true Coronian. Judging by her clothes and appearance, this woman tried to pass herself off as one.

Her eyes narrowed. "Maybe I'm a different Coronian than those you've known. Maybe I don't follow every custom of my culture."

"Then, why dress and look the part? Or maybe you aren't Coronian at all." Tam arched a brow that didn't seem to faze her, either. "Maybe you're a Native."

Jax smiled. "I noticed that, too." He looked pleased that they were in sync. "She's no Coronian, even if she's not Native."

Being on the same page as Jax hadn't happened often. They'd rarely been so before Kiann. His face etched in a frown. Jax better be right about this woman being a lead to Kiann's disappearance, because otherwise they were damned.

"What?" She glanced from side to side at them. "What did you notice?" She sounded bored, as if nothing they said made any difference, but her hands fisted. Again, not something he would have noticed offhand. She wasn't as coolly collected as she wanted them to think.

Tam reached out to grab her wrist. A band of gold resided there. A thin strip, barely noticeable with her dark skin. That didn't fit. Coronians were dark, but would never wear such body markings beyond a heartstone. "That's Native henna. I should know. We work with it in cloth. Your mannerisms aren't truly Coronian, no matter how much you pretend and try to make them look Coronian." Too much didn't add up for her ancestry to be authentic. "When he threatened you, you went Native, not Coronian."

"Because I wear body art, it doesn't make me Native, or make me know anything about the woman's kidnapping." Her com went off with a beep from the seat beside her. She didn't move to answer the communication.

A damning move. Why wouldn't she answer? Because she didn't want them to hear?

"Going to get that?" Jax reached for it before she could pick the com up. "Or should I answer it?"

She moved to grab it back from him with a quick move that Tam didn't see coming. She moved rapidly like a psi-cat. "Stop that."

"Why?" Jax angled the communicator back, keeping his hands on the box-like radio. "Worried they might tell us something that you won't? Like what you know about Kiann."

"Who took Kiann? Was it Marses?" A foregone conclusion, but Tam wanted answers. His chest constricted. If Marses got his hands on her, they might lose her for good. "Are you a bounty hunter and after her, too?" Tam folded his arms in front of his chest. They'd never thought Marses would hire anyone else with his secretive ways. But maybe he had. Desperation took many forms and might have made the man do something rash. "Don't you realize what you've done?" He could spit, he was so mad at losing Kiann. "You've deprived Ebolia of its true line. Its true ruler." *And deprived me of my second mate.* No, he would get her back. He vowed it to himself.

After assessing the woman, his eyes met Jax's, which resembled a wounded animal's.

With that, Tam had surprised her, he had no doubt. She didn't show much of a startle, only a slight one that he only saw because he was again paying close attention. The woman was good at controlling her involuntary reflexes. She affected a bored look. "Kiann's not of the line. She's of the Royals, but not of the house that sits on the Ebolian throne."

"Then who is she? If you know so much about her." Jax held onto a seatback with tightly gripped knuckles. He looked ready to charge the woman.

Tam put a hand on his shoulder to stop him and hold him back if need be. They had to find out as much as they could from her. "Who did they tell you that she was? Some maniac?"

"A cousin in the Royals. Once removed." She lowered her voice to a whisper level. "Crazy one at that." Before either of them could react, she snatched the com away from Jax. "This is L. I'm fine. T lost. Abandon." She clicked it off before a reply could come.

"They lied to you. Played you." Tam's heart raced again with the knowledge there were bounty hunters after them. They at least had a start on finding her. They had to find her soon. Did this woman know who'd taken her? Even a suspicion was better than any clue they had right now. His eyes narrowed. He was now on the same page with Jax. She'd tell them what she knew.

"No one played…"

Jax moved forward with a hiss of his tongue. "Stop the charade. It's getting old."

"Going to grab my throat again?" Her fists came up in a defensive posture. "Don't try it, or you'll be sorry."

Yep, this wasn't a gentle Coronian. An air of danger surrounded her. An element of unpredictability. Not something common to Natives, either, making him reassess his original estimate. It didn't matter, except if she could give them information about Kiann.

"Only if it will make you listen to reason." Jax glared at her with purple fire roasting in his eyes. "You're a bounty hunter. A Native bounty hunter. You may not have taken Kiann, but I'm betting you know who did. And you're going to tell us who it was."

He'd never seen Jax so angry. Jax's whole body tightened in his rage.

They were both lost without their new mate.

She eyed them with wary eyes. "Then answer my questions. Is Kiann crazy? Mental? Stupid? Dangerous?" She folded her arms across her chest. "To herself and others?"

"No. None of the above." She suggested the story that Tam was sure Marses had used. It made sense he'd paint Kiann with a brush designed to make bounty hunters bring her in. Tam tried to think of the best words to reassure this woman that Kiann wasn't what she'd been told. She appeared reasonable, even if she did seem cold-blooded. "She's only dangerous to a pretender to the throne."

He'd committed treason against the current ruler of Ebolia. He didn't care. Marses had the throne under false pretenses. Tam and Jax would expose him for the villain that he was, and save the woman they needed to be with.

Her lips pursed together. "What are you two doing with her? You were cozy before she dematerialized."

"We're her mates. She escaped Marses to find her heartstone. Your employer kept her from finding the missing piece of herself for years." Tam moved closer and kept his words even, making her hear each one. Maybe he could reason with this woman. She was the only link they had to Kiann; therefore, he had to. "I said, he kept her from her heartstone." Of all the crimes one could do to a person besides murder, that was one of the worst. The act would keep someone from their destiny.

She didn't bat an eyelash at his speech with the talk of heartstones. She was colder than Tam thought. "I never said he was my employer."

"You don't have to." Jax gripped the seat again. "He's the only one who would hire you or someone else. He's desperate to get Kiann back under his control, so he can take out his competition."

The ship shimmed again with a blast. Several people screamed. Considering what the ship had already been through, panic ensued.

The pilot's voice came over the speaker. He sounded harried and impatient. "We have been fired upon *again*. This time, the ship firing says they want Besela. A Coronian on board. They will let everyone else go. Are you willing, Besela?" The pilot and copilot were probably at this moment offering sacrifices up to whatever God they believed in that she'd go peacefully.

There was only one Coronian onboard.

Tam's gaze darted back and forth. If she made it off the ship, they'd never get their answers. But how could they stop her? He prepared for a fight.

"Sons of bitches never listen," she muttered under her breath as the pilot hesitated. "I'll go."

One of the others must have taken him news of Besela's acceptance because he continued, "Okay, we'll dock with this ship. Hopefully the rest of our trip won't as be as eventful as this first leg." His teeth sounded as though they gritted together on the last part.

Before Tam could grab her, the woman grabbed her bag, then looked back at Jax and Tam as she moved to the front of the transport. "You aren't scamming me? Kiann is who you say she is? Do you have proof of her lineage?"

Tam tapped his chin. Did they have anything they could pull as proof? Not yet, but give him time with a computer, and he could find some. Maybe the woman could help them find Kiann and get the ball rolling to place her in power. Then they could be mates. His throat constricted. They'd had so little time together. Surely the Fates couldn't be cruel enough to give them a mate and take her away like this. "I can find proof, if you give me a chance. We aren't scamming you. Kiann is the true heir to the throne."

"If you're deceiving me, it won't go over well." She glanced between him and Jax. "Not well at all."

"I give you my word as a Native." Jax bowed his head. "We tell only the truth. And not the truth of leaving things out, but the whole."

"I know." She bowed back to Jax. "I'm going to regret this." She didn't say it loud, but Tam heard her words. "Come on."

"What? Where?"

"Come with me. I'm not making the invitation again. You want to find Kiann, come with me."

After a shift of his gaze to Tam, Jax nodded, indicating that they would accompany her to wherever she was going. Jax hadn't needed to ask. They had to find Kiann.

Their only lead was this woman. Tam wasn't about to let her get away. That meant traveling with her to whatever destination she led them to. Tam refused to think about how Kiann was doing. *Please let her be safe.*

Jax grabbed their bags, including Kiann's, and off they dashed to the front.

The copilot motioned to Besela. "We're ready for you to depart. Please come with me."

"These two are coming with me, too."

The copilot's eyes widened. "This is highly irregular. I must prot—"

"Deal with it. Unless you want to be fired on again. The two fools out there will, unless you hand me over, and I'm taking these two with me." Besela sidestepped beyond him to the temporary access tunnel they'd arranged to dock with the ship outside their transport.

Tam and Jax followed behind her loping gait. She reached down to scratch her hip. Her whole hip moved.

Tam stared. Had he seen what he thought he had?

Maybe she wore an elaborate disguise to alter her appearance? He'd figured there must be something, but he'd never seen anything like what she must be wearing. She carried off a Coronian body almost perfectly.

Tam made it into the shuttle, and the door clamped shut behind him so the transport could take down the temporary loader. The pilot would act quickly, glad to be away from the trouble.

A momentary spear of anxiety ran up his spine. They'd gone with a woman they didn't know. Away from any leads they might have about Kiann from where she'd disappeared.

It had to be the right decision. Kiann's life depended on their actions.

"By the way." She didn't turn around to face them but walked a step into the small shuttle. "My name's not Besela. It's Layla. I am a bounty hunter." She pulled down her hair from a ponytail. Long hair in the Native tradition. She turned to face them with a grim expression. "A psycho named Mercurior beat us to the punch and has your mate." She pushed through a door. "Orion." She waved to the shuttle controls. "Balt." She motioned to the side. "I'm back. I have company."

Tam blinked as an Amador sitting off to the side stood to his full height with fire in his rust-colored eyes, resting under his green hair. Oh, damn. Balt was bigger than Tam and Jax put together. If he wanted to, he could pull them apart and hardly break a sweat.

Jax stepped closer to him, as if to protect him. The gesture would be futile, but Tam warmed at Jax's thoughtfulness. The man could pull him in half, like a psi-cat with a *mouselet*.

A man with gills pulled out a phaser and turned from the shuttle controls. "Layla, what the shit is going on? Who are they?" Orion looked at Tam and Jax with a discerning green gaze.

Green eyes on one and green hair on the other. How color-coordinated. And now they'd die with green in their vision.

"If they're telling the truth, their mate is the true ruler of Ebolia."

The gill guy's eyebrow quirked. "Mates?"

"Yeah. And he—" She jabbed her finger at Jax. "—is a Native. He's telling me the truth or what he thinks is the truth. She's not crazy."

The big man folded his arms in front of his massive chest. "You fucking sure, Layla?"

"Damn sure. I knew all that platinum was too good to be true, especially when he hired Merc. Orion owes me that Tenaglian whisky." She headed back to a door. "I'm changing. Be right back. You four get acquainted."

All four men stared at each other.

Tam held out a hand to show he was harmless. He didn't want trouble with these hard-looking men. "Nice to meet you. Where would Merc take our mate?"

Chapter Twelve

"Fuck me if we'll find her here." The big man moved in front of Jax as they disembarked from his ship. Though he looked casually around, he was on alert. Everything on him tensed before he relaxed. "And that rat fucker."

Jax nodded to show he listened, but his mind was consumed with thoughts of finding Kiann. If only they could fast-forward time to when she'd already been rescued.

He surveyed the small rock they'd landed upon—an outpost on an Ebolian moon with few people and even less civilization. The perfect place to dispose of something you didn't want to come up again.

Icy tendrils ripped through him.

Kiann was that something.

They would be in time to save Kiann. He would get his chance to be with her and show her he wanted to be her mate.

They'd decided to split up once all the pleasantries had gone forth. Tam had hacked to find a document that proved Kiann was who she said she was. She'd been in the photographs of her father's funeral, identified as his daughter. They'd gotten lucky that the photos had been through Butler's outfit and still existed.

The proof showed her as the true agent of the realm. It worked as evidence.

Or at least, it had been good enough for Balt, Orion, and Layla to put their talents together to help them. At no charge. A move that made Orion shrug his shoulders. Layla had kissed him, and his gills had flapped open and closed.

Tam taken those papers with Orion and Layla to get them plastered on the airwaves. They had to get the news out, and the sooner the better.

Please let them get there, and up and running in time.

They had all the leverage they'd ever have to save Kiann. It had to work.

Balt and Jax had headed to the moon, flying under the radar, where they were supposed to bring Kiann when they'd found her. It was assumed Merc had the same rendezvous point. Would she still be there? Had Marses taken her somewhere else? Or done the deed already?

Wouldn't he know if something had happened to Kiann? Surely he'd feel it within himself if anything had happened to her. She was his mate, for curse's sake. Granted, they hadn't bonded, but she was still within him and had been from the first. No matter how much he'd tried to deny her.

What had the psycho done to her while she'd been in his care? A shudder ran along Jax's spine.

The more Jax heard about Merc, the more murderous thoughts he had. And the more worried he became about Kiann's safety. The man apparently thrived on pain. He'd delivered Orion to Ansel. That spoke volumes. If Merc was a sadist, Ansel was the cursed head of all of them.

Orion had remained stoic about Merc and his time with Ansel, but rage had simmered in both of his mates.

Much the same way the emotions swirled within Jax for his mate now. He could usually be on an even keel. Not about this. He wanted to do something illogical.

He patted the gun at his side. His collection would come in handy. Rarely did he use them, except for target practice. Today, he might have his chance to use them for the good of his mate.

Tam had protested once that he should be the one to rescue Kiann, but he was the diplomat. His presence would be better suited to access the media. He'd known his savvy, even though he wanted to be the first one to get to Kiann, hence the token protest.

Jax vowed to him he wouldn't let him down in the rescue operation. Nor would Jax let himself down.

"You don't talk much." Though he spoke quietly, Balt moved quickly for such a hulking person around a corner as they headed for the one place marked on the planet as having a building. "You remind me a lot of Layla." He cracked a grin that overtook his whole face. "When she's not in disguise."

"We are both Natives." Neither lived by the full code of their people. Amazing how the races were all judged against the perfection of their race, which didn't exist. Each had quirks the generalities of their races didn't publicize. "How did you three become mates? Was it difficult?" As different as they all seemed, it had to have been a struggle for them.

Maybe the big man could give him insight about why he'd been such a jackass to Kiann.

The Amador regarded him with an intense gaze. His green-hued hair blew in the slight breeze that drifted over the small area. "You have no idea. It's not easy to join three different people. You three are as different as we were...are."

That Jax did know. His airways constricted. Boy, did he ever know how difficult mating could be. The simple Fates had been said to have senses of humor in their plans for everyone's lives.

Not that he'd ever imagined Tam before their mating, but accepting their mating had been easy. This one hadn't been. He'd been a fool and had paid a fool's price.

Only Kiann didn't need to pay for his stupidity. He'd sacrifice himself before he allowed her to settle his debt.

What he wouldn't give to go back and accept her with willing arms from the beginning. He wouldn't make that mistake again. She would be their mate in all ways when this was done.

"We're nearing the facility." An old warehouse that had been left when miners had abandoned the rock years before. Balt held a finger to his lips as they ducked behind some garbage containers.

A man strode into view after exiting the warehouse. He held several reams of platinum. He leaned down to kiss them. His blue eyes gleamed under the light of the sun that warmed Ebolia, only no warmth entered those eyes. They were colder than the ice caps of Nativia.

Mercurior.

Balt didn't have to identify him for Jax to recognize the man. The man who'd taken Kiann from him.

He looked mean. Even his smile looked nasty, as if he'd kill you as soon as stand beside you.

If he'd hurt Kiann, Jax would be seeing him again. Soon.

Jax flexed his arm muscles. If only he could see Kiann now, but discretion might buy them a way inside.

Balt tapped Jax and motioned him around the side of the building away from Mercurior.

They watched Merc's shuttle take off. Good riddance. His departure also left them with one less enemy to deal with.

Merc's departure left whoever was in that building alone with Kiann. It looked as if she'd just been delivered. A boon. Whoever had her hadn't had her long. Balt had said their ship could fly rings around Merc's because he'd loaded it down with technical gizmos, so they'd arrive soon after he did, despite his big lead.

Maybe Marses hadn't had time to hurt her.

Jax picked up the pace. They had to get in before anything happened to her.

They both sidled to a window, and Jax tried to peek inside. The panes had been coated with black, making it impossible to see past the murk.

"Fuck. It's been painted." Balt sidestepped him, looking in as well. "It's not metallic coated, so they can't see us, either."

There was no way to see what was going on in the warehouse before they broke in. That had them at a disadvantage.

A woman's scream rent the air, breaking the quiet stillness with a piercingly high decibel, along with a crash that came from inside.

Balt looked back at him with an alarmed expression. "Now, wait a minute…"

Jax couldn't wait. He had to get to her *now*. She was being hurt. He couldn't stand his ground. He wouldn't let her be put through any more.

Grabbing his phaser, he took off at a run for the wooden door, ignoring Balt's muttered epithets to come back.

"Ah, fuck." Balt's lumbering strides followed him, but he made no move to stop Jax's movements, which was good, because Jax wasn't stopping for anything or anyone. He'd have laid the Amador low had he tried to restrain him. He wouldn't rest until he had Kiann safely in his arms.

Jax kicked once at the door. Twice. Three times.

The stinking door still stood there between him and his mate. His foot throbbed from the pounding against strong metal.

Balt rolled his eyes and kicked once with his massive leg in full motion. The door splintered and burst open.

Of course, any element of surprise was now gone, and a weapon had been aimed at their heads. A solid cannon held by a man that Jax didn't know.

Marses sat in a chair near the man holding the weapon. He arched a brow at them. "Who are you?"

Kiann struggled to her feet even with her hands bound behind her. She'd been struck on her face. A handprint shone vividly on her pale cheek. "I don't know who they are, Marses. Probably some crazy citizens. Get them out of here."

Not the rescue reaction Jax had expected.

* * *

Kiann shivered. Her hands ached from where they'd been pulled tight behind her. Her cheek smarted like stinging *spinies*, creatures that resided in the sands of Ebolia. Their sting could be aggravating. She refused to look at Jax and the green-haired man. She wouldn't reveal anything to her stepbrother. If she looked at them, she might crumble to the floor. If she looked at them, everything would show in her face about what Jax meant to her.

What was he doing there? He never should have come after her. He should have left well enough alone. Was that a bruise? Had he been hurt?

She averted her gaze. She couldn't give anything away.

"Who are you?" Marses's voice snapped with impatience. He hated to repeat himself, which was what had gotten her smacked. Not that he would spare her pain. Oh no, he planned to make sure she never left here. At least, alive.

"They wandered here, I'm sure that's all. Let them go." She kept the pleading note from her voice. "They're innocents."

Jax meandered closer. "We heard a scream."

"It was nothing." She spoke quickly. "A misunderstanding. Now, please go." She didn't expect Jax to listen. But she had to try. Her sacrifice would be nullified if he got himself killed. Her hands clenched together where they'd been bound.

"Foolish Kiann." Marses clucked his tongue several times. "Running away has made you even stupider than before."

She swallowed, keeping her eyes averted, but she could see enough to know that Jax's body clenched after Marses's comment. *Don't. Please, Jax.* Marses could insult her all he wanted as long as he didn't take Jax.

"I'm sorry you've stumbled into our business." Marses waved to the other man. "But, now I'm afraid, you need to drop your weapons."

The big green-haired man rocked back on his heels. "Oh? Why is that?"

Before anyone could answer, Jax aimed his phaser and shot the other man in the shoulder. A preemptive action.

The man fell to the ground in agony from the burn.

The green-haired man descended on him in a second, taking the weapon.

Jax had a weapon? Kiann's head reeled from this turn of events. He'd had them, so she'd been told by Tam, but she'd never expected to see him use them. He was a good shot, too. He'd disabled the man without killing him. The action had been deliberate. It hadn't been a lucky shot.

She looked around for anything she could use to help Jax defend himself against Marses. But with her hands still bound, getting to any sort of weapon wasn't going to be easy.

More tongue clucking.

Kiann swung her head around.

Marses now had a phaser of his own aimed at the two men. "Drop your weapons and move away from his."

Her heart quickened its pace. Jax was in danger of getting fried. Marses had his weapon set to kill. He'd planned to kill her with it once he'd interrogated her as to who she'd met on Settler's Mine. He'd planned to say brigands had done the deed, robbing her and murdering her.

A shudder raced along her spine with the knowledge of how she'd been about to die. No, she wasn't going to die here on this rock, not with Jax here ready to fight for her. She'd waited too long for that to happen to give up now. New resolve guided her actions.

The green man didn't move, but Jax aimed his phaser at Marses. "Don't make me shoot you."

A cynical smile passed across Marses's face. He leveled the weapon before aiming it at Kiann. "Drop it, or I'll shoot her."

The big man's voice was rough as he spoke. "Why should that matter to us? You heard her, we don't know her. We're scavengers. Don't care if you kill the female." With a vicious grunt, he stomped the wounded man's hand before he could reach for the weapon. "We'll move on without care."

"Cut the bullshit." Marses shook his head. "Please, spare me. I'm not as stupid as Kiann."

Jax's voice was almost unrecognizable. "No bullshit. I will shoot you."

"And I will shoot her. You can't get me before I get her." Marses's finger pushed on the trigger. "You two are too good for scavengers. You got the best of my head guard. I knew

Kiann had fucked some poor men—and deluded them with her 'visions,' I'm sure." He rolled his wrist. "One was a Native. I'm guessing that's you."

"Fuck you." Jax's gaze never wavered.

Her gaze was desperate as she tried to keep an eye on the situation and look for something to help. Jax's use of curse words showed how angry he was. Anger made people do irrational things. He needed his wits about him to fight Marses, so that wasn't good. She couldn't stand here helpless without doing something to help her mate. Her hands strained against the bonds that held her tightly.

"Lower your weapon."

They were at a standoff. One that wouldn't end well. Kiann weighed her options. She couldn't pick up anything, but she could use her body. She didn't want that gun used against Jax.

Taking a small swallow, she took two small steps toward Marses that he didn't even notice. Arrogant SOB. He'd counted her out of the equation because he thought her helpless and dumb. His mistake would lead to his defeat.

She took off at a run toward him and plowed headlong into him, knocking them both to the ground.

"You bitch." Marses tried to keep his hands on the weapon, no easy feat with Kiann on top of him, bucking against him.

She slammed her head down into his, knocking stars to come floating around her head. She'd almost knocked herself out with the blow.

Marses screamed in both rage and pain.

Jax was there in an instant to take the phaser from Marses's hands. He yanked her up, making her even dizzier. "You little fool."

"I couldn't let him hurt you." Her words came halting and with difficulty. Her head pounded, and her eyes watered great globs of tears. But Jax was safe for now. He tenderly checked over her head as Marses continued to roll around the floor, holding his. If only she could hurt him more. Keep him from the pieces of himself like he had her. But she'd never be that cruel.

"B. Come in." A woman's voice sounded on the radio.

The green man picked up the link. "Yeah?"

"Turn on your newscast. Over and out."

"They did it. They fucking did it." The green-haired man sounded jubilant. "Good fucking timing. Marses, you are going down."

"What did they do?" Marses froze on the ground as he peered up at them, hands still wrapped around his skull. "Who did what?"

Balt lowered his com link and projected the image on the wall. "Watch this, fucker."

"...To sum up our biggest story, the heir to the throne of Ebolia has been living in seclusion all this time in the palace of Marses the Royal. Her identity has been authenticated. The Royal's people had no comment about Marses keeping her prisoner, not allowing her to search for her heartstone, or a possible deception leading to an attempt on her life..."

An old picture of Kiann flashed on the screen as the commentator droned on. Not her best snapshot, but it showed the world that she existed. The words told what had happened.

Kiann closed her eyes. They'd succeeded. Her face had been plastered from here to Signapore, the capital of Ebolia. Her story had been posted all over the place. Everyone knew she existed.

Marses could still touch her, but there would be questions about her existence. His rule of Ebolia would be in question. No matter what happened, he'd have to face up to what he'd done to her.

There was so much she'd wanted to confront him for. Now there was need.

She was finally free.

"You messed with the wrong person's mate." Jax's hand tightened on his weapon as he positioned himself in between Kiann and Marses.

Even now, Jax sought out her protection. Her body warmed for the first time since Merc had captured her.

Marses's eyes grew wide as he yammered, "No. This can't be. I planned this. Carefully. Fucking Fates."

Jax glared down at him as he untied Kiann's arms, which had been tied too tightly by Merc. He rubbed her arms to help the circulation return. Her skin tingled with his gentle touch. "Don't make me hit you again. You're going to get what you deserve."

"Don't. He's not worth it." Kiann rubbed her hands together, trying to get feeling back in them.

"Never try and fuck with Fates." The green man approached them. "I'm Balt, Kiann. And I think you're going to be famous."

Long as she was famous with mates, she didn't care.

Chapter Thirteen

Jax turned to Kiann, who didn't look directly at him. "Tam should be here soon." She hadn't said much since things had gone down. She'd hardly spoken any words at all. She'd been checked over to make sure she wasn't hurt, and no serious injuries had been located. They'd been taken to a secure, small outpost on Ebolian soil where Balt had left them to themselves. They'd be safe from the press there as they waited for Tam and what came next.

"Ummm," she said noncommittally from her spot in a huge chair made for two to sit in. She didn't seem that excited about anything, which was curious after escaping Marses.

"I'm sure he's eager to see you." He cursed himself. Why couldn't he talk to her? Instead, he kept harping on Tam's return. There was much he needed to tell her, wanted to tell her. And yet, he couldn't find the right words. His chest rose and fell with a deep breath. He needed to tell her what a fool he'd been. How he should have run with this mating from the start. Not easy words to say.

"Maybe."

"Oh, he will be." Jax moved to sit by her on the edge of the chair. "I can assure you of that. Same as I was." He managed to get the last sentence out without choking on the words that hung like bones in his throat. Where was his courage?

"Were you?" Her face lifted, and she looked up at him with eyes that contained shadows. If only he could look into them and tell her state of mind. Instead, a blankness stared back at him.

A look that he wanted to drive away. "I was." He grabbed for her hand, and his wound up on her leg. He traced small circles on the pants she wore. A chance to touch what he'd almost lost. He couldn't pull his hand away from her now that he'd started touching her. "I thought…I'd lost you."

"I can't believe you came after me. I never thought you would." Her voice broke in the center, but she recaptured her voice by the end.

He'd been terrified he wouldn't make it to her in time. "I'm glad I found you." Glad she was his mate. More than she could ever know. This next hour marked the time he'd spend to make it up to her.

"What happens next?"

He continued to trace tiny circles on her leg. He needed his hands to stay on her. The contact grounded him and helped him find the words to say to her. "Marses is going to face some hard questions about what he did. People don't take kindly to a person being kept from their heartstone. And you are the true heir." He smiled. "I think you have Queen in your future."

"No."

"No? You don't want to be Queen?" That would put a wrench into things. Everyone would expect her to take over when Marses was deposed. And he would be deposed. Jax's hand stilled. He didn't care what she did, but the road away from what they'd started would be a hard one.

"That wasn't what I was asking about when I asked what happens next." Her gaze shifted down to watch his hand on her leg. She wouldn't meet his eyes. "And whether I'm Queen or not has a lot to do with what I asked."

"What were you asking?" He traced circles again. Whatever she decided, they'd be there for her.

"What happens with us? To us? As mates."

His hand tightened before relaxing. "Well, I've always wanted to travel." He shot her a smile. "Being the mate of the Queen of Ebolia will have travel involved." He would move his business to Ebolia. Henna clothing could be made anywhere. All he'd have to do was get the henna sent his way. They'd be set. Tam wouldn't mind, either. He'd like to wander. He'd always wanted to know more about his heritage.

"I'm being serious." Her head still didn't lift.

"I am, too." He reached up again and didn't miss her hand this time. "We're going to be mates in all ways. You'll need patience." His mind flashed to himself and Tam, and how difficult they could be at times. "Lots of it." She had no idea what she'd gotten herself into being mated to the two of them.

"You want to be the mate of a Queen?" Her voice trembled as if she couldn't believe what she'd heard.

"I want to be *your* mate. Big difference." He stroked his fingers through hers, glad to have this chance with her. Few second chances happened in life. He intended to take full advantage of this one. "It doesn't matter to me if you're Queen or not. That's your decision. All I know is that you're my mate."

"What changed?" She still sounded skeptical, as though this might be taken away from her at any moment. The way Marses had taken her life away. He'd have to do his best to reassure her. Maybe spend the rest of his life doing so.

"When you were taken—right in front of my eyes—I realized I would miss you." He shrugged. It ranked as the worst moment of his life, even above standing outside of the warehouse and wondering if she was alive or dead. "That I had come to need you in my life without realizing it." He'd never forget what they'd been through. It would remind him to treasure all his moments with his mates.

"Are you sure?" Her gaze finally lifted to his face to stare at him. "Sure about being with me?"

"Completely." He leaned over to press his lips to hers. "Totally." Another light kiss. "Definitely."

"Being mate to a Queen won't be easy. And we were…"

He lowered his lips to hers again, pressing his tongue along the seam to her lips. She opened, albeit reluctantly, and his tongue dipped between her lips to play. Her shy responses thrilled him. He lifted his mouth from hers. "Nothing you want is ever easy. The question is, is it worth it?"

Her mouth trembled.

He wanted to kiss her and make everything better for her. He wanted to hold her in his arms and keep her safe from everything. And this time, he would. Without reservations. "You are worth it, Kiann. Worth everything to me."

A single tear ran down her cheek as her lashes fluttered closed.

He dipped his finger to catch her tear on his fingertip and lift it to his mouth. Salty. He'd make sure she never cried over him again. Ever.

He lowered his mouth to take hers again, kissing her deeply. Exulting in her sounds of pleasure. Her movements soon turned from shyness to desire. She responded to him as if they'd been lovers for years and kissed him back in the way he liked, without any uncertainty.

He needed to be with her. Within her. This all-consuming need encompassed his very being. He experienced that feeling all the time with Tam. Now he understood Tam's desire to be with her at any cost. She brought up those feelings in both her mates.

He tangled his hands in her hair. The silken threads wisped around his fingers as if the strands were a cloud. He ate at her mouth, deepening the embrace. He didn't merely kiss her, but gave her his soul in return, in the hopes she'd give hers back to him.

And give back to him she did.

When he pulled away, they both were panting and breathless. His heart pounded so hard he could barely hear anything over the sound. "Time to show you how worth it you are to me." He stood up to pull his shirt over his head.

* * *

Whatever Kiann was about to say got lost in her exploration of the roped muscles of Jax's bare chest. She couldn't form anything comprehensible so chaotic were her thoughts. Not that she hadn't seen his chest before, but this time, the bared skin struck her in the gut, taking away all powers of speech.

Probably because he was about to make love to her.

Jax was about to take her. The man she'd doubted would ever accept her as a mate. Now, he had. He was about to make her his.

She swallowed, mouth dry, as he unbuttoned his top button on his pants. All the air whooshed from her lungs as she noticed the bulge under his waistband. No question what that was, or how much he looked forward to this. Maybe as much as she did. Nah...

His gaze caught hers. Held her captive with its snare. His eyes expressed everything he must be feeling. They let her see into his soul and told her how much he wanted this. She couldn't escape his gaze and didn't want to. She wanted to stay wrapped up in it for hours. In him for hours.

He peeled off his pants. His cock sprang free with a soft bounce. Kicking the pants off his feet, he stood before her in all his naked glory.

What glory he had.

She'd been speechless before. That was nothing compared to this. Her mouth salivated. One gorgeous hunk of man stood before her with blond hair, muscles, and a thick cock, standing up in honor of her. She took in the whole picture with unrestrained glee.

Jax wanted her.

He smiled as if knowing what she was thinking.

Her face heated. She wasn't used someone knowing her that well. Or a naked man. With him and Tam as her mates, she'd have to get used to both of those on a regular basis. It wouldn't be a hardship; she'd have fun with the learning curve.

He moved forward, dropping to his knees. He put one hand on her leg, stretching it out. "You need to be naked."

She'd been so caught up in his disrobing, she'd completely forgotten to start with herself. "Yes. Yes, I do." She made no pretense about what she wanted. There was no sense pretending she didn't want the same things he did. Forget the same page, they were on the same letter.

One thought distracted her.

If only Tam were here.

Though in a way, it would be good for herself and Jax to get to know each other like this first. To make things right between them and try out intimacy with just the two of them. Then, they could all be together without any issues.

Together forever.

She reached up and pulled off her tunic shirt in a quick motion. Somehow the all-consuming modesty that might have lingered in her fled. Except a smidgeon of unease remained.

Men and women had different builds. Jax had been attracted to mostly men. A shiver ran down her spine, but not from cold, from an attack of shyness. What would he think of her body? Men and women were built differently. She had parts bigger than theirs, and they had parts she didn't. Would he find her different body attractive? As much as he did Tam's? She'd seen him look at his lover. She selfishly wanted that look for herself.

Reaching around herself, she unhooked her bra before dropping it from her arms. She piled it beside the chair.

She couldn't lift her head to find out what he thought. Maybe not knowing was better. She should've switched off the lights.

Finally, she looked up to find his gaze centered on her breasts. He lifted his head, and she saw wonder in his gaze.

Yes, he did. He liked what he saw.

A sigh broke free from her lips.

He remained turned on. His hard cock was the evidence of that.

He yanked on her pants, helping to glide them down her legs. Off her ankles they came, along with her underwear. Leaving her naked, still resting on the chair.

Again, she found she couldn't look at him. Couldn't see what he thought of her fully unclothed body.

A soft touch landed on her knee. A warm hand skittered up her leg with little caresses. The touch urged her to look and see what she might find on Jax's face.

Steeling herself, she slowly moved her head so she could see him. So she could see for herself his reaction.

His eyes glazed over with passion. With desire. For her. A shudder ran through her at seeing how much he responded to her.

He parted her thighs with knowing hands. "Open for me." He didn't mean her mouth. She was about to grant him access to her most private parts. And she couldn't wait to take this to the next level. To take him inside and love him with her body.

She separated her thighs as far as she could, though she was puzzled what he had in mind. He wasn't going to take her in the chair, was he?

That would be uncomfortable. Did she care? Not as much as she wanted this to happen.

But something wasn't right. Wasn't he supposed to set up to drive his cock into her? Instead, he stayed in the same position, only moving his hands down.

After running over her inner thighs, his fingers delved into her wetness. He touched with circular motions as his fingers slowly drove down onto her clit and inside of her. His touch was expert, seeming to know how to start and get the most from one little flick of a finger. He started light, barely caressing.

Her hips bucked at the surprise of his fingers touching her there and the slightness of his touch. It tickled. She'd not expected he would play before he took her, not like this. This careful foreplay took her by surprise.

His fingers felt much better than her own had when they touched there. Just like Tam's had. Her entire pussy electrified, as though anything that touched her would snap her with electricity. The shock of this moment with Jax, along with the adrenaline of what had almost happened, had combined. It would not take much to send her over the edge. She stood on the brink of a precipice, and only Jax could take her over.

As if he knew her need, he moved slowly and deliberately for several seconds, but then picked up the pace as she moistened and slickened under his questing digits. Had he been rougher, she'd have gone over. Jax wanted to prolong this moment. He was no longer gentle nor slow, but it wasn't quite enough to take her over the edge.

She bit her lip. What a frustrating man. Every part of her cried out for her to come. And yet this careful touching kept sending her higher just when she thought she'd reached the peak.

He knew how to stretch this moment and increase her arousal.

Two fingers strummed on her clit as his thumb wandered in and out of her. He set up a rhythm destined to give her maximum pleasure, but not bring her too close too soon. The man dragged things out like a pro.

Hard to believe this was his first time with a woman.

She was his first time.

Her eyes closed. Just like she'd been Tam's. It would always be a special thing in her life. She'd never dreamed about being anyone's first.

She leaned her head back against the chair, unable to support its weight any more as she gave herself over to the sensations. Soon, desire spiraled within her, peaking up to a crescendo that kept her whole body tensing...

Until his fingers stilled.

"What? Why did you stop?" She didn't mean for it to come out so testily, but hell, she hadn't wanted him to quit. She rested at the brink of something that stayed out of her reach, but she needed to find. Her whole body quivered in anticipation.

"Am I doing this right?" He sounded concerned. Genuine. "Hurting you?"

Pain was the last thing on her mind. What had prompted the question? Her body tensing. He'd not known what it was from. "The pain is only when you stop." The words came through gritted teeth. She'd been close to going over a sweet edge. "And you're doing fine."

"Oh." He laughed on a whisper. "I've never done this before. I thought I might be hurting you. Your body…"

"Just start moving again." Frustration moved through her. Time that natural talent got back to her nether parts. They swelled and ached for him to come back. "You're not hurting me." Her breath came in a pant.

Instead of putting his fingers back where she most wanted them, he leaned forward until his face was in front of the apex of her thighs. "Spread more."

More? She was almost spread-eagled as it was.

Before she could protest, he put a hand on each leg and helped her widen her position so that she spread across the chair.

She was a wishbone. What would his wish be?

He'd better wish for taking her all the way.

What the hell was this position for?

Her answer came as his mouth descended. Stupid question. She needed to become more sexually aware.

A moan escaped her lips and coherent thoughts left her as his mouth met her. "Ohh."

A satisfied grunt sounded from him in reaction to her vocalization before his tongue licked up her slit and back down it again.

A warm, wet tongue that had plans for her.

Her body tried to go boneless, hard to do when sitting in a chair. She couldn't take much more of this pleasing torture. If she didn't orgasm soon, she'd go crazy.

His tongue flicked across her with rapid-fire motions, dragging across her clit, plunging into her opening. He left no surface unlicked or untried. Deliberately, he circled her clit with intense pressurized movements.

She whimpered. Her fingers dug into the chair arms. So close. If only she could pass over whatever barrier kept her from her orgasm.

As if he knew she needed more, he gave it to her. He suckled her into his mouth, drawing as much of her in as he could.

So good. But not enough. Why? Her head fell back. Her thoughts raced.

This was Jax doing these things to her. The man she'd never expected to fall for her, had. Jax's fingers were on her sex. *Jax. Jax. Jax.*

Her body exploded on a torrent of need. A waterfall of want that lifted her to the ceiling and up beyond the world she knew into the stratosphere.

She fell back to the ground, still in the chair, with his mouth still on her, his tongue grinding across her clit mercilessly.

It didn't take long to start up another intense climax that left her head swirling and her breath panting. "Mercy..."

He pulled his head away and looked up at her. His mouth shone with her essence on his lips. A full tongue slipped out to take off those drips as though he couldn't bear to lose any of her cream.

"Oh, my Goddess." She swallowed, head still back against the chair. It would be a while before she could move any part of her.

"I guess you enjoyed."

She snorted as she lifted up her head, which still had a dozen imaginary weights attached to her neck, pushing it down against her muscles. The impediments would fall off in a minute when she recovered. "Yes." More than she'd ever thought possible. "I very much enjoyed."

He leaped to his feet with a smile on his face. "I'm glad."

She pulled one of her legs down.

"No. Stay there." He positioned himself in front of her, placing his legs over the chair arm, too.

His face scrunched up as he slid back from the chair. "Ow. That won't work." He looked puzzled.

She laughed, unable to help herself. He must think himself a contortionist. That position would have put him in charge of the sex. They would have to go to the bed for that.

He growled.

"I don't think we'll both fit on the chair." She made a move to get up, but his body blocked her.

"Yeah, we will. Just need to rearrange ourselves." He grabbed her hips and swung her around his body with a strength she hadn't suspected. She knew he was strong, but damn, he bore all of her weight as if she weighed as much as a feather. He didn't strain to maneuver them both into position, but had smooth movements. He sat on the chair and draped her over him. "Now this will work."

She nodded. His tip already knocked at her entrance. A shiver ran down her spine. It was like the position that she'd taken Tam in. "I think so." Like Tam had, he put her in control of her own pleasure. The mastery of her sexual exploits tantalized her with its treat. The treat was being able to control the way she took him.

Jax, logical man, man of control, Native, had put her in control of him. Him.

She shivered. Knew how special this moment was. For him to cede control to her was a big deal. Now she had to work on making him lose control during their lovemaking.

"I know so." He kissed her with a fierceness that surprised her. A wild abandon that didn't seem to be the controlled Jax she knew.

She made him this way. Made him grow wild with desire.

Thrill filled her with icy chills.

She did this to him. Not anyone else, except Tam, could cause this reaction. And she owned Jax's reactions.

Nothing could be sweeter to her than that.

He touched her back and hair as he made a soft sigh against her lips. He moved her into a position to ride him.

She lowered herself carefully over the chair's arms and slipped herself over his hard cock, sheathing him with her warmth.

Every centimeter forward made her pull back halfway and start again. She took her time easing him in. There was pressure, but like last time with Tam, no pain.

She leaned her head back as the tightness of her engulfed his hardness, and rocked bit by bit until he was seated within her.

Both her mates had been within her from the time she'd first met them. They'd seated themselves so deeply in her psyche, she hadn't even been aware of it, until she'd been willing to do anything to save them. She would have died so they could live. She couldn't have stood knowing they weren't in the world.

No wonder Jax had run from that depth of a bond.

Understanding filled her with the completeness of the act, which brought them together.

Her life had gone from bad to good in one fell swoop. Great, in fact.

But it wasn't complete.

The moment wouldn't be until Tam joined them. She and Jax would have this moment to cement their relationship in the threesome, but they wouldn't be whole until all three found their way.

Up and down, she bounced on Jax.

His hands lowered to grip her hips. Beads of perspiration popped up on his face, which tensed in the utmost concentration.

She bore down on him as hard as she could, clenching her muscles around him.

He let out a groan. "You're killing me."

"I hope not." She let out a small laugh. "I like you alive." She liked him within her like this, so close to him that she felt it when he breathed or swallowed.

His hands gripped even tighter as he tried to push her more fully down on him and seat himself more in her depths. He also tried to control the pace by pushing on her to make her move faster or gripping her to make her slower.

Jax didn't want to lose that iron control he had, even when he'd given her the keys to drive their encounter.

"Stop that." She stopped her motions, freezing in place.

He froze. "Stop what?"

"Trying to control this." She arched her head back. "You put me in charge. Don't take that away."

He frowned apologetically. "Sorry. I can't help it."

She took her hand and grasped his. Put them down on the chair instead of her body. "Keep them there."

Three blinks of his eyes showed he heard, but he didn't comment. Unacceptable.

"Keep them there, or I will stop this." She'd take the control from him, one way or the other. Next time, he could be on top, but knowing him and Tam, she wouldn't get the chance often to drive their sexual encounters. She would seize this moment—this opportunity—to be in charge.

"Kiann…"

"I'm serious. Touch me and this ends. I'll pull off." She gave him a determined look. Let him know she meant it.

He licked his lips. His hands clenched on the chair as his head bobbed up and down in a nod.

"Say it." Hearing the words aloud would help him remember what he'd agreed to.

"I won't touch you. I'll leave you in charge." His breath caught after the last word. "Just start moving again."

The comment made her movements frenzied as she started to rock back and forth against him again.

He kept his promise, keeping his hands to the side.

Every movement was hers. Every clench of her pussy around him, she did. Every nuance of the pace was hers.

Oh, how she liked to be in control. Her wetness seeped as her arousal grew again, inching toward that high peak of pleasure.

Over and over again she went up and down, until in one blinding beam of light, she came with a mutter of his name.

His hands raised, but he quickly shoved them back again.

The orgasm wouldn't stop as it hit her. Everything went red against her vision.

Soon after she'd recovered, with her body pounding down against him, his whole body tensed as his seed came spilling forth.

He'd come inside her. She'd brought him to the breaking point, taken away his control, and taken him over the edge along with her. Her tongue came out to lick dried lips.

His forehead descended to hers and rested there for a minute. His arms snaked around her now that they were done. "You did kill me. Now you must bury me."

She giggled. "Dead men don't talk." Somehow she'd never expected this teasing in the afterglow, especially from Jax, the serious one.

Everything felt right with this closeness, with this world. Like it was supposed to be.

He wiggled under her as a shiver from an aftershock rippled through him. "Sure they do. I am."

"You're one good-looking dead person," the voice spoke from across the room.

They both turned their heads to the doorway. Tam sat on another chair with an arched brow, looking completely at ease.

Now, things had come full circle. A ripple of even stronger correctness spiraled through her.

She was a part of something she'd never been before, an accepted piece to their puzzle. Things were falling into place. A smile lit her face.

If only she could open herself up and show them both how she was feeling inside. She'd have to do her best to show them with her body.

She'd spend the rest of her life doing just that.

* * *

"How long have you been there?" Jax made no move to dump Kiann from his lap, but cuddled her closer to his body. She snuggled in.

Tam couldn't hide his smile. Damn, what sights he'd seen.

His mates making love in a chair. Jax giving over control of the sex to Kiann. Yeah, Tam had done that so she'd be more at ease, but Jax didn't often take a position where he was on the bottom.

Tam had enjoyed watching every minute of the act.

His cock stretched out in a long length, harder than he'd ever grown before. He'd never wanted two people more than right now. "Long enough to know this chair is damn uncomfortable. Yours must be, too."

Jax chuckled wryly. "That it is."

Tam held up a key. "They gave me this. They said you two were up here." His smile grew larger. "When I walked in, you two were otherwise engaged." He tossed down the key. "I locked the door. No one will disturb us for now. For a while at least." Eventually they'd have to face Ebolia and their people. But right now, they needed this time away from everyone else to be with each other.

Jax picked up Kiann and straightened from the chair. He walked to the bed and tossed her on the middle of the mattress.

"You two couldn't wait for the bed, I take it?" If only Tam'd been there from the start. He'd seen enough, though, to know how Jax had given up control and lost what little *he'd* had left.

Jax shrugged as he gazed at Tam with love evident in his eyes. "It was a spur of the moment thing."

Jax and spur of the moment never went hand in hand. If Kiann could make him more spontaneous, it would be a wonderful thing for all of them.

Yes, she'd changed their whole existence from the moment her stone glowed for them. For the better. They'd needed a change.

They'd needed a woman in their lives. Never would he have thought it, but she worked for them.

He'd met a few happy all-male couples who had been quite content. He and Jax had been both, too, but things were even more fulfilling. The change came from finding their mate. Whether male or female, she would have changed their lives.

Kiann pushed up on her hands and surveyed them both. She looked decadent on the bed with her tousled hair, her swollen lips, and her damp thighs. She had that "I've had sex" look. "Tam, welcome back."

Tam lowered to the bed to press a small kiss to her lips. "I'm glad to be back and see you."

He hadn't known if Jax and Balt would make the outpost. A desperate race against time had him blowing up every ten seconds at Orion and Layla, which was probably why they'd gone with him instead of sending Balt. Balt would have broken him in half for his emotional outbursts.

Orion had just smirked, and Layla had threatened to taser him.

He'd hated being separated from his mates, but that had been the only way to save Kiann. Now, the only way to keep her safe had worked. He had both his mates in front of him, and he might never let them go.

Jax joined them on the bed on the other side of Kiann. He placed a hand on her back, stroking Tam's in the process.

"You done good." Her voice became a whisper as tears misted her eyes. "Thank you—both of you—for what you did for me."

"I'm your mate. Saving you is what I'm supposed to do." Tam wrapped his arms around her, and Jax joined them. They stayed that way for several minutes.

Tam termed it basking in the love of his mates, snuggled up like a psi-cat to a heater.

Then, Kiann broke away to look behind her at something. "I thought men needed recovery time?" Her face smoothed out in surprise.

Jax looked as bland as possible. "We do."

"He doesn't need much." Tam's cock grew heavier, knowing that Jax must have grown hard again. "At all." He wanted to be inside them both. The way they were inside of him all the time.

She shook her head. Then, a mischievous look bloomed on her face like a flower to a sun plant. She had something on her mind, which from the look, probably meant good things for Jax and him. "Tam."

"Yep." His name flowing from her lips sounded like the angels from fairy tales he'd read as a child. He couldn't wait to hear her scream it in the middle of passion. That would sound even better.

"Are you recovered from traveling? Do you need rest time?"

He blinked at her a moment. Was she kidding? "Nope. I'm fine." More than fine. He was ready to go.

Her head bobbed from side to side. "So, do you…"

"Yep." He didn't let her finish. No need. Clearly, they both had the same ideas. He wanted them both. Now. To complete their bonding as mates.

"Yeah," Jax echoed him.

They both gazed at him. Kiann's face showed surprise again.

"I got what you were talking about to Tam. You're not that subtle."

"Good." Tam's speech conveyed more than the simple word said, and they all knew that it did.

Jax had accepted their mate. His understanding of what she hadn't spelled out confirmed that. Kiann was safe. Time for them to bond and consummate all the crazy thoughts he'd been having.

Jax ran a hand up his arm.

Kiann lowered herself backward so they both had to scramble to lie back with her. "How does this work?"

"What do you mean?" Tam reached out to tuck a stray tendril of hair back off her face. His hand moved down and stroked her cheek. She was soft. He could lose himself in her supple curves.

"We don't have assigned positions, if that's what you are asking." Jax shifted his weight, and the bed shifted. "We work it out together."

She bit her lip.

She was nervous about coming together as a threesome. Why wouldn't she be? She'd only read about the positions and probably not much. Hell, he was nervous about being in a ménage sexual position.

But they'd work it out together.

Tam moved his hand to cup her chin and reassure her. "As we will work out everything else from now on."

"Okay."

Jax caught Tam's gaze and lowered his head. He pressed a kiss on Kiann's neck, nibbling it softly.

Her eyes rolled back.

Tam lowered his mouth to her, exalting in her taste. As always, she tasted of nothing he'd ever had before, yet it was a flavor that he knew. One that was familiar to him, as if he'd known it all his life. The same with her. He might not have known her long, but she touched something deep inside that had possessed him forever.

He ran his hand down her body, caressing her breasts, which were heavy in his cupped hands. He pinched nipples that pebbled under his ministrations.

His hand lowered over her flat belly to push into her mass of curls. She was so wet, she dripped. The earlier sex had lubricated her up.

"Curse it all. Lubricant." Jax's thick voice broke through Tam's thoughts. They must be in tune. Tam thought about lubed up and so did Jax.

Tam shifted his weight and got up to reach in his pants' pocket. He tossed Jax some lube, which he caught.

"Should have known you'd be prepped."

First time Jax had ever said anything to him about his state of preparedness. Usually Jax was the prepared one. He cocked his head to the side. "She's pretty wet."

Jax nodded. "Yeah, but not enough for…everything."

A shiver ran through Tam. Jax intended to take this all the way. Make them a true threesome in this sexual encounter. It would be a damn fine way to spend a few hours. Days. Months. Maybe years.

Tam wore too many clothes. He'd barely realized it when he'd sat down on the bed, but he'd never stripped.

He tore his clothes off so quickly, he probably set records. A button fell off and clinked to the floor. No matter, there'd be more buttons.

Came back onto the bed to see his mates' shining faces looking up at him. Nothing got better than this. Not for a lifetime.

He kissed Kiann wildly, then reached over to kiss Jax. Jax tasted of a woman's flavor. Their woman.

Longing swamped Tam. He'd never wanted anything more than the two of them.

Kiann opened her thighs. "I need you. Now. I need to become one with you."

He was more than happy to oblige. Tam took his time, entering her slowly, exhaling as he thought of boring facts and figures to keep the pace light. He had to take his time.

Double penetration was a tricky affair. Jax would have to prepare her so she wouldn't be hurt.

Wetness and tightness surrounded him.

He lay on his side as she did, giving them a new position and new sensations. He couldn't move as much as in other positions, so it kept her acquainted with some power over the act.

His whole world narrowed down to these two people and nothing beyond them.

Jax moved against her back. He must have already lubed her up and prepped her while Tam was taking entry. He'd make sure she was ready. He'd use his fingers and the lube to stretch her bit by bit. Then, he'd press himself inside.

Jax's hand pressed into her shoulder. He would take things slow and move in little steps at a time.

He'd taken such care the first time he and Tam had made love. He'd take no less here, so Tam could predict what he did when.

Tam held still, moving only when she needed the distraction. Holding back was torture, but their orgasm would be the reward. Once Jax was in her, they could time their movements at the same time. Take her by working together.

His body was coated in a sheen of sweat.

Kiann shuddered against him. He knew she was being pierced in two places at the same time. He stroked her face as he moved against her, thrusting his cock in deep. She whimpered, but the sound wasn't one of pain, only pleasure.

Still Tam held himself back.

Jax grunted as his head lolled back.

He must be fully encased within her.

As was Tam.

She was the uniting force between them, so it made sense she'd be between them in the ultimate form of possession for a threesome. She was the cog that drove their wheels.

Their mate. Their love. Their future.

Everything drew down to this moment of becoming one with the woman who completed their mating. The woman he wanted to keep safe from all hate or harm. The man he loved more than life itself.

Along with the man who shared this woman, his bed, and his life. The man he loved just as much as the woman between them.

Jax moved first, slowly easing back and forth. The tense lines took over Jax's face as he tried to keep himself in control.

Tam found a rhythm to match, keeping his thrusts in timed to Jax's pulls out.

Kiann writhed between them. Looks of pure pleasure strained across her face.

Tam saw the exact moment when Jax lost control. His movements became frenetic. His hands clutched at Kiann, pulling her as close as he could, pounding into her with a slapping sound that Tam could distinctly hear.

Tam matched him stroke for stroke, pace for pace. He increased his thrusts as Jax did and slowed down as Jax did.

Kiann was the first to slide over the edge of bliss. Her face contorted as her body spasmed. Wetness seeped around Tam's cock. She moaned both their names. "Goddess, hurry."

He had to force himself to hold together. He wanted to split into a hundred pieces and let the orgasm sweep across him. His teeth gritted as he recited something about henna. *Had to last, had to last, had to last.* He had to make sure both his mates hit what they were entitled to.

Jax orgasmed next with a yelp.

Tam had never heard him hit that note before. He rocked his body against Kiann as Jax did. Each stroke took him in and out of Kiann's clutching depths.

Knowing his mates had come to their pleasure already, Tam allowed himself over to the bliss side of the beach. Exaltation kept his orgasm going long after it should have finished. He jerked in response to the shudders rocking his body.

Jax shuddered with an aftershock. "You're my life. Both of you."

Kiann's smile lit up the galaxy. "You two are mine."

"Same with me, perlin. My life for you." Tam nodded in agreement.

Her hand stroked up his chest. "What's a perlin?"

"Technically, it means 'little cat' in my father's language." He ducked his head at her quizzical raise of an eyebrow.

Jax stretched. "He uses it as an endearment. Not often, though."

If he used the words often, they wouldn't be special. "You both are my perlins. My everything."

"I like your word. Perlin." She tested out the sound, looking as comfortable as a psi-cat resting in a sunny window.

"It's okay, you know. Time for you to live now." The words popped out of his mouth without a reason. He had no idea why he said them. Redness colored his sight for brief instant.

A tear ran down Kiann's cheek, which he wiped away. "Past time."

Tam cuddled her closer. He didn't ask what the words meant, nor did Jax, but she seemed to know. Such was the way of an Ebolian seer.

When they'd cleaned up and lay in each other's arms, stones glowing in the darkness, drifting to sleep, red again swamped Tam's vision. Red clouds with a woman in the center, hanging on to two men. Her face radiated her joy as the cloud men laughed at something she'd said.

His gaze shifted to Jax and Kiann, but neither of them spoke if they'd noticed he'd had a vision.

He didn't need a dream to tell him what he'd discovered.

The woman was his future. His life. His passion.

Jax was his and so was she. They belonged together. No vision could ever capture what she truly meant to them both.

Morning would come too quickly for the Queen and her mates. They'd better be well rested for what the day would bring. Much responsibility would be thrust upon all of them. After all, Kiann had a planet to take over.

A hand brushed against his cock, and it sprang to life again.

Or maybe they need only be partially rested.

ᴗTHE ENDᴗ

Mechele Armstrong

Have you ever wondered, "What if crayons have a kingdom?" Mechele Armstrong did at age five. Now, turning the imagination of a wide-eyed child into intense spellbinding stories for adults, she is winning over new fans every day.

Writing stories and poetry as a hobby, she graduated from Virginia Commonwealth University with a degree in Religious Studies and Social Welfare. Although there were challenges with work and family, the need to write and be published, to share her passion for books was always there.

During a rainy weekend at the beach reading several romance novels she fell in love, not with the hero, but with the genre again. So began a two-year adventure of doing what she loved most, creating worlds with strong heroines and enchanting heroes that will keep you turning pages until the end.

Using the Internet and the local Romance Writer's Association, she learned and refined her craft. Living in Virginia with a husband, kids, dog, and fish, she finds time to share her vivid imagination and ability to tell stories of adventure, love, lust, and everything in between.

Find Mechele at http://www.mechelearmstrong.com, or email her at mechele@mechelearmstrong.com.

TITLES AVAILABLE In Print from Loose Id®

DARK ELVES: DISCOVERY
Jet Mykles

DARK ELVES: SALVATION
Jet Mykles

DARK ELVES: TAKEN
Jet Mykles

DAUGHTERS OF TERRA:
THE TA'E'SHA CHRONICLES, BOOK ONE
Theolyn Boese

DINAH'S DARK DESIRE
Mechele Armstrong

INTERSTELLAR SERVICE & DISCIPLINE:
VICTORIOUS STAR
Morgan Hawke

LAST HOPE
Moira Rogers

LEASHED: MORE THAN A BARGAIN
Jet Mykles

ROMANCE AT THE EDGE: In Other Worlds
MaryJanice Davidson, Angela Knight and Camille Anthony

SHARDS OF THE MIND:
THE TA'E'SHA CHRONICLES, BOOK TWO
Theolyn Boese

SLAVE BOY
Evangeline Anderson

THE PRENDARIAN CHRONICLES
Doreen DeSalvo

THE LOVERS: SETTLER'S MINE 2
Mechele Armstrong

THE RIVALS: SETTLER'S MINE 1
Mechele Armstrong

Publisher's Note: The print titles listed above were previously released in e-book format by Loose Id®.